Southern Hexes

A MAX PORTER PARANORMAL MYSTERY

Stuart Jaffe

Southern Hexes is a work of fiction. Names, characters, places, and incidents either are the product of the author's imagination or are used fictitiously, and any resemblance to any persons, living or dead, business establishments, events, or locales is entirely coincidental.

SOUTHERN HEXES

Cover art by Mari Morgan

ISBN 13: 978-1-963517-09-5

First Edition: April, 2023
First Hardcover Edition: February, 2024

For Jill and David Stone

Also by Stuart Jaffe

Max Porter Paranormal Mysteries

Southern Bound
Southern Charm
Southern Belle
Southern Gothic
Southern Haunts
Southern Curses
Southern Rites
Southern Craft
Southern Spirit
Southern Flames
Southern Fury
Southern Souls
Southern Blood
Southern Graves
Southern Dead
Southern Hexes
Southern Hart

Nathan K Thrillers

Immortal Killers
Killing Machine
The Cardinal
Yukon Massacre
The First Battle
Immortal Darkness
A Spy for Eternity
Prisoner
Desert Takedown
Lone Star Standoff
The Puppeteer
Blowback
Prime

The Ridnight Mysteries

The Water Blade
The Waters of Taladoro
Waterfire

The Parallel Society

The Infinity Caverns
Book on the Isle
Rift Angel
Lost Time
Pages of Glass
The Bold Warrior
City of Infinity

The Malja Chronicles

The Way of the Black Beast
The Way of the Sword and Gun
The Way of the Brother Gods
The Way of the Blade
The Way of the Power
The Way of the Soul

Gillian Boone novels

A Glimpse of Her Soul
Pathway to Spirit

Stand Alone Novels

After The Crash
Real Magic
Founders

Short Story Collection

10 Bits of My Brain
10 More Bits of My Brain
The Bluesman
The Marshall Drummond Case Files: Cabinet 1
The Marshall Drummond Case Files: Cabinet 2
The Marshall Drummond Case Files: Cabinet 3

Non-Fiction

How to Write Magical Words: A Writer's Companion
For more information, please visit ***www.stuartjaffe.com***

Southern Hexes

Chapter 1

THE LENGTHY FARMHOUSE ATTIC smelled of old newspaper and rotting wood. Though a full week into November, a strong afternoon sun pressed against the house, thickening and warming the air. Still, Max Porter shivered. He raised his phone overhead to splash light in the darkened corners. His breath shallowed and his pulse thumped hard. Searching for a ghost had yet to become routine — thank goodness.

Max's partner, Marshall Drummond canvassed the rest of the building. Being the ghost of a 1940s detective, Drummond could move faster through the house — not having to bother with walls, doors, or stairs. But Max had to handle the attic. This was the spot their potential client, Mrs. Lowell, had heard all the noises coming from, and that meant she needed to see an actual person inspect the area. A bit ironic considering Drummond was far better equipped to locate a problem in the attic — or anywhere in the house. After all, he could see all ghosts and Max only saw Drummond. But Max stumbled ahead, clenched in preparation for hitting a cold spot, hearing an ear-splitting moan, or feeling an icy blow to the chest that could send him skidding across the dusty, splintered wood.

Each step creaked the floorboards. Max swallowed dry. He spread the phone's flashlight across an old dresser, a bicycle with two flat tires, and a stack of boxes marked *X-Mas Decorations.* Didn't look like anybody had decorated for the holiday in years.

"You find anything?" Drummond said, poking his head through the floor.

Max yipped and jumped back. Heart hammering, he scowled at his partner. "That's not funny."

"Would it have been better if I said *Boo!* and waved my hands around?"

Shaking off the sudden fright, Max turned his attention back to the attic corners. "Maybe wear a sheet over your head next time. Improve the view."

"I'll invest in some chains to rattle, too."

In a more serious tone, Max said, "Any ghosts in here besides you?"

"Not anywhere in this house. But I think I've found the lady's problem."

A few minutes later, Max stood on the farmhouse porch and gazed across several wide pastures. Tall, dead grass waved through the land and a few sweetgum trees dotted the open spaces. Once a horse farm, a thriving one judging by the stables good for at least a dozen horses, the place had become a gentle retirement property. A breeze wafted through the yellowed grass while three turkey vultures spun circles off in the distance. Max closed his eyes and tried to grab the soft sense of peace he knew surrounded him. But this wasn't his land, and he had come to work.

"My Vincent used to do the same thing." Mrs. Lowell pushed a screen door open and walked to a group of wicker chairs around a coffee table. She carried a tray with two glasses and a pitcher of sweet tea, her wrinkled hands shaking but determined as she slowly made her way. "He could spend hours just a-standin' on this porch with his eyes closed like some kind of statue and the rest of him open to this wonderful place like the birds themselves. He loved it here."

"It's beautiful," Max said. Not even the echo of a dog barking in the distance could break the sweetness in the air. "Like a dream."

"It was his dream to live in a place like this. Most of our time, we lived in cities. Crammed, little apartments costing more than a decent mortgage. That kind of thing. But Vincent had grown up on a dairy farm in South Carolina. Land was in his blood. So, when his mee-maw passed away, we came into a good chunk of money, and with that, we came here."

She poured two glasses full of sweet tea and offered one to

Max. He had learned to enjoy many of the South's cultural quirks — including grits with salt and butter — yet he still couldn't embrace this concoction. Eating two spoonfuls of raw sugar would have been easier. But Max did not want to be rude, so he sipped the tea and did his best to hold back from wincing.

"I never had an interest to live here, you know." She settled in one chair as she stared across the grass. She wore a blue blouse and a floral skirt, several rings and a necklace, and she had put on makeup, too. Even her hair looked as if she had spent time getting it the right shape — a rather ancient coif that reminded Max of the 1980s and Nancy Reagan. "This place had always been his thing, and now I've got to carry the weight of it. You see? I'm the one left behind, not him. I guess that's why he's haunting me now."

Finally. Max had refrained from pushing the old woman into the point, but relief washed over him as she turned her focus to the reason she had called. Perhaps she had sensed that she could only stall for so long. He felt a tinge of guilt — clearly, a lonely, old woman stuck out here by herself who needed a little company — but from the moment he had driven up to the house, Max knew the place wasn't haunted.

To be fair, he didn't *know* for sure, and he did feel genuine nerves up in that attic, but after inspecting numerous homes for ghosts over numerous years, he thought he had developed a radar for it. Still, he had agreed to check out what he could and trusted Drummond to handle the rest. With the answer in hand, Max now had to play out the last part of his visit like a silly children's program where the adults all knew how the story would unfold but had to endure it until the end.

Mrs. Lowell gulped down half her glass of tea. "The noises have been going on for quite a while now. I've looked up in the attic, but I can't find what makes the sound. Always from the attic. The first night after it all began, I dreamt of Vincent. And every night since I hear those noises and dream of Vincent."

That sounded interesting, and for the first time since arriving at the farmhouse, Max considered that there might be an actual case here. Not because of the noises or the dreams, but because they happened together. Perhaps he had missed something.

"Don't fall for it. There still ain't anything here," Drummond said, slipping through the walls after a final once over of the property. His pale, ghostly visage matched the chill he brought with him, and Max thought he saw Mrs. Lowell shudder. Then again, she might be jittering from the half-pound of sugar she had ingested.

Drummond threw open one side of his coat and thrust a hand in the pocket. His other hand tipped back his Fedora as he surveyed the grounds spreading into the distance. "Nice place."

Mrs. Lowell set her glass down with a clink. "I must admit that I never once considered the possibility of extraterrestrial interactions until I saw that piece on the local station. I watch WXII."

Drummond snickered. "There it is."

"Not *extraterrestrial,*" Max said, his heart sinking. "We deal with the paranormal, the supernatural."

"Yes, sir, I don't usually watch the news programs anymore — get my facts off the internet — but when the Winston channel runs a special Halloween show on ghosts of North Carolina, you better believe I was gonna watch that — what with everything with my Vincent. That's when I saw you talking about some of the spooky homes in Old Salem, and I thought to myself maybe that's what I got going on here."

Drummond drifted away, but before passing through the porch railing, he said, "I can't stand to listen to another of these crackpots. I'll wait in the car. Take my advice — get paid and get going."

The offer to appear on the Halloween special had come from a client, a producer for WXII-12 News, that suffered a small issue with a haunting in her wine cellar. The Porter Agency had no trouble fixing the matter, and she was so grateful, she suggested doing the special. At the time, Max thought it would be good, local exposure. He figured most people would dismiss him, probably forget him, and that was fine. But a handful of those experiencing real paranormal problems would reach out. Free advertising. Better than free — she had insisted on paying him for his time.

Ever since that thing aired, though, the Porter Agency had been overwhelmed with calls. Almost all of which turned into nothing serious or simply nothing at all. Like this one.

"Well, Mrs. Lowell, I'm pleased to tell you that you are not being haunted."

"I'm not?"

"No, ma'am. I checked the attic and the house, and I promise you that there isn't a ghost anywhere on the premises. What you need is an exterminator. You've got mice in the walls."

"Mice?"

Max gestured to the large pastures. "The weather's getting colder, and the field mice are looking for a warm place to stay. If you don't get some traps and bait and such put out soon, I suspect you'll have a very noisy winter."

"But my dreams of Vincent."

"You loved him, and you miss him. Once you got it in your head that he was trying to talk with you, the dreams were almost inevitable." Max mostly believed that last part. But if Mrs. Lowell called them again with a real ghost problem, he would have the team start with those dreams.

"Oh dear, I feel so embarrassed." She looked more disappointed than anything.

"No need. Strange sounds coming from the walls is a good reason to call us. While I do have to charge you for this visit, you'll find hiring pest control is a lot cheaper than having us clear a house of a ghost."

She nodded before turning a sheepish smile his way. "I have one more little question, if you don't mind."

Minutes later, Max drove away from the old farmhouse to the sound of Drummond's mocking laughter.

"An autograph?" the ghost said. "Well, well. One appearance on television and suddenly you're a big star. I should be honored to share a car with you."

"You should've been honored before the tv thing."

The ghost continued to snort and chuckle while Max turned toward home. It didn't take long for Max's silence to chill the levity. They both stared at the road as the sky ahead turned gray. By the time Max pulled into a gas station, raindrops formed big splotches on the pavement.

"Just what I need," he said, getting out to fill the car.

"It's only rain."

"It'll make the day seem longer, and I'm done with today."

"Look, partner, I know how you feel about these cases, I feel it too, but you got to admit, the money's coming in. You and Sandra deserve some relief in that department."

Max screwed his face tight. "Ever since that stupid tv show, all we get is one phony call after another. I mean I agree that getting paid several times a day to check out a house or listen to an old lady or both is easy money, but we don't do this for the money."

"Bull. Everybody is in it for the money. Remember, I lived through the Great Depression. It's easy to say you don't care about the money when you got some. But trust me — when it's all gone, I mean all of it, suddenly every penny is a fortune worth dying over."

"All I'm saying is that if we really wanted to be rolling in dough, then we'd have picked a different career. I'd be a lawyer or a doctor."

Drummond snickered. "You'd have to have made it through law school or med school for those."

"You don't think I'm smart enough?"

"Oh, you're plenty smart. Research is your thing and you'd have hit the law books and whatnot like nobody's ever seen. But I can't picture you cutting open a body and you're too honest to twist the law to suit a client."

Max noticed the cashier watching him through the store window. He had grown to know the look on that woman's face. She saw him talking to, gesturing at, and having a conversation with the empty space next to him. Maybe she would dismiss it, assume he had an earpiece and talked on the phone, but more often, he caught the cockeyed stare from people — the giveaway that they thought he might be more comfortable in a padded cell.

He finished with the gas and got back in the car. The rain fell harder, drumming the roof like a thrash band on speed. At least whenever a storm hit this hard, it passed over quickly.

Easing into the passenger seat, Drummond shook off the water that could not possibly accumulate on him. “I feel it, too, you know. It’s frustrating to be spending every single day going from one non-case to another. But each visit is money in the bank, and I’m tired of seeing you and Sandra and the Sandwich Boys struggle. That’s all I’m saying.”

“I appreciate that. I really do. But we’ve had loads of money before, and we’ve been near homeless, too. Where we are now — well, I’d rather be dropping a few rungs on the financial ladder than wasting more days like today. What’s the point of taking these stupid cases when real people with real problems need our help, but we can’t find them because we’re squandering time collecting fees for nothing?”

“Sounds like you need a break.”

“Don’t you?”

“Yeah, but I’m dead. I don’t get tired like you.”

Max brought his appointments up on his phone. “Still one more today — Dwayne Fincher.”

“See that? It’s only a little after lunch and you’re almost done.”

“That’s because I need to help my mother the rest of the day.”

“Oh. Sorry.”

“I know you’re joking — half-joking, anyway — but she’s got her infusion today at the hospital.” He shook his head. “I’m done. That’s it. I’m canceling Fincher’s visit. We’ll deal with him another time.”

In a gentler tone, Drummond said, “Good idea. Family’s important.” His mouth turned upward, and his eyes shined. “Besides, this way I can be done for the day, too. There was that car crash last week that killed a few lovely women. Entering a beauty pageant, I think. Maybe they didn’t move on and need a hand to guide them through the afterlife in the Other.”

“Always thinking of others, I see.”

“That’s what I’m about.”

Max laughed. Harder than necessary, but it felt good.

Chapter 2

A FEW HOURS LATER, Max paced a curtained-off section of a hospital room while Mrs. Porter sat in a special chair that propped her arm up for the MS infusion treatment she needed. The first few times, she had gone to a treatment center — a big room with numerous chairs and a handful of MS patients all getting taken care of together. Max thought his mother would find comfort in speaking with others who were going through the same thing. Maybe even make a friend or two. But seeing people in wheelchairs, people who were blind in one eye, those who couldn't speak or needed help with basic functions threw her into a week-long depression. From that point on, he paid for a private room.

The infusion IV procedure required nearly four hours and had to be done twice a year. While she could have brought a book or a laptop or any number of ways to entertain herself during the long treatment, she had insisted on Max being there. Every time.

"What if something bad happens?" she had said.

Max didn't mind, though. Not really. With all the new cases flooding The Porter Agency, it had become increasingly difficult to make time for his mother. This way, at least, he could guarantee they would spend a few hours together.

During this particular hospital visit, however, Max found it hard to concentrate on her. He kept hearing the desperate voice of Dwayne Fincher, his last appointment for the day. When making the call to cancel, Max assumed they would simply reschedule. But Dwayne choked and coughed and breathed hard as if a machine on the verge of breaking apart. He only relented when Max explained that his mother had multiple sclerosis and needed his help for her treatment. Max didn't like playing that card — it left a slimy sensation on his heart — but doing so shut Dwayne down. The conversation petered out, and Max agreed to meet Dwayne first thing in the morning.

Picking over the month-old magazines in the hospital room, he sat on the small couch next to the infusion chair and waited for the nurse to check Mrs. Porter once again. They seemed to flow in every few minutes to ask how she felt, to measure her pulse, to smile and promise it wouldn't take much longer. At first, Max thought they had seen him on that Halloween special and wanted to be near his small bit of fame. Soon, though, he understood that they watched his mother closely because of her age.

That his thoughts would first jump to his television appearance as a reason for anything soured his stomach. He should never have done that stupid show. It had spoiled the pleasures of the casework and had polluted his own thoughts. Of course, like Drummond had pointed out numerous times since the show aired, the money generated had helped them tremendously. He couldn't deny the strange joy of seeing his credit card bill in the mail and not feeling his heart quicken, not breaking into a cold sweat, or not developing a hard lump in his gut. Still, a part of him would gladly return to their financial struggles if it meant they could sit back, wait, and deal with a real case again. One that mattered.

"— which is why I've started using a cane at home." Mrs. Porter stared at him expectantly.

Max flashed a smile as if he knew what she had been saying. "A cane?"

"I've made sure to hide it in the closet when you've come around. It's embarrassing. But you heard the nurse just now."

"I suppose." He hadn't.

"Suppose nothing. I can't pretend things aren't getting worse, and you need to be aware of what's going on, so you're not caught unprepared. At my age, with this horrible disease, it's getting worse all the time. I could go at any moment." She lowered her voice just above a whisper. "Sometimes, I can feel

Death standing nearby."

"Don't say that."

"I've lived a good life. A long one, too. Long enough. Though I wouldn't mind some more years to enjoy. But what really bothers me is this stupid MS. I've lived a clean life — cleaner than most people. Rarely drank, rarely smoked. Why do I have to spend my final years suffering in pain and hooked up to this machine and hobbling around? It makes me want to yell at Death to hurry up already and get it over with."

"Mom —"

"Oh, wipe that worried look off your face. I don't mean that. I'm just frustrated and well, I thought you should know."

"That you think you're going to die soon?"

"Look at you. You're all flustered. No, honey, I'm not dying. Not yet. It's hard, though. You don't understand what it's like to always be tired, always have this disease hanging over you. It's like being haunted by a ghost that rarely ever leaves you alone."

"I might know more about that than you think."

"That's on a good day. The bad days are getting worse. I get vertigo and sometimes I have to concentrate just to catch my breath. I get these horrible chest pains. I told the doctor and she said they're called MS hugs. Isn't that terrible?" She rolled her lips in as her eyes glistened. "Then a few days ago, I woke up like usual, but I couldn't move. My bones were cement. They just refused to move. They were under this terrible weight."

"Why didn't you tell me about this?"

"I'm telling you right now. It took me a few hours to get moving."

"Hours? We've got to watch you more."

"No, no, no. I get my fill of worrywarts from PB and J. The last thing I want is more of that false concern. Fact is, I'm dying. If I have anything to say about it, you'll leave me alone for most of the time I have left. I'm not going into a nursing home. Don't make me do that. I just want to finish standing on my own two feet, as they say."

"I didn't say —"

"It starts with everybody pitching in, giving me their time, everybody being kind and concerned, but eventually, taking care of me starts conflicting with your life — your work, your family, your whatever. You'll sit down one day and think that you can't keep it up, that I need more care than the family can give me. That's when you'll come to me with a smile and a brochure for some place where people shuffle off to die. Well, I'm saying that I won't do that."

Max put an arm around her shoulder, careful not to jostle the IV, and kissed her head. "Don't worry. I know you don't want to go to a home. You've made that clear every time. I promise we won't do that to you. We'll figure something out."

Sniffing hard, she said, "Sorry. I didn't mean to go on a tangent. That wasn't anything I wanted to say. I was talking about my cane. I need that cane to get around better. But then, we all need help from time to time."

Max knew she referred to something else — perhaps from an earlier part of her speech that he had missed. He sat next to her, his mind swirling over all she had said, but he must have taken too long to conclude her meaning. With an impatient grunt, she tapped his knee with a sharp fingernail.

"When the Grim Reaper hangs over you, the world comes into focus. The things that matter finally start to actually matter — and that's the people in your life. Those that you love. Like PB."

"What about PB?"

"You're smothering him."

"What?" Max clamped down the surprised screech that raced up his throat, turning the word into a high-pitched yip.

"He's a young man now. He needs advice, guidance, not rules."

"What are you talking about? Did he say something to you?"

"He doesn't have to. I raised you, didn't I? I know a thing or two about parenting. I watch what's going on and I listen. PB spends enough time with me that I can figure out what's really happening in your house."

Max fought the urge to stomp around and bellow about personal privacy, about the quality of her parenting, about every little thorn between them. But when he looked straight at her, he saw her hair had gone from grey to white, her wrinkles had loosened more and deepened further, and she had purple-black bruises on her arm from the IV needle. She seemed to shrink before him — no longer a powerhouse of brutal energy that could dominate his thoughts and fears, that could reduce him to a child with a mere handful of carefully chosen words. Before him now, she became an elderly woman. A woman who, on a bad day, couldn't move her body and agonized she would be bedridden in her final years.

With a calm pat on the shoulder, he said, "You don't have to worry about PB. He's fine."

"You're not listening. PB is going to graduate high school soon, and right after him comes J. That's a big deal for most kids, but these boys started out living on the streets. They never thought they would ever see a day like that."

"And we've made sure they know how proud we are of them."

"Stop interrupting and open your ears." Her mouth barely parted as she growled out the words.

Max's skin prickled. He stopped from making a comment.

She continued, "PB looks at his brother, and he sees that J is a good student, that J is taking all the steps to head for a successful future. Whatever J dreams of doing, he'll have a decent shot at doing it. J's already on a good path. But PB still doesn't know where he fits in. He comes to my home, and I can tell. The questions he asks me, the things he wants to talk about — he's got no direction and he's afraid he won't ever find his way. You need to show him."

"I try to encourage him to try new things, see what he likes, but I can't force him —"

"He looks up to you, and he should. You're the reason both those boys are getting a chance at a real life. You pulled them off the streets. You gave them jobs, a home, a family. Look at your own success."

"You're scaring me with all these compliments."

"Nonsense. I compliment you plenty. It's that you don't ever hear me unless I'm saying something you'll want to use against me later. Always has been that way. If I say that I'm proud of you, then —"

"You've almost never said you're proud of me." Shocked by his own outburst, Max folded his hands and faced the window.

"If I was sparing in my praise, it should mean all the more when I do give it. And I'm telling you now that I'm proud of you. I've never quite understood what you do, but seeing you on television is proof enough. You've made something of yourself."

That stupid tv show. Max closed his eyes. If he could have blotted out the entire world, he would have. Despite the arguing, for a brief moment, he thought he would feel flush with his mother's pride. But no joy arrived. The things he had accomplished, the life he had built — it all remained the same from days before. Being on a television show had drummed more business, but nothing else had changed. Yet to his mother, seeing him on a television show suddenly made it worthwhile, validated him to her.

Worse, she only found room to praise him because he was the face on the show. However, Sandra was an equal partner in the Porter Agency — not to mention his wife. Without her ability to see all ghosts and her ambition to become one of the few good witches around, they would never have achieved any level of success. Of course, they had a third partner in Drummond, but Max guessed that a ghost could not be filmed for television.

He shook his head. How could he possibly offer PB any real guidance when he couldn't figure out his own life? Saving him from answering the question, Max's phone rang. A peek at the screen — *Dwayne Fincher*.

But before he could send the call to voicemail, his mother said, "What are you doing? This is a hospital. You're not supposed to have a cellphone on in a hospital."

"I'm not sure that's still a thing."

"You listen to me. I know. It messes with the equipment. You could kill somebody."

"Sorry, but it's a business call. The price of success." Before she could start in on his impertinence, he hurried into the hallway and answered.

"You've got to help me," Dwayne said, sounding more frazzled than during their previous calls.

"Calm down. I'm sorry I had to cancel last minute today, but—"

"Things are getting worse."

"Like we discussed, I'm going to see you tomorrow."

"What if I don't have that long? This thing is going to kill me."

Max continued to believe Dwayne's call amounted to nothing more than another waste of several hours resulting in a relatively easy paycheck, but part of him heard something else. A level of desperation — no, a level of fear — unlike the other non-cases. When Dwayne said he might be killed, he believed it.

"How about I move you to the first appointment in the morning? I can meet you at eight o'clock and we —"

"No, no, no. You've got to come help me now. Tonight. Please. I've been cursed."

Max paused. Ever since he had appeared on television, the endless non-case calls were for haunted houses and noisy ghosts and a few false claims of possession. But nobody had said they were cursed. Either his fanbase had suddenly broadened or Max faced a real situation.

"Okay."

"What? Really? Oh, thank you so much."

"I have to finish what I'm doing and get a few team members together, but we can meet you later tonight. Where do you live?"

"Come to my office. I've got to try to get my work done, if the curse will let me."

Dwayne blubbered more thanks, texted the office address, and ended the call. Standing in the hospital corridor, Max thought he had made a mistake. A curse that stopped a man from working in the office? On the one hand, he had witnessed some awful and awfully specific curses. On the other hand, why would anybody go to the trouble of putting together a curse only to make it so a guy couldn't get a job done? Sure, it might lead to him being fired, unable to get a new job, maybe even end up homeless. But that was so subtle. Curses were used to harm someone and let them know they were being harmed, that they had messed with the wrong person and would regret it for the rest of their life.

Just last year, a cult group called the Brotherhood had attempted to curse Max by making his hand kill anybody he touched. That was a serious curse. Dwayne's problem sounded so minor, a mere inconvenience, that Max's instincts said there had to be more. After all, the curse didn't stop Dwayne from the task of calling the Porters, Dwayne hadn't mentioned being unable to think or write or speak. If the curse had simply put stumbling blocks in Dwayne's way towards accomplishing basic work, then Max felt sure it would escalate. Whatever the curse did, Dwayne had only experienced the surface.

Chapter 3

OVER THE NEXT SEVERAL HOURS, Max flipped between the idea that Dwayne Fincher would be another waste of time and that Dwayne Fincher would be horribly cursed. When he thought of the latter, he fluttered with excitement — a real curse meant a real case — and chastised himself for taking delight in another's misfortune. It would be best for Dwayne to be a liar, crazy, or simply mistaken. Then Max could collect the visitation fee and go home. Boring, true, but at least nobody would be a victim of the supernatural.

Except Max didn't get involved in these cases for the boredom. He didn't stay in the weird world of a paranormal detective to play it safe. In his past, Max would have had difficulty admitting that much, but he had been doing this long enough to know that there was a bit of an adrenaline rush when he closed a case. Defeating the bad guys, protecting people from ghosts and witches, discovering all the strangeness of the world that flows below the surface — it thrilled him. It kept him coming back to the job even when he nearly died doing it. Besides, if Dwayne needed real help, the kind of help only the Porter Agency could provide, then whether or not Max received a burst of happiness from taking on the bizarre didn't matter.

The tense silence in the car confirmed that Sandra and Drummond held similar debates in their heads. When Max parked on a side street and headed toward Winston Tower — one of the tallest buildings in Winston-Salem — that same tension grew stronger. Walking into the building and riding the elevator to the ninth floor, only deepened the sensation. By the time they entered the Law Offices of Hostetler and Chase, Max felt ready to burst at the slightest provocation.

Until he saw Dwayne pacing the office lobby while his wife sat in a chair, rubbing her hands against her skirt. The terror painting their faces, the apprehension bouncing between them, overshadowed any excitement Max felt or anything he sensed from Sandra or Drummond.

"They're here," Dwayne's wife said, bolting to her feet. She was tall, but then Dwayne towered over them all, and her figure struck Max as extremely controlled — not too thin, not too curvy. In fact, her clothes, her hair style, even her expression all hit him the same way. Right then, he understood that whatever Dwayne's role in this office, the man had greater aspirations, perhaps even political ones, and he expected his wife to fulfill her role as his ideal mate, camera ready with poise and a winning smile. She put out her hand. "Thank you for coming. I'm Nell."

Her thick North Carolina accent probably helped at all the state hobnobbing parties, but she would have to tone it down if they wanted to get more national consideration.

"Please," Dwayne said, "my office is down this way."

He led them through a maze of desks and hallways designed to feel imposing, impressive, traditional, yet also contemporary. Old wood corridors with large oil paintings gave way to offices that boasted standing desks, flatscreens, and more glass than seemed prudent. Especially with the way Dwayne and Nell shuddered through every step.

Max glanced back at Sandra. His wife shook her head. No ghosts around here.

Gazing all around, Drummond said, "I picked the wrong career. Even when I was alive, the lawyers had all the money. Bankers, too. Heck, even with the Great Depression hitting a lot of them hard, you better believe they were first to recover."

They stepped into a more conservative office than the others they had passed. Carpeted, dark woods, tall bookcase with legal cases bound into thick volumes that nobody needed to use since it all had been digitized long ago. A photo of Nell on the desk and two potted plants by a window that gave a view out at the city with Route 52 cutting across in the distance.

Dwayne sat and splayed his fingers on a wide blotter next to a stone paperweight. "Thank you for seeing me so late."

"It means a lot that you're taking our case," Nell said.

Sandra settled in a chair opposite him. "We haven't agreed to take the case yet. This is what we call a *courtesy visitation.* It's a chance for us to determine if there really is a case."

"There is."

"A lot of the times we get called in for all sorts of strange things that end up having very simple and normal explanations."

Nell tapped a single fingernail on the desktop. "You think he's making this up?"

"Not at all," Max said, mustering the smile he had worn all day long. "But you might be mistaken as to the cause."

Dwayne looked to his wife. "You see? I told you we shouldn't have called them."

"Something very wrong is going on," she said, "and it is beyond what any normal person can see or do anything about. We've got to try."

Max said, "We're already here, and when we last talked, you sounded quite eager to have us visit. So, let's hear what's been happening and figure it out from there."

Nell walked behind her husband and placed her hand on his shoulder. He reached up and laced his fingers with hers. An unconscious move that Max recognized from his own marriage — these two had been together a long time and built a strong connection, a true love between them.

Dwayne paused to collect his thoughts. Then: "Sorry. It's all so hard to believe. But also not hard. Not when you see what's been going on. I guess it began with the car."

Wiping at her eyes, Nell sniffled. "That damn car."

"I've had it for years. Got it as a high school graduation gift and never really needed another. It was a tank of a car. I've driven it across the country twice, up and down from Connecticut to Florida dozens of times, and even once took it into Canada. Nell always wanted me to get a new one."

"But he always says *Why fix what ain't broke?* I suppose I never really wanted him to get rid of it anyway. I mean, after all, we honeymooned in that car."

He squeezed her hand as he looked from Max to Sandra. "I'm sure you can guess what happened."

Floating toward the door, Drummond said, "I'm thinking the car died from boredom. Do we really have to listen to this?"

Max had no trouble staying focused on Dwayne. He had plenty of practice ignoring his ghost partner while others were in the room. Besides, he knew that Drummond paid close attention to every word spoken, every gesture made.

"It's likely," Sandra said, "that your car finally showed its age."

Dwayne nodded as if expecting this answer. "The first time the engine stalled, I thought the same thing. But soon it became one problem after another. The engine, the brakes, the windshield wipers, or a clunking noise that no mechanic could figure out. I eventually had to get rid of the car and buy another. But that one had the same series of unending problems."

Nell said, "Then came the house."

"Like the car, it started slow."

"The wine."

"Yeah. We got into wine for a while, and we have a little rack of about eight bottles. Good stuff. Expensive. One night we opened a bottle and it tasted awful. We tried the next and the next. All of them had gone bad. Smelled and tasted like vinegar. Then my record collection — classic LPs — they all started skipping. Our dog managed to pull my best suits off the hangers and peed all over them. Then he ran away. By that point, these bad things expanded to my work. I do contract law here, and I'm one of the best in the firm. I know that sounds arrogant, but you must understand, I've got a reputation around here for exemplary work. I'm meticulous. Terrible in the courtroom — I hated trial work — but get me at a desk with paperwork, and I'll bury the competition. It's no surprise that I was being considered for partner."

Max said, "I take it things went wrong with that, too."

"Mistakes started creeping in," Dwayne said as if this was the worst part of the entire ordeal. "Typos, at first. More than I'm known to make. Then a few papers not properly filed by the deadlines."

Nell said, "He would come home and vent about it all, and I have to admit, I thought maybe it was all cause of what'd been going on with the car and the house. Maybe he couldn't sleep enough and that caused his work to slip. Stress — that kind of thing."

"I thought it, too. But then came a big meeting. One of our top clients had flown in from Texas for an important negotiation with the State about bringing in a new factory and warehousing. North Carolina wanted those jobs, and our client wanted every concession they could wring out of the State. I had to be there. Even if I wasn't up for partner, I had to be there. It meant everything, and I'm not a moron. I set my alarm three hours early to make sure I got there."

With a huff, Drummond said, "Let me tell you what happened. He didn't make the meeting."

"You can guess what happened. I didn't make the meeting." Dwayne didn't see Max choke down a laugh. Instead, he flattened his hand on the desk and struggled to keep from letting his tears flow. Then: "The things that went on that day to block me from that meeting — it's not natural. My alarm never went off. I scuffed my good shoes. The toaster shorted with sparks, and we had to put out a small fire in the kitchen. I tried to call the office, but our phone batteries were dead. I went to send a message with my laptop, but it kept locking on the home screen. My car took ten minutes to start, and when I finally got on the road, there was an accident involving a truck carrying adult toys. They were spread all over the highway, stopping traffic in all directions, and since it was a ridiculous thing to spill, the reporters showed up to slow progress even more. By the time I got to the office, the meeting had ended and not very favorably. The client was ticked off, my firm was ticked off, and any chance of being made partner went out the window. Now, any single one of those things happening, even a few of them, would have been bad luck. Sure. But all of them?"

Sandra crossed her legs and leaned over her knees. Years of marriage to this lady told Max everything — she didn't buy the story. In a placating voice, she said, "A lot of things in this world seem improbable but turn out to have very ordinary, mundane explanations."

With a sharp turn, Nell said, "How could you possibly explain this?"

"Let's start with the obvious — do you have any enemies?"

"He's a lawyer. What do you think?"

Patting her hand, Dwayne said, "I don't practice criminal law. When a client gets angry with me, they take their business elsewhere. Simple as that. Worst thing they might do is try to sue the firm."

Drummond slipped next to Max. "Would you please be direct with the guy? If I lose my date, I'm going to hover over your bed and sing drinking songs all night long."

Unable to respond, Max raised a questioning eyebrow.

"Not that date. There's a waitress from 1982 who likes me, and I've learned that in the Other, it's a good idea to have a backup. Before you give me another look, you should believe me that every ghost in the Other plays the same game. I'm sure both ladies have their own backups, and I don't want to start being second choice. What? We've got a lot of time to pass."

Shifting in the chair, Max said, "Your clients that aren't enemies but dislike you — or anybody else that would have a grudge against you — any of them involved in witchcraft?"

Dwayne shook his head. Didn't pause. Didn't cock an eyebrow.

"Have you bought an old book or an antique recently? Bought it sometime near when this string of bad luck became most notable?"

Nell shook her head.

"What about strange symbols?" Sandra stood and meandered around the office. Though she looked like she was moving in order to think through the problem, Max knew she hunted for a witch mark or a casting candle or any other evidence of witchcraft.

Dwayne said, "Nothing like that. It's just been one catastrophe after another. But I swear, there's no reason for any of it. It doesn't make any sense."

"Does the name Cecily Hull mean anything to you? Is she one of your clients, perhaps?"

"Never heard of her? Nell?"

"No." Nell clutched her husband's shoulders like a shield. "Please, help us."

Sandra stopped in front of the desk and inspected the picture of Nell. "I don't know if this is a case for us. There's nothing that points to the unnatural." Placing it back, she picked up the stone paperweight.

As if receiving an electric shock, Sandra flung backwards. She let out a short screech and tumbled to the floor, her muscles firing off uncontrolled. Max rushed to her side while Drummond flew overhead.

"What's happening to her?" Nell said, her eyes wide. "Should I call an ambulance?"

"No," Max said, as he helped Sandra sit up. "She's okay, I think."

"Still no ghosts," Drummond said. "But when she touched that thing, there was a heckuva light show for me."

Nell nudged her husband. "Get her some water."

With a stunned expression, Dwayne rushed out of the room. Max put a hand under Sandra's head and leaned in close. "Are you okay?"

She nodded. Then shook her head. "I don't know."

"Don't know what?" Dwayne said, entering with a coffee mug of water.

Nell took the mug and handed it to Sandra. "Don't pester her. They're supposed to ask the questions. Right?"

Rubbing her hands, Sandra stared at the paperweight on the floor. "Fine. I'll ask you one. Where did you get that?"

Max reached for the stone with caution as if it were a piping hot pan on a stove. But he felt nothing radiating off it. With one finger, he poked it — still nothing. He picked up the paperweight and rolled it in his hands. No symbols, no markings, and no pain.

"Mr. and Mrs. Fincher," Sandra said with more force. "That stone — where did it come from?"

Dwayne shared a shocked look with his wife. "It was a gift."

"That's right," Nell said, all her smarmy doubt trembling. "From Roy Malone."

"We went to college together, roommates, and he was best man at our wedding. Roy's my best friend."

Struggling to her feet, unable to stand straight, Sandra held Max's arm tight. "We'll take the case."

Chapter 4

SANDRA SLEPT POORLY THAT NIGHT. Touching that stone had left her weak. Over the hours since, Max could tell she felt bruised and sluggish. He listened to her shifting and groaning, unable to find a comfortable position. Twice she rose to use the bathroom and needed his help getting there without falling.

The following morning, Max put together breakfast and let Sandra sleep in. She woke anyway, said she felt a little better, but after struggling to get out of bed, she agreed to rest. Thankfully, they had no appointments and didn't expect any calls, but that could always change. If any came, Max would turn them away. They had a real case to work on now. At least, it seemed like a real case.

Driving home after their meeting with the Finchers, while Max fretted over Sandra's condition, Drummond had devised a plan to figure out the truth.

"Simple enough," he said. "We follow them."

"That's it?" Max said.

"With Brenda and Osorio as part of the team now, our options have improved. Might as well start using them. As a cop, Osorio will know how to tail somebody throughout the day. We'll put him on Dwayne since that's the most important. Brenda should follow Nell Fincher. And I think J should go after Roy Malone."

"You want one of my boys to follow the guy responsible for the magic stone?"

"It ain't ideal, but we need somebody who can perceive the paranormal and Sandra's not looking too well right now. I've got to go into the Other and ask around, hit up my contacts, see if there's any information I can find. That'll take me longer than usual. Things have gotten a bit cold towards me lately when I start poking around on a case. Apparently, the ghosts in the Other are less inclined to help a detective when he keeps getting them involved with witches. That leaves J."

"What about me?"

"You don't see everything. Just me. Besides, we need you to dig into the research."

But after breakfast, after Osorio and Brenda's enthusiastic acceptance of their assignments, Drummond's plan hit a snag. J couldn't do the job. He had joined an SAT study group, and Max refused to encourage the boy — no, the young man — to skip his education. Max refused to even entertain the thought of Sandra filling in. Not after such a sleep deprived night and her weakened state. He would have to do it himself.

Except then PB volunteered.

"I don't know," PB said with a shrug, "I guess I should see what you all are really doing. And when my brother needs help, I'm there to help. Anything for him."

"Glad to hear it," Max said, beaming a bit of pride. He and Sandra had bought a 2010 Mazda hatchback to give PB some freedom. It was good that the young man wanted to give back a little.

A slight change in assignments — Max put PB on Nell Fincher so that Brenda could follow Roy Malone. She didn't have the gifts J and Sandra shared, but she knew enough witchcraft to notice the signs. If Roy was behind all this, Brenda should be able to pick up on it.

With the team in place, Max settled into his makeshift office — the alcove off the kitchen — and tried to enjoy researching in quiet. He powered up his laptop, got out his notebook, and rolled his neck loose. Comfortable.

He stared at the screen, not sure where to begin. His eyes drifted towards his phone. If Sandra needed anything, they had agreed that she would text him rather than yell. She was only a few rooms over, but he didn't want her exerting unnecessary effort. No texts on his phone. Perhaps he should go check on her, just in case. But he pushed the thought out of his mind and focused on the computer screen.

He needed four minutes longer before he managed to start in earnest — a trip to the bathroom, a glass of water, and pressing his ear against the bedroom door in case Sandra had fallen and weakly cried out for him. When he finally got to work, however, the act of research consumed him. It always did. Even when, like this time, he had so little to go on.

He began with some broad searches for stolen stones. Most of the results concerned quests in video games like *Pokémon* and *The Witcher*. There were a few articles about stones swiped from archeological digs and a few diamond thefts, but nothing anywhere near North Carolina nor anything connected to a curse.

After numerous variations on the terms, he changed his approach slightly and started investigating witch stones. These results tended to link to sites selling crystals or explaining the wonders of crystal therapy. Even a few of the most reliable witch sites he knew had little to offer beyond the use of stones in various casting techniques.

Max still prepared for the possibility that Osorio and the rest of the team would return with news that Dwayne Fincher's story didn't hold up. He was conning them for some reason — hoping to cash in on debunking a television fraud, perhaps — and no real case existed. Except Max couldn't deny that something had harmed Sandra. Even if Dwayne had ulterior motives, the weird nature of that stone could not be denied. All of which meant that Max needed to perform the most basic steps he would with any client.

He started searching into Dwayne Fincher's life. If the man was not what he seemed, Max would find out. If he was legit, Max would find that out, too. Perhaps most importantly, assuming the case was real, understanding Dwayne could lead them to understanding why somebody wanted to curse him and who that somebody might be.

Unlike delving into witches and spells, Max found it easy to uncover a normal person's life. Most people put too much personal information on social media, and much of the rest could be discovered with a handful of legal but invasive websites. In short order, he had a strong fix on Dwayne Fincher.

The man had been born in Mason City, Iowa to a dentist father and dental hygienist mother. A good student with enough extra curriculars to impress most colleges but not so much as to run the kid ragged and never let him enjoy his youth. Undergrad at Iowa State. No major run-ins with the police, though his name did appear amongst a group of partiers for a disorderly complaint during pledge week — no charges filed. No frat, either. Wasn't clear if they didn't want him or if he turned down any offers that came. After graduation, he went on to Loyola School of Law in Chicago. Based on his grades, he kept his nose in the books.

"Pretty uneventful life, huh?" Max said to the screen.

Sifting through yearbooks and social media photos, Max rarely came across evidence that Dwayne dated anybody. There was one picture from a friend's wedding in which Dwayne had his arm around a beautiful red-headed woman. He looked quite drunk. She looked quite unhappy.

Fresh out of law school, he worked as an ADA for Chicago handling the simplest of cases. He successfully prosecuted five convenience store robberies but managed to get most defendants to plead out long before he had to face a jury. He left for a corporate job less than two years in.

"You weren't kidding. You really hated trial work."

The details of Dwayne meeting Nell proved easiest of all to find. Years ago, Nell got into recipe blogging. She would start each dish with a picture of the food, a quick description of what would be entailed in making it, and then a long, detailed story about why she wanted to make it before finally providing the actual recipe. Thousands of words telling the world about how each meal connected to the love of her life — Dwayne Fincher.

According to the blog, Dwayne had bounced around several places before landing a job with a firm in Charlotte, North Carolina that handled a lot of banking deals and related contracts. Nell worked as a teller in one of his client's banks. She wrote:

> *When he walked in, my heart just froze. I couldn't breathe. I never really took for gospel the idea of love at first sight, but let me tell you, dear readers, this man proved it to me. I'm not a bold girl, yet I could hear the church bells already, and they were fading as he walked toward the exit. Now, I've never been the daring type when it came to men, but I hurried over to him and handed him a slip of paper with my number. Wouldn't you know it, he called me.*
>
> *For our first date, I wanted to wow him so that he knew we were meant to be. That's why I told him we wouldn't be going out for dinner or anything typical like that. I would make him a meal he would never forget. After all, the way to man's heart is through his stomach, right? And that's why I made him the exact recipe below.*
>
> *I'm sure you all want the dirty details, and maybe someday I'll share more, but I will say this much. The meal was a success, and so was the dessert. If you need any proof, look no further than the wedding ring on my finger.*
>
> *Before I get to the recipe, let's talk about the importance of sourcing each ingredient.*

Max imagined that for Dwayne, meeting Nell had been like stepping into a hurricane. The man had so little experience with dating that Nell's strong approach must have taken his heart from that first meal. If he had been a virgin — something Max thought very possible — then all reasonable sense went out the window once they slept together. Whatever the *dirty details*, their publicly filed wedding certificate put the official start to the marriage seven months after that first date.

From that point on, Dwayne and Nell acted like a power couple. They steadily rose through the ranks of North Carolina society, and as their popularity and influence grew, so did their prospects. The firm opened a branch in Winston-Salem and promoted Dwayne to head up the contracts division there.

He had not been bragging when he said that he was among the best. His reputation brought in bigger clients and being made partner was a foregone conclusion. A few years there and he would have had no trouble taking a stab at Governor or Congressman. Heck, he might have wanted to try for Senator.

Max peeked at his phone — no texts from Sandra. He sat back and tapped his chin. Dwayne's story played out normally. Quite successful, but nowhere did Max spot any reference that might have suggested witchcraft or anything unusual. If Dwayne had called upon forces other than disciplined studying and hard work, he had done an incredible job of hiding the evidence. No, there wasn't anything off here. Dwayne had earned his accolades.

As for enemies — that part Dwayne had oversold. He had claimed to have plenty from being a lawyer, but Max couldn't find a single complaint. No malpractice charges. No sudden vacations or unexplained absences that would have been used to cover up a bad situation. Nothing to hint at an overly dissatisfied client. Not until the curse had kicked in, anyway.

He saved his notes in a new file for the Fincher case and thought more about the curse. Sandra had a small but growing set of rare and valuable books on witchcraft. All witches built their own personal library of tomes, after all. Perhaps she would have something helpful.

But after spending twenty minutes searching through her books, he concluded that if the answer could be found there, he lacked the skills. It wasn't simply a question of research ability. Rather, most authentic witch texts, especially ones outlining the casting of spells, were written in codes, in ancient languages, and sometimes, in coded ancient languages.

Not wanting to disturb her rest, Max waited another hour until he heard his wife rumbling around their bedroom. When he approached her, he felt both hopeful and disheartened. She seemed better, certainly recovering, but she had not bounced back completely. Other times when Sandra took a blow of magic energy, she reacted as if struck hard with a fist. It hurt, sometimes for days, but she always pushed on without complaint. The fact that she willingly agreed to bedrest, that she made little effort to force her way into the case, troubled Max. Whatever they were dealing with was far more dangerous than they normally faced.

After explaining what he needed, Sandra groaned and sat up in bed. He motioned to gather her books, but she waved him off.

"There's nothing in those that'll help," she said. "The only curses I've ever read about deal with binding ghosts or locking them to our reality in some way. Then you use that energy to do whatever you're trying to do. There are countless variations, but the thing about witchcraft is that at the core of it, all we're really doing is shifting natural energies around. Taking them from one source and using them in a different way. But that paperweight I touched — I never once saw anything to suggest it had magic at all. If I had, I wouldn't have picked it up. Or I would've been more cautious."

Max sat on the corner of the bed. "Drummond said there were no ghosts around that office."

"Even if the energy came from a ghost miles away, there would have been a visible line of energy connecting them. When we first started all this years ago, I had never seen such a line, but that's because I didn't know what to look for. I'm getting better at it. You sort of have to *feel* its existence before you can see it. But even if I missed it, Drummond would have caught it right away."

"Then maybe this really is all a hoax."

"I didn't get zapped by a hoax."

"No, but that's a good word for it. Maybe Dwayne rigged that paperweight with some kind of electric shock."

"You don't believe that."

Max shrugged. "What are we dealing with then?"

"I'm not sure." She reached out her hand and waited until Max slid close enough to touch. "But if there's an answer in any book, I know where to find it."

A lump formed in his chest. "You can't go there. Not in your condition."

"I agree. That's why you'll have to go."

He swallowed that lump down into his gut. "Really? You want

me to go to that witch library?"

"Don't call it —"

"I know. *Don't call it a library.* Fine. Haven House. You want me to go to Haven House and deal with those witches who would love to boil me alive and eat me to the bone."

"They're not that bad."

"Those are the oldest, old-school witches that I've ever met."

Sandra kissed Max's hand. "They're also the ones who will be able to tell us about what we're facing. Don't worry. I'll call ahead and let them know you're visiting for me."

"If you can call ahead, why not just ask them on the phone? Save me the trouble of going out there and playing mind games."

"Because, as you pointed out, they're old school. They won't discuss details of witchcraft on the phone. Or the internet or text message or anything like that. All knowledge is passed either directly from witch to witch or through their closely guarded books. That's it. Now quit complaining. This is what has to be done, and if you won't go, then I'll have to do it."

Standing with his arms up, he said, "Fine, fine. You win. I'll go. I don't like it — in fact, I hate it — but I'll go."

"Relax, honey. You know how to behave around witches. There's nothing to worry about." Her face tightened. Then: "But bring Drummond with you. Just in case."

Max sighed. "Of course."

Chapter 5

MAX SAT IN HIS CAR after the winding drive to Haven House. He had felt the dread rise with each mile towards Lexington, off the main strip onto a row of houses, to the end where the woods covered over all, through a narrow drive beyond the last home, onto a winding dirt road, until finally reaching the centuries old stone building. Staring at the house, he swore it stared back.

It had been kept in immaculate condition and modernized along with the world. The polished wood porch and dark wood door with stained glass inlays could have been built yesterday, while the roof boasted solar panels, and the front lock required a security code. Max had no doubt that several complicated spells protected the old building, too. A cozy place ready to destroy any threat that came its way.

"You going to keep watching her from afar or you going to ask her out?" Drummond said, hovering over the passenger seat.

"I didn't come all this way just to turn around." But part of Max liked that idea. Even encouraged that very thing.

"You'll be fine. Those witches love Sandra. They treat her like a daughter they never had."

"Yeah, but I'm not Sandra."

"You're her husband."

"Somehow I think that only makes it worse."

Drummond snickered. "Maybe so. But you still have to go in there and do your job. Might as well get to it."

"Easy for you to say when you'll be out here the whole time."

"It's not my fault they have ghost wards around the entire place. But I promise you that I will be here. I won't leave until you do."

"Watch what you promise. If I die here, you'll be stuck

forever."

"First, my verbal promise is not a legally binding contract, and it's certainly not like a spell. I won't actually be stuck here. Second, if you die at Haven House, there is no possible way they'd let you move on. You'd be a ghost, and we'd be able to float out of here together."

Max frowned. "Is any of this supposed to make me feel better?"

"Just get going." Drummond pulled his Fedora over his eyes and leaned back in the air.

The ghost never truly slept, but the action made the message clear. The conversation was over. Time to work.

Leaving the car and approaching the porch, Max's legs wobbled. He had met these witches once before, and that experience had left him wishing never to enter this place again. Though they had not outright attacked him — they wouldn't when Sandra was there, too — he witnessed enough to warn him away. They were older than any person should have been, and they housed books that went beyond simply offering information. One book had tried to seduce him like a Siren, lead him into cracking his mind upon the rocks of mystical insanity. At least, that was what he thought had happened. No telling for certain. But he could not deny the sense of threat permeating the place from wood to stone to glass to the very nails that locked it all together.

He walked up to the front door and raised his fist to knock. Sandra had refused to give him the door code. She said doing so would break the confidence she had established with the witches. Besides, if he used the code and walked right in, they would be startled and might react poorly. Max agreed with that much. He did not want to find out what those witches would consider *reacting poorly.*

None of that matter, though. Before he could bang his fist against the door, it opened. An elderly woman with dark skin and white hair answered — Madame Novak. Thick glasses rested on her crooked nose, and she pointed a boney finger at him.

"Max Porter," she said, her voice as crinkled as her skin. "I knew we'd be seeing you again."

"Sandra did call ahead, didn't she?"

"Oh, yes, she did. But I meant from before." Stepping aside, she gestured into the house. "Come, come. Let's see if we can help you out."

Max had to admit that if the place had not been a sanctuary for witch knowledge, if it had simply been a forgotten library, he would have loved it. Converted from an old farmhouse, the layout had gone unaltered for over a hundred years. Narrow staircases, uneven doorways, and odd-sized rooms suggested a smaller home that had been added onto over the decades as the farming family aged, married, and multiplied. But where once the hallways led to bedrooms, living rooms, playrooms, and more bedrooms, they now contained a labyrinth of endless bookshelves stuffed with various dusty tomes, handmade grimoires, and brittle treatises.

"As I understand the matter," Madame Novak said, leading Max at a gentle but steady pace through the confusing array of stacks, "you and our dear Sandra have had a nasty experience with a cursed stone."

"That's right. But we haven't found evidence that connects the stone to a ghost or a specific witch or anything."

"It's a good thing you came to us. Madame Fein and Madame Weir and, of course, myself — why, we are some of the most knowledgeable witches still alive. There was a time, long ago, mind you, that I couldn't make such a boast. But other witches have grown too old to stay young and passed away. Moved on. But the three of us, well, here we are, still kicking around, as they say."

That was an understatement. Max had seen the photographs of these three witches with their full coven — some from the 1950s and a few from the 1970s. But as he followed Madame Novak through another series of twisting corridors, he noticed other photographs framed on the walls. One caused him to stop. It showed the three witches in front of a less modern version of Haven House. The year 1912 clearly marked in the corner.

"Oh yes, that's a good memory," Madame Novak said, the

scent of old newspaper wafting off her. "The day we first came here. Not to work, of course, we were too young, too novice, but it was our first visit. Back then, the coven did not let its baby sisters go to Haven House often. Too dangerous."

Max could feel her watching him, feel her waiting for him to ask the question. But he stayed quiet. He had seen magic used to lengthen a man's life well beyond the hundred and twenty or so years this photo made her. Best not to engage on any topic beyond his main purpose for being there.

"Come, come," she said, less pleasant, more grumble.

At the end of another aisle loaded with books on either side, they stopped in front of an old woman with kind eyes and a grandmotherly smile. Madame Fein. Max remembered how this little witch — maybe reaching five feet on a good day when she could straighten her bent back — played up her sweetness and gentleness. But the unbalanced pile of gray atop her head and the waddling shuffle she added to her walk would not fool him. She was a witch. He liked her more than most witches, but he still kept his guard up.

She patted his arm. "Good to see you again. Madame Fein is always happy for return customers."

Madame Novak bent closer to Madame Fein's ear. "No, dear. This is Max Porter."

"Oh?"

"Sandra's husband. Remember? She called about the stone that's cursed."

"Yes, yes. Of course. Madame Fein doesn't forget. You leave him with me. I'll make sure he gets what he should."

The witches shared a look that sent ice down Max's spine. The thought that he should run out of that house and never come back sounded like the epitome of wisdom right then. But Sandra counted on him and not simply for the case. She had to know what they dealt with to protect herself from being harmed again. Forcing a deep breath, he gave a slight bow to Madame Novak as she left him with Madame Fein.

"Come along now. Madame Fein has all the answers and most of the questions, too."

She chuckled as she led Max to a narrow door. This opened to a cold staircase leading downward. A claustrophobe's nightmare — the stone walls and ceiling barely gave him enough room to move. He hesitated, wondering if this abyss stared back at him with the same apprehension.

"Ho ho, not so brave a man as Sandra boasts. Afraid of a little dark." She reached over and flicked a switch. Bare, dusty bulbs lined the ceiling all the way to the end of the stairs. An oddly long distance — had to be more than one floor's worth of steps.

He climbed down, staying several stairs behind Madame Fein. Though his nerves eased under the lights, he could still hear his pulse hammering in his ear. He had experienced strange, seemingly impossible places before. One witch had lived in an underground apartment beneath a double-wide in a poor section of Lexington. And Madame Ti, the head witch working for Cecily Hull, had an entire layer beneath the Winston-Salem sewers. Despite having been to those places and others equally bizarre, Max felt each step downward like an electric jolt straight through his foot, up his leg, and into his gut — an instinctual warning to get away from here. Yet he had one passing thought of Sandra, and the will to go down another stair emerged.

At the bottom of the stairs, where their footsteps sounded muted — buried — they walked a few paces around a curve that ended with a metal door on the right. Madame Fein tapped a keycode into a wall-mounted pad, and a loud clank followed. Max startled.

"Just inside here," she said. "Our little private study."

They entered a wide circular room with a low ceiling and sunken floor in the middle. The old stone walls looked like Parisian catacombs, and Max wondered if any deeper into these tunnels the stones would have become skulls. Along the curved edges of the room, three dark wood desks had been set up, each with books and papers, reading lamps and padded chairs — a beautiful rolltop from Drummond's time, a converted hutch that had been decorated with fingerpainted handprints on the sides, and a rustic slab of wood like a facsimile of a desk that had not quite succeeded.

As Madame Fein tottered toward the rolltop desk, her footsteps echoing on the stone floor, Max looked closer at the sunken section. About the size of a basketball half-court and made of highly-polished wood, someone had gone to great artistic lengths to create a permanent casting circle worthy of these powerful and respected witches. But what would they need such a large circle for? Even as the thought popped in his mind, Max decided he never wanted to find out.

To the left, another metal door. A marble placard inlaid with the letter *W* had been mounted above. On the right, the same but with the letter *E*. Max checked above the door he had come through, and no surprise, he saw the letter *S*. Across the room, on the north end marked with an *N*, there was no door. Rather, an enormous fireplace dominated that space, and set upon the glowing red embers, he saw an object that dropped his jaw — a cauldron. An actual cauldron. Straight out of fairy tales and nightmares, black cast iron, large enough to boil a grown man alive.

"Wait here and Madame Fein will return." The old woman headed for the eastern door. She paused and turned her grandmother smile on him. "Be a good boy and don't touch anything. A witch's study is not the place to become curious."

When she left, she closed the door and the loud clank of a lock engaged. Max jumped but kept his mouth from uttering a shocked cry. Several wooden benches lined the walls, and he dropped to one. His breathing tightened. He had placed his head in the lion's jaws and sat there waiting for the beast to chomp down.

"Stop acting paranoid," he said, his voice louder in the open space than he intended. Of course, being paranoid did not mean they weren't out to get him. But though he had no faith in these witches, he trusted Sandra infinitely. That alone kept him from bolting.

He surveyed the room, imagining all the spells cast in that wooden circle. Decades of spells. They coated the air like a unique scent. Probably soaked into the walls. He would have remained on that bench, nervously waiting, frantically thinking about horrible spells and the twisted minds that created them, but he heard bubbling and his eyes darted right to that cauldron.

"No, Max. You don't want to know."

But even the sound of his voice betrayed the lie. The desire to know, to have answers, had served him well, had propelled him in all his research. The desire to know gave him purpose and prospects. The desire to know fueled him and the Porter Agency.

Careful to avoid touching the casting circle, Max stayed on the outer-stone ring. He scurried toward the cauldron, noting the lack of odor. Thank goodness. He would have hated to smell something cooking, something that made his mouth water, and then learn it was a horrid concoction of … well, he didn't want to think about that.

Steam rose from the boiling liquid and up a chimney. The heat from the cauldron and the low, glowing red fire beneath pumped out in waves. Max approached as if facing off a cornered animal. He wanted to be ready for anything. But *anything* could really mean *anything* in this case, and how could he be ready for that?

As he moved close enough to peer over the cauldron's lip, as he saw the water bubbling in a vigorous simmer, he clenched his teeth and tightened his fists. Bones. Large bones bounced into view before submerging again. Human bones? Possibly. Or a bear. Or a wolf. He couldn't picture any of the three old ladies taking down such large, aggressive animals, and he didn't want to picture them digging up a grave. But he could see the latter as clear as an illustration in an old horror novel by Poe or Lovecraft. A graveside image with one witch standing half in the ground and shoveling while the other two lick their lips and rub their hands under a cloudy moon.

"You again," a voice like grinding rocks said as thudding steps entered from the western doorway. Madame Weir shambled toward her desk, mumbling to herself, never looking right at Max. She wore all black that matched the dark shadows hiding her missing eye. The other, a pale gray ball, glowered wherever she gazed. "You don't belong here."

"I'm sorry," he said, speaking fast and shaky. "I mean no

disrespect. Your sister, Madame Fein, she brought me here."

"My room," Madame Weir said, still working her way to her desk, still not looking directly at Max.

"Again, I'm sincerely sorry to cause you any concerns. Once Madame Fein returns, she can show me out of here, and I won't bother you again."

"Mine," she said, raising her hand while pinching her fingers.

She repeated a phrase from an ancient or dead language, the words tumbling faster as her clawed hand pulsed to the rhythm. The air around them tingled. Or perhaps Max merely felt his own fear stinging his skin. Either way, he understood the reason why — Madame Weir was casting a curse.

Chapter 6

MAX STAGGERED BACK AGAINST THE STONE WALL. Whatever curse she planned to put on him, he refused to stick around for it. That was lesson number one when dealing with witches — don't hang around while they cast a curse. Probably lessons two, three, four, and five, now that he thought about it.

The east and west doors were closest, but he had no idea where they led. Not a good idea to get lost in the witch's own lair when trying to avoid that very witch. But in order to reach the south door which led upstairs and out of the house, Max would have to walk right by Madame Weir or race around the room counter-clockwise. To pass her meant getting closer to her. To walk around her meant giving her more time to curse him.

A third alternative popped in his mind — one that must have come from spending too much time with Drummond. He could punch her. A quick tap to the head that would daze for several minutes. At least enough to get back to the main floor and possibly reach the car. Even if he didn't make it that far, she would have to start her curse all over again which meant he'd have bought even more time.

Of course, that came with a major downside. Pissing off a witch. Then again, she looked mighty pissed off already.

"Ho ho," Madame Fein said, returning through the eastern door. "What trouble have you gotten yourself into?"

She carried a book in one arm, its tattered cover flopping against her side, and worked her way to the nearest desk. Madame Weir paused, never looking anywhere but straight ahead yet clearly listening to the arrival of her sister.

"I didn't do anything," Max said. "I've just been waiting here like you said."

"If that were true, you would still be where Madame Fein left you. But you are not at Madame Fein's desk, you are standing near the fireplace."

"Is that why Madame Weir is upset? I swear I didn't touch anything."

Madame Fein shuffled over to her sister and placed a hand on her shoulder. "It's okay. You go on, now. Madame Fein will handle this man."

"My room," the gravel-voiced witch said.

"Mine, too, don't forget. And right now, he is our guest."

Madame Weir cocked her head toward Madame Fein. "Guest?"

"Sandra's husband. You remember Sandra?"

"I like Sandra."

"We all do."

With a grunt, Madame Weir turned away, walking back through the door she had arrived. Max let out a held breath, and his goose-pimpled skin eased. Until Madame Fein patted the book she had brought and said, "The answers you seek are all right here. So, what does Madame Fein get in return?"

Max's stomach dropped. He should have expected this. Witches never do anything for free.

He fought back the urge to spit on the floor or flip the bird or even shake a fist. Negotiating with a witch would only lead to trouble, but if it had to happen, it started with this first reaction. Since Haven House had what he needed for the case and for Sandra, it clearly had to happen. Swallowing down all his frustration, he opted for a simple nod as if there could be no other way for them to proceed. Madame Fein watched him like a wolf sizing up her next meal. His skin prickled once more. At this rate, his skin should stay prickled permanently.

As this witch moved toward her desk, breathing hard with each step, Max gave serious consideration to leaving empty-handed. Sandra knew other witches. Surely there would be at least one out in the world more like her — a witch seeking to be good. Or, at least, a more helpful witch.

Except none were like Sandra. That's what made her special

to the witch community.

Max could go to Cecily Hull or Madame Ti, but that brought with it a host of other troubles, none that were any better than dealing with these witches and several that were worse. Besides, other than Sandra, all witches he could approach would want to strike a deal for the information, and that deal would be ugly. At least the Haven House sisters cared about Sandra, a fact that inclined them to being somewhat fair with him — maybe not Madame Weir, but the other two for certain.

Sandra. Perhaps he could use their affection for her.

"I'm here on behalf of my wife. She's the victim of this cursed stone and in no shape to travel all this way. That's the only reason I came. Sandra needs your help."

"And you think that should exempt you from paying? What kind of witch would Madame Fein be if anybody could be allowed to get magic for free? Our kind has spent centuries trading on the one thing we have that the rest of you want. If not for such deals, we'd never have survived. No, no. Madame Fein will tell all you need to know in exchange for a promise to help us here at Haven House on another occasion."

Max forced down the scoff that threatened to emerge. "There is so much wrong with your wording. I can't accept that."

"What did Madame Fein say wrong?"

"First, you said you'd tell me all I *need* to know. That's not good enough. You will have to agree to tell me everything, not just what you want to share or what you think I need to hear. Also, I won't promise anything so vague and undefined as to help you with something at some point. No. That's no good."

"But your wife —"

"My wife is a smart and kind woman. She'll understand if I can't make a deal, and she'll be angry with you, not me."

Madame Fein stabbed a bent finger at him. "You're not so stupid. Madame Fein will give you a better offer."

"A fair deal is all I ask."

She thought for a moment. "Madame Fein will answer all about Sandra's condition, and for that, you will bring a clip of hair from the culprit. There you go. Specific and clear. No vague words. Deal?"

"I appreciate your efforts." Max hated to point out the big flaw, but he figured he best not ruin the Porter's relationship with the Haven House witches by agreeing to something he couldn't deliver — not if he wanted Sandra to ever speak to him again. "Forgive me, but the only problem I see is that I can't get this hair for you until I know who the culprit is, and I can't do that until I have the information I came here for."

"Madame Fein trusts you to honor your deal even after our talk. When your case is over, you will bring Madame Fein what she asks for. Or you will face serious consequences."

Max went over the wording of the deal in his head. Then he went over it again. Then once more. But each time, he could not parse out any trick. Unless he wanted to turn the deal into an exercise in paying lawyers to add in as many slippery terms as possible, he thought his best course would be agreeing, learning all he could, acquiring the small bit of hair, and putting to rest everything connected to this case.

Despite his reasoned approach, he still felt a sense of defeat when he nodded, a wriggling worm of doubt that he may have made a mistake. The knowing grin that rose upon Madame Fein's lips guaranteed he had lost at the game they had played. The mistake became glaring — he simply didn't know all the rules.

Before he could despair, she opened the rolltop desk and set the book in her arms down. With a relieved sigh, she scooted onto the chair, swiveled to face him, and indicated the nearest bench with a tilt of her head. She waited.

Well, he had made the deal. Might as well get the information he came for. The rest of it he would handle later. He trudged to the bench hoping what he would hear did not make his efforts worthless, and he wondered how many people felt buyer's remorse instantly after making a witch deal.

Madame Fein folded her hands in her lap as if about to educate her grandson on how to make the best chocolate chip cookies. "Now, then, young man, the first thing you must understand is that you and Sandra are not confronted by a curse but rather a hex."

"I didn't realize there was a difference."

"Ho ho, there very much is. To start with, you must understand that the word *curse* is used carelessly all the time. Anything bad that happens around an object and people will say it's cursed. But in the witch world, specific words hold specific meanings."

"Like the way it has to be connected to a ghost or a witch?"

"Yes. But only for some curses. There are countless ways for a curse to exist, and that is important. Your wife is no amateur anymore. She's even moved beyond a novice, but she still has much to learn. The realm of curses is one of the widest and deepest of witchcraft subjects. Some witches have spent more than one lifetime trying to find the bottom. Yet it seems there are always more ways to create a curse."

"Gee, I'm so surprised."

She snorted. "Madame Fein always likes good sarcasm."

"Glad to be appreciated. So, if I got this, Sandra was hit by a hex."

"Not quite. In the most basic sense, a hex is performed by an amateur while a curse requires the true skill of a seasoned witch. But it is far more than that. A curse, when properly enacted, will harm the target in some specific way. A witch would not curse a man with simple bad luck. Such a curse would fail to work. A real curse has specific purpose. To make the man suffer to always lose the flip of a coin, for example. To always fumble a lie. Or even to always betray those he loves. The more specific, the more effective a curse will be."

"I take it that a hex is none of that."

"Hexes are primitive. Some religions in the world honed a stronger version by creating hex bags or mojo bags."

"I thought mojo was good."

"Mojo is merely a word for magic. It can be good or bad. Like a casting circle, a hex bag helps focus the spell. That's important because hexes are easier to cast but harder to control. They tend to be vague. That's one of many reasons you must always use a curse when dealing with ghosts and not a hex. A hexed ghost might cause you more harm than you cause it. No telling when a simple word like *other* has so many extra meanings to a ghost."

Max wanted to take notes so he didn't miss any details but knew enough witch etiquette to stay still. He would have to rely on his memory for now. "So, this stone paperweight was hexed, not cursed, to give Dwayne Fincher bad luck. But because a hex is less controllable, the bad luck has spread beyond a few inconveniences in his life. Is that about right?"

"There is more."

"There always is."

"The deal was to tell you all, not just what Madame Fein knew you would need."

Raising both hands, Max said, "My apology. Please continue."

"A typical hex for bad luck would cause one or two instances before the energy within it dissipated. But from what you have said, this hex has gone on for weeks and when it has jumped from the car to the house to the office, it appears to have gained strength. It even struck out at dear Sandra when she was not a target."

Max's face pinched as he thought through each new piece of information. "That's not supposed to happen with a hex. You said it's a weak, amateur spell. Shouldn't it have fallen apart?"

"Madame Fein thinks you are getting smarter. Now, for the stone to hold the kind of energy it does, energy that has started to grow with usage, and for it to be unconnected to a ghost or any visible signs of a witch, suggests that it probably has been naturally cursed at some point in the past."

"Do I want to know what *naturally cursed* means?" Before he could rephrase the question, he froze with his mouth half-open. Then: "Hold on. How did you know about there not being anything attached to this stone?"

"Sandra, of course. She told us what you would want to know so that we could have it ready for you when you arrived."

Max fumed but bit back all the things he wanted to blurt out. Instead, in a clamped tone, he said, "All of this walking me around, bringing me down here, having your sister threaten to curse me — all of this was to get a deal out of me when you already had agreed with Sandra to give me the information. Is that right?"

Her grandmotherly eyes flashed the evil lurking within. Adding a saccharine music to her words, she said, "Madame Fein is a witch, after all."

He never wanted to deck an old lady more than at that moment. No matter how wrong, a swift punch to her jaw would have felt wonderful. The consequences would have been horrible, not the least of which would be not getting all they needed to help Sandra. So, Max pushed down his anger and offered a pleasant nod. "Please, tell me about natural curses."

"Yes, now." She opened the book she had brought with her, its pages crackling as she turned them with great care, and read for a short time. It felt long, though. Long and slow and tortuous. Max simmered at the point of interrupting her, of demanding that she stop with this game, but held back. She probably wanted that reaction, probably could use it against him in some witchy way that he had yet to experience. As if sensing she had reached the height of his discomfort, she said, "Just reviewing. Madame Fein wants to make sure all she says is correct."

The satisfied smirk on her face burned into his chest. Once more, he had to fight the urge to lash out. While he succeeded, he also revised his impression of this woman — he no longer liked her.

"Natural curses are caused by a ghost." She closed the book.

"But there's no —"

"Let Madame Fein speak," she said, raising her hand. "Ghosts are formed in many ways, but the most natural way is through tragedy. A mother that dies during childbirth is a clear example. Here she is expecting a great and joyful moment, then poof — it's all over. Confused, angry, mournful — she may find it difficult, maybe impossible to move on. So, she stays, and a ghost is formed. This much makes sense to you?"

"Yeah, I got it."

"Ho ho, don't get snippy when you're so close to all the answers. But now that Madame Fein thinks on it, you should consider how you feel against what you want. For that is similar to what happens with a natural curse. You see, some tragic deaths that should have resulted in a ghost — well, they don't. The soul moves on but the anger, the sorrowful energy remains behind. This is rare. When it does occur, it is usually connected to children or the truly innocent souls. Those types that would not fully comprehend such a sudden death. It can also occur to a less pure adult so filled with rage that despite moving on, that inner-fire continues to burn. Now, Madame Fein feels certain that you understand from your dear wife that witchcraft is all about energies. In all cases of life, energy seeks out a balance with the world, a place to fit in properly. You see?"

"I think so. Normally, this energy would be part of the ghost." Max glanced at the book, wishing he could study its yellow-brown pages but knowing the words would be coded gibberish to him.

"Yes, but because the soul has moved on, there is no ghost. This energy must attach to something, so it locks to the first available thing it can find."

"The stone."

"In this case, it seems so."

"But doesn't energy usually fall apart. Like the hex energy, it dissipates."

"Weak energy, yes. But energy like this, formed from extreme anger or pain or confusion, it will hold together much longer. It feeds into itself and can grow stronger. That is something which appears to be happening with this stone."

Max tapped his chin. "If this stone has a natural curse, then why have we been discussing hexes? How is that part of it all?"

"This is the last thing Madame Fein will share, so pay attention. A naturally cursed object, like this stone, would not simply bring bad luck upon a person. It would often be a more violent, rage-filled reaction. Objects that have been linked to murders throughout centuries are more likely to be this kind of curse. If your perpetrator meant to simply hex an object that would be given to the target — a stone paperweight — to cause bad luck but picked this particular stone, one already the victim of a natural curse, the irony is delicious. The interaction between the hex and the natural curse is what would cause the increasing strength and undirected nature of the bad luck. That includes the violent shock sent to Sandra."

"That's a ridiculous coincidence."

"Oh yes. It all seems quite on purpose and quite old. Something done in the early days of witchcraft. Or even before. Perhaps a beginner trying to work from an outdated text."

"Somebody willfully put a hex onto a curse. Probably an amateur, somebody messing with things they don't understand, somebody like that. How do I stop it?"

Madame Fein rolled her eyes. "You don't. You're just a man, after all. To stop a hexed, naturally cursed object would require a strong witch."

"But it can be done?"

"Of course."

"Sandra's a strong witch. She can do it."

"Maybe. Maybe not. She is a strong witch in training. But it won't matter because you must know where the stone came from. You have to put it back in its correct place — part of rediscovering its balance."

"But it could be done."

"The strange and bizarre occur all the time in the world. This would hardly be the strangest or the most bizarre. But we are now drifting out of our deal. Madame Fein has provided all the information on hexes and curses in this matter. The spells for ending such things were not agreed upon."

For the first ten minutes of the drive back to Winston-Salem, Max did not say a word. Part of him replayed the entire conversation with Madame Fein, making sure he recalled it clear enough. Most of him replayed the rest of his experience in Haven House, wishing he could forget it fast enough.

But eventually Drummond's patience wore thin, and he pressed Max to talk. Once Max started, the whole story spewed out. Everything from Madame Novak opening the door when he arrived to Madame Fein closing it when he left.

"I can't believe what I'm hearing," Drummond said.

"I know. It'll be difficult but we have to find where that stone came from to break this hex."

Drummond grabbed his hat and slashed it through Max's head. "Not that."

A fast shiver rippled through Max from the ghostly pass. "What then?"

"You made deal with a witch? Are you insane?"

"I had to. At least, I thought I had to at the time. But I was careful. It's a very specific deal."

"Listen, partner, I've had plenty of run-ins with witches like these in my day, and not a single one ever made a straight deal with me."

"Oh, so you've made deals with witches, too."

"You know I have. That means you can learn from my mistakes."

Max glanced at the ghost and noticed real concern on his dead face. "Should I have let it all go, learned nothing, and be stuck worrying for Sandra's health and safety?"

"Of course not," Drummond snapped. He replaced his hat and settled back. Softer: "Of course not. I just … I hate to see you getting roped into all this like I did."

"It's not my first time tangoing with a witch."

"That's my point. Each time, the deals get worse, more complicated. Each time, your reason for doing the deal seems more valid. Until one day, you're tied to a chair, murdered, and your ghost is bound to your office for eighty years."

"Good thing I don't have an office, then."

Weak laughter filled the car that rippled its way into stillness. When they arrived at the house, Max shut the car off and faced Drummond. "We probably shouldn't mention the witch deal to Sandra. Not yet."

"You want me to lie to her?"

"No. I will tell her. I won't lie to her. But right now, she's still recovering. And if she finds out what happened because she couldn't be the one to handle those witches —"

"She'll feel guilty."

"She might even go back to Haven House and try to change things with those witches. Or she might try to find some spell to break the deal. One thing's for sure, she won't be able to leave it alone. Right now, she needs to get better and work on the case. My end of the witch deal is best handled by solving this case and getting that clip of hair, so let's do that."

"Can't say I agree, though I suppose I understand." Drummond shrugged. "Nah, you're being stupid again, but if you want to be a coward about facing your wife, that's your business. I try not to get between you two when it comes to your marriage."

"Since when?"

With a tip of his hat, Drummond said, "I'll see you later."

The ghost vanished, and Max entered the house through the side door. He walked into the kitchen to find PB standing by the table, ready to punch a hole through the wall. Or maybe through Max.

Chapter 7

WAITING FOR PB TO EXPLAIN WHAT TROUBLED HIM, Max scanned up and down the young man. No bruises. No blood. All his limbs appeared to be in the correct places and working properly.

Stabbing his finger to emphasize the different parties involved, PB said, "I spent all day following that pampered housewife because you wanted me to do it and you know what happened? Absolutely nothing. I wasted the whole day. Is this what you do all the time? Follow around people for no good reason? It's idiotic."

Taking a seat at the kitchen table, allowing himself a breath of relief, Max switched his thoughts into parental mode. PB was acting like a teen — which he still barely was. "You weren't doing this for me. It was to help out J, remember? Anything for your brother."

"And I did it, didn't I?"

"Not really. You're supposed to still be following the lady."

"What for? Do you know what she did all day?"

"I don't. That's the point of the job."

"Oh, you need all the exciting details." PB overacted enthusiasm. "Well, let's see. After her husband went off to work, she sat on her big couch in her big house and watched tv. Shopping channels, if you have to know. Is that exciting enough? You want more? You'll love this — once the maid service arrived, she left. You know what she did next? Shopping. Oh, wait — first, she went through the drive-thru at McDonald's. Sat in her car to eat it, looking all around like she was sneaking off to shoot up or something. Then she bounced from one store to another, getting clothes and crap. After that, she went to more stores for more shopping, and I left her doing that because that kind of woman takes hours for it and would've eaten the rest of my day."

"What else did she do?"

"How the heck should I know? Doesn't really matter. She's a bored housewife with no real purpose in her life. Not the criminal mastermind I thought I'd be following."

"Well, I'm so sorry that the job didn't meet your high standards." Max paused. Getting sarcastic wouldn't help matters, and clearly PB was upset about something. Max doubted that a little boredom was the problem. But before he could probe for the truth, his phone rang — Jorge Osorio.

"Hey, boss," Osorio said. "I got good news. I know exactly what's going on in this case."

"I'm listening."

"I'm driving to your house. Get everyone together so we don't have to go through it over and over."

Max started to protest when PB stormed out of the house. He cut the call and rushed to follow, but PB drove off down the street.

Crap.

It took two hours to assemble the team, but that gave Max time to bring Sandra up-to-date on PB. She had slept through the yelling in the kitchen. Not surprising — in the last few years, Sandra had started sleeping through anything. Max wondered if that change came as a result of all their hard, exhausting work or as a by-product of becoming a witch. Casting spells often wiped her out in the short term. Maybe it had more residual effects than they realized.

As the team gathered for the meeting, J called. He was having dinner and catching a movie with a few friends from his study group. PB was out, hopefully blowing of steam in a safe way. That left a bit more space in the cramped living room for the Porter Agency to congregate.

Brenda arrived first. She had originally been a client, but after that case, this middle-aged woman with a wide, dark face and a stocky build joined the Agency. She had a warmth about her, a contagious optimism that Max had not noticed originally but later felt whenever they met. She also liked her cigarettes, so she stood on the driveway puffing down her last one before the meeting started.

Max helped Sandra to the couch. She didn't really need him now — he guessed one more day of light rest and she would be completely back on her feet — but he still treated her like a fragile piece of crystal. She slapped at his hands as he tried to help her sit.

"I can do it," she said. "I'm not an invalid."

Drummond appeared next, giving Max enough time to tell him about PB. After explaining it all, Max admitted that he thought PB would come back for the meeting. He had hoped, anyway.

"Give the kid some breathing room," Drummond said. "He's growing up and that means he's got a lot of life to figure out."

Sandra said, "Maybe I should text him."

"Sheesh, do the two of you ever listen to me? Let the kid have some space."

Brenda came into the room with a bright smile that matched her pink outfit. "He's here. Coming up the drive right now."

Detective Jorge Osorio, a plump man with a thin mustache, long ponytailed hair, and a leather satchel over the shoulder, entered the house. He nodded at Max and Sandra, gave Brenda a slight bow, and sat in one of the old chairs opposite the couch. As they exchanged the usual pleasantries, Osorio dug through his satchel, his one hand wearing a leather glove.

That hand could never touch anything again — not without causing serious damage. Another curse. The same one intended for Max and meant to cause a far worse outcome. But Osorio ended up taking the brunt of the damage, and to date, Sandra had yet to find a way to reverse the spell.

As he produced a small notepad with a bent cover, Osorio shifted in his seat and juggled his belongings into a comfortable position. Max noticed the way the pad shook. Both Osorio and

Brenda — the new members of the team — fidgeted in their seats as they watched for a sign of how to proceed. Max could have smacked his head. Of course, they would be nervous. This marked the first real case they had been on since joining. Until now, they had been called in for minor matters that could be handled in a few hours. With all the spurious cases that had come of late, most of the minor matters were truly minor and truly not paranormal.

But this case — this was the real thing. Neither one of them had been through a full case with the Porters yet. Not as fellow teammates.

Max had planned to let Osorio speak first, but clearly it would be better to take the lead here. He could show them how he weaved his findings into a coherent narrative so that everybody followed with ease. He could teach through example that there was nothing to fear about speaking to this crowd. They weren't bosses and employees. They were all equals and needed to treat each other as such. Besides, the Agency didn't pay Osorio or Brenda, so no reason to think like that.

Max moved to stand when Sandra stretched her legs across his lap. She gestured to Osorio. "Seems like you've got the most to tell us and you're all ready to go. You okay with kicking this off?"

"No problem," Osorio said, flipping his notebook open with a short motion of the wrist. "I won't bother you with all the basic morning routine. If you want that, I'll tell you later. But I think it's best if I get straight to the point — Dwayne Fincher is having an affair."

Drummond cocked his head towards Max. "You should take some notes. This man knows how to give a report."

Before Max could retort, Sandra wiggled her feet and threw in some puppy eyes. Max started a foot massage as he listened to Osorio skip all that background that might have been important, certainly would have been interesting, and could have been crucial toward comprehending the full picture. But nobody else appeared miffed, so Max kept quiet. People just didn't appreciate good research anymore.

"First thing, I will say this — the man really does have bad luck. Took him twenty minutes to get his car running and he almost hit a deer on the way to the office. I suspect he would have, but he's probably extra cautious considering the curse and all." Osorio glanced at his notes. "At 10:47 am, less than three hours into his work day, Dwayne Fincher leaves the office. He hops in his car and drives east — out of the city, away from his house, away from his work, off towards Greensboro. Takes Exit 210 and stops for brunch at the Carolina's Diner off the main road. A woman showed up ten minutes later. Beautiful woman. Looked like a model. He acted all upset, and she placed a hand on his arm in a comforting way that only people real close do. They talked well into the lunch hour. Then his bad luck hit again — a waiter dropped an entire tray of drinks on him. Dwayne and his lady had a look between them, one that said *Hey, let's take advantage of this opportunity*. She drove off. A few minutes later, he left, and I followed him. We ended up at her house. Nice place. Contemporary with plenty of windows to watch through. He took off his clothes to get them cleaned in her washer. But after some kissing and giggling, her clothes came off too, and they ended up in bed to the tune of *Afternoon Delight*."

Brenda said, "Not for real. I mean the song. I know the sex was for real."

"Sorry. They played that stupid song loud. Ticked me off. But as big as all that is, I've got something bigger to tell you. While they were messing around, I had time to search the house address online. Guess who the woman is."

It hit Max right away. "Jill Malone."

"Bingo."

Sandra said, "Dwayne is sleeping with his best friend's wife? No wonder Roy wanted to curse the bastard."

"This puts my day in a different light," Brenda said. After indication from Osorio that he had finished his report, all eyes turned to her. She scooted to the edge of her chair and straightened her posture. "I got nothing nearly as thrilling as Jorge's story, but I did my job and followed Roy Malone all day. Knowing about his wife, though, makes things like the simple morning breakfast routine and the kiss at the front door before he left for work all a bit strange."

"Strange?" Osorio said.

"Most folks cheat on the other because things are bad in the marriage, and whatever's causing the bad, sex is the first casualty. But there they were, all smiles and kisses. I didn't think anything of it at the time, but now it feels very performative."

"You think they knew we were watching?" Max said.

"Not us. But maybe somebody. Maybe anybody. Jorge wasn't lying — that house has so many big windows a blind man could've watched them. Maybe she's figuring that at some point Roy would find out and hire a private detective to take pictures."

"Then why screw Dwayne in that house when it would be so easy to get those pictures?"

"Why cheat in the first place? People are dumb and do dumb things. They like the thrill of getting away with something. I don't know. I'm just telling what I saw. Anyway, Roy drove off to work and pretty much stayed in his office all day. The only thing I wanted y'all to hear about seems a lot more important now. See, during his lunch break, while his wife was home bumping with his best friend, Roy Malone drives west on 40, out of the city — not just downtown, the whole city. Heading towards Statesville. Didn't go as far as that but nearly so. He pulled over by a gravel depot thing. Y'know, one of those landscaping places with huge piles of gravel and sand and mulch and stuff. Just sits there for a while, staring at the trees. Then at one point, he drives away, goes all the way back to Winston, cuts through the city and goes north on 52 to Exit 114. Pulls into a motel. A Day's Inn."

Sandra said, "He's cheating, too?"

"I thought he might be, but that's not what happened. First thing, he didn't go into the front office to get a room — he already had one. Just walked up to the room on the far end, second floor, and had a key to get in. Spent about thirty minutes in there before he left. No other cars around, and I waited to see if anybody came out after he had gone, but nobody did. I even knocked on the door and peeked in the window. Couldn't see anything. The room was dark. Whatever he's doing in there, he ain't messing with another person. After that, I caught up with him back at his office, and he just went about a normal day. Finished his work, headed home."

"Thank you," Max said. "You both did a great job."

"Uh-oh," Sandra said with a grin, "I know that tone."

"What?"

"Brace yourselves, everyone. Max is ready to tell us all he learned through his research."

Trying hard not to appear deflated, Max detailed Dwayne's life as far as he knew it. When it came time to talk about Haven House, he held back everything except for what pertained to the case — hexes and curses. He could feel Drummond's gaze, a chilly reminder that a lie of omission was still a lie and that he should not lie to Sandra. Right then, he knew he would tell her everything. He should have done so the moment he got home, and he would do so soon. He had to. An unpleasant conversation, no doubt, but likely to bring them closer and strengthen their bond.

"Seems to me," Brenda said, snapping Max's focus back to the meeting, "that we should be looking at the Brotherhood of the Rising. They're the ones causing lots of trouble lately. I don't say that just because they were behind everything with me and what happened to Jorge. Max said that this hex of a natural curse is supposed to be old stuff. Like early-witchcraft days. That's what the Brotherhood gets involved with. Right?"

Sandra said, "Yes and no. The kinds of spells they use are old, archaic craft, but this case is not really their style. It's too small."

"Plus," Osorio said, "after what went down the last time, they don't have much of an organization right now. What is the Brotherhood at the moment? Just Mr. Carroll really. If he has the ability to rebuild that group, I think it'll be a few years at the earliest."

Brenda said, "Then we're back to the scorned best friend. Whatever the case, we need a plan going forward. Isn't that how y'all work?"

Setting Sandra's feet aside, Max stood, puffing with a surge of purpose. They did have a way of doing things at the Porter

Agency, and they should follow it. "Okay, enough speculation. Here's what we'll do. I'm going to hit the research hard, investigate everybody involved in this case. Osorio, you stay on Dwayne Fincher tomorrow. That guy has secrets, and we need to know if he's got more. Brenda, you follow Roy. Be careful. If he knows anything about this affair, even if he's not behind the hexing, he could still be dangerous. As for Jill Malone, chances are the two of you will see her while staying on your targets. We should have a better picture tomorrow of how things really are going on with these people, and if we need to follow her next, we can. Drummond, with Sandra still mending, I'd like you to take on Nell Fincher."

"The boring one?" Drummond said. "Gee, thanks."

"I can do it," Sandra said.

"Doll, that's not going to happen. Max is right this time. You got at least one more day to make sure you're ready."

Osorio and Brenda did their best to look comfortable while the Porters chatted with a ghost. Seeing their odd expressions, Max said, "Sorry. You'll get used to it."

With a slight squirm, Osorio put his notebook back into the satchel. "I can take another day off, but that's it for now. Don't get me wrong, I'm happy to do the work, but I can't be your go-to-guy whenever you need a full day of tailing people done. I start taking work off that much and I lose my job."

"Yeah," Brenda said. "I've got bills to pay."

"We know," Sandra said. "The money from Max's tv gig and the cases it's generated has helped us get out of the hole, but it isn't as much as you think. If the day comes that we can afford to bring one or both of you on full-time, you better believe we'll make that offer."

"Even part-time," Max said. "We appreciate you volunteering, but you should get paid something for this. We know that."

"I appreciate that," Brenda said, "but it don't change that I've got to work. I'm sorry, but I can't go following anybody tomorrow."

"That's okay. We understand." Max could feel Sandra's

eagerness, but he refused to risk her health. "New plan — Osorio and Drummond stay on the Finchers. If we get nowhere new, we'll switch to the Malones the next day and I'll take over for Osorio. Meantime, I can research the Malones and we should be fine."

Drummond brought his hands together with one clap. "Let's get started."

Max raised an eyebrow. "It's nearly ten. Everyone get a good night's sleep. We'll start in the morning."

"Oh. Right."

Chapter 8

FLOPPING INTO A SEAT AT THE KITCHEN TABLE, Max picked at the leftover scrambled eggs from J's plate. Handling the morning routine on his own exhausted him before the day had even begun. Even with PB and J both being older teens, both able to get ready for school without incessant prompting, both full of energy yet acting too cool to show it, somehow Max still found the whole experience overwhelming. Mostly because of the questions he wanted to ask and the answers he feared to hear.

His questions for PB had a lot to do with the previous night. When did he get home? Where had he gone? Did he want to talk about their argument? But PB inhaled his breakfast, slung a bookbag over his shoulder, and hurried outside — telling J not to take too long or he'd be walking.

Max's questions for J were less intrusive, but then, J tried to hide far less. That got Max worrying he had failed to treat the boys equally. Was PB's flash of anger a result of feeling an inequity? Maybe he had an honest grievance with Max after all.

Closing his eyes and arching his neck back, Max allowed a soft groan to escape his lips. He needed to bellow his frustration, but Sandra had slept in and he didn't want to disturb her. She would be pushing herself hard enough soon. No reason to get her going earlier than necessary. Besides, he had research to do.

After clearing the table and rinsing the dishes, Max returned to his office alcove and fired up his laptop. Today's target — Roy Malone.

Much like his backstabbing best friend, Roy had posted an enormous amount of his life onto social media. More accurately, it appeared that Jill Malone did most of the posting, even on Roy's account. The pre-Jill period of Roy's online life was rather scant. However, Max knew lots of tricks to find out what he wanted, and after some dedicated searching as well as plenty of sifting through photos, posts, and articles, he had sketched out an idea of who they dealt with. It wasn't pretty.

Roy Malone grew up in Winston-Salem, and based on the few family photos Max could find, the man's parents were devoted Wake Forest University alumni. The Malone family had a living room decked out in Deacon images including a cardboard standup of the top hat-wearing fellow situated next to the letters WFU — each one looked about five feet tall. March Madness basketball was showing on a large television, and the entire room had been painted in Wake Forest's purple and gold.

Not surprisingly, Roy went to Wake Forest for college — probably wasn't given a choice. Got a poly-sci degree, then turned right around and went back for an MBA. With those two degrees completed, he slid right into working on complex property deals for an investment brokerage. He worked hard. Throughout most of his twenties, his life centered around work and little else. Other than the mandatory appearances at home during Wake Forest sporting events.

Beyond one photo on Dwayne's account, Max could find little evidence that Roy had any social life. But the two had become friends, and since both men revolved their lives around work, they appeared to blow off steam together. If this singular photo was typical, they relaxed by getting drunk.

Then Dwayne introduced Roy to Jill. Blonde, perky, straight-tooth smile, and a model's complexion — she looked like she had stepped out of an L.A. photo shoot. At the time, she had worked for a bank and that brought her into Dwayne's circles. He was already married and trying to do his best friend a good deed by setting them up. But perhaps even then, Dwayne simply wanted to find a way to keep Jill around.

From that point onward, Roy's photos became a collage of Jill. Pictures of her at the beach, in a wedding gown, riding a horse. Pictures of them together blowing out candles, costumed as a pirate and princess for Halloween, and dressed to the nines for some fancy party. While Max still thought most of these posted photos were Jill's doing — they all showed her in the perfect light, the perfect head tilt, perfect everything — he had to admit that Roy's page had a certain devotion to her. The man loved his wife, adored her, coveted her. After all, once he met her, she was the subject of all his photos. Not another woman in sight.

Max jotted down a few notes. The act of writing helped make the thoughts stick in his head and gave him a visual view of progress. The more the pages filled with notes, the closer the answers felt.

A car door thumped in the distance bringing Max out of his research tunnel. The street tended to be quiet during the day — a working-class neighborhood had few people sticking around home. In fact, Max often thought he and Sandra were the only two on the block that worked out of the house. But that couldn't be. There had to be some mothers, some elderly folks, and some tele-commuting their jobs. At least a few folks in this area had to be laid off, fired, or perpetually unemployed.

Shaking away his wandering mind, he refocused on his research by opening Jill Malone's social media accounts. The first thing to jump at him regarded her career. Years after her marriage to Roy, she would leave banking and follow her passion — photography. She even opened a gallery downtown.

The next thing to catch his eye was her photos. Even a novice could see the differences from Roy's page. While she may have curated his choices, her pages portrayed a woman living a full, happy life. There were some of Roy, of course — enough to say she was married — but most often, her pictures displayed the whole gang. Her, Roy, Dwayne, and Nell — all going to a rock concert or line dancing or drinking around a small table.

To the average person, nothing would have appeared wrong. A tight group of friends who loved to spend time together and did their best to enjoy each day. Like most people, this online portrayal of perfect happiness masked the rest of the days — the normal days, the boring days, the sit in the car eating fast food with guilt days.

To Max, however, the photos told a different story, one easy to see once their backgrounds were known. Because before Jill entered their worlds, Dwayne, Nell, and Roy lived quiet, rather mundane lives centered around stressful work and climbing the corporate ladder. But once she joined them, that was when the outings began — the Vegas trip, the birthday bar bash, and the Caribbean cruise.

In many of the group photos, Jill clearly gazed at Dwayne. Some of these gazes held a friendly, innocent laughter. But most showed her longing, her desire, her lust. Max marveled that she would be so blatant. Then again, he would never have picked up on it had he not already known.

"Or maybe I'm not giving the male of the species enough credit." After all, Roy had figured it out and he wore the blinders of love.

A scuffling noise pulled Max's attention. Better not be mice in the walls. He shook off the thought. He needed to look into Nell Fincher, figure out how she fit into this group. The mice could wait.

But a car door slammed again, an engine roared to life, and the vehicle peeled out as it ripped down the street. Max hustled to the front windows in the living room — too late to catch a glimpse of the car but fast enough to see exhaust rising in the air and still hear that engine blasting. He stood at the window as if he could will the driver to zip back this way to be identified.

A minute later, he turned back to the kitchen feeling foolish. But a little refreshed. Maybe his mind had needed a break. It had happened in the past. An intense research session would be followed with him finding excuses to zone out in front of a book or a window or even simply sitting in a chair. His thoughts would ramble over nothing specific as deeper in his mind, in a part he did not consciously access, he digested whatever he had learned.

At least, he liked to think of it that way. But that had not happened to him in a long time. Years, in fact.

Only a few steps to the door, and his skin broke into a sweat. He stopped. With his fingers shaking, he checked his pulse on his neck. Racing. An odd mix of herbs — rosemary and fennel — filled the air. Was he having a stroke? No, that was burnt toast. Heart attack? No, that was sharp chest pains down the left side. Something was wrong, though.

He reached the hallway, and his eyes stung as if blasted dry even as they watered from the discomfort. Thinking of calling for Sandra's help, he turned to look at the bedroom door. The house flipped. Or maybe he fell. Vertigo?

I'm dizzy. That's all.

Could be food poisoning. He had gone through that before, and it certainly gave him sweats and chills and nausea and dizziness. Except he hadn't eaten anything unusual or questionable, and he wasn't nauseous — although, the spinning hallway tried its best to start up that symptom.

Stumbling to his feet, he opened his mouth to call Sandra. His throat constricted. No sound came out. He went into the bathroom. Cold water on his face. That sounded good. He would splash the water over his head, too. Then get Sandra and probably go to the hospital.

But when he stood at the sink and turned the faucet on, he glanced in the mirror. Blood. Running lines from his eyes, dribbling from his nose, seeping from pores in his forehead. He opened his mouth to cry, and blood slopped out, splashing in the sink.

His heart kicked harder, slamming against his tightened chest. The muscles in his legs wobbled while the rest of him contracted with sharp pain. He moaned.

The temperature around him — or in him — rose fast. Sweat mixed with blood into a thin slurry. His shirt stuck to his back as he cupped cold water from the faucet and dashed it against his face. But he hardly felt anything. He couldn't get enough water from the small sink.

Bumping into the walls, he returned to the hallway. His mind clouded as he made his way to the kitchen. Bigger sink in there. Colder water, too. No, same water. He needed Sandra. Of course, but he needed the water first.

He stuck his head in the sink and turned the faucet as far to the cold side as it would go. Barely cut into the heat. He tried to call Sandra, but another blob of blood splashed out of his mouth.

The freezer. Nothing colder in the house.

He turned too fast from the sink and the kitchen wheeled around him. His back banged against the hard floor, and for a breath, he stared at the ceiling, watching the tiles roll in a circle. From the floor, he trembled to his knees and crawled to the refrigerator. Thankfully, they had a model with the freezer section on the bottom. But even as he opened it, he knew it would not be cold enough to soothe the vicious heat pumping through his body.

Sagging to his back, tears welled in his eyes. He was sure they were tears and not more blood because he could see clear enough. But what he saw growing out of the ceiling and through the walls finally chilled his feverish bones.

Worms. Blood-soaked worms with pale dead skin. They pushed through the drywall as if birthed.

Whatever had controlled his throat, whatever had kept him from calling to his wife, could not hold back the horrified screech that erupted from his lips. He wailed. As the worms grew longer, they stretched and writhed, seeking purchase throughout the kitchen like tortuous vines.

Sandra burst into the room, saw Max, and her face dropped in pain. He managed to lift his hand, to point toward the ceiling. When her eyes followed, everything about her changed. She stood straighter, stronger, and took a few seconds to survey the kitchen and Max.

"Stay calm," she said with a firm voice. "I'll handle this."

Watching her stride out of the kitchen, he wanted to relax into a warm sense of relief, but he also wanted to grab her, refuse to let her leave him alone even for a second with those tangles of nightcrawlers. Some reached halfway to the floor. A few had extra heads giving them stranger, more chaotic motion.

Sandra returned with a piece of chalk in hand. She batted away a few of the worms before helping Max to sit up. "Can you stay like this on your own?"

He nodded. He wasn't actually sure that he could, but she wanted him to, so he would do his best. Clenching his stomach muscles, ignoring the stabs shooting up his chest, he focused on not falling to his back. Stay seated. That's what Sandra needed.

As a worm slid against her head, Sandra grabbed the thing and wrenched it down. She tossed it into the corner, picked up her chalk, and drew a tight circle encompassing herself and Max. Whispering a spell as she lowered to her knees, she wrote along the edge of the circle. Witch symbols — many Max had seen before but there always seemed to be new ones popping up.

Watching her work helped him stay focused. Worms flopped onto the linoleum and slithered toward them, but Max saw no concern in his wife's behavior. She held still, continuing to mutter the strange languages of the witch.

He tried to blot out the scratching sound as more worms burrowed through the walls. To avoid seeing how close these creatures came to the circle, Max lowered his head and gazed at his hands. But blood bubbled around his nails, trickled off his fingers, and stained his pants. His head pounded in time with his heart.

Sandra leaned back and shouted one final phrase.

Max had no clue what the words meant, but he certainly witnessed their effect. Like the rippling wave of a bomb, the air around them blasted outward. Tinted yellow, it spread fast, and wherever it touched a worm, that creature disintegrated. Their dust floated through the air, settling throughout the kitchen. But they were gone. The scratching noise in the walls was gone, too.

And the pain. Max felt fine. He looked at his hands. The bloodstains were there — it had not been a hallucination — but the wounds had closed. No more blood seeped out of his body.

Turning to face him, Sandra smiled. "It's over." She held his cheek and used her thumb to rub away some of the blood and tears.

"Did any of that hurt you?" he asked.

"I'm fine. Really. Let's see if you can stand up."

With her help, Max rose to his feet. A bit shaky with adrenaline but otherwise, he stood. "I'll be okay." He massaged his chest and hoped his heart could handle his anger. "I definitely want some payback."

Sandra kissed his cheek and chuckled. "That's my man."

He grunted as he reached for a chair. "Maybe I'll get payback after I sit for a few minutes."

Chapter 9

TO MAX'S SURPRISE, wiping worm dust off the kitchen counter, the kitchen table, and the refrigerator had a calming effect upon him. Restoring order. That seemed a likely reason, but he never considered himself much of a psychologist. Whatever the rationale, he knew that sliding those piles of dust into the trash can lessened the horror of what he had seen. And felt.

"That was maybe the strangest part of it," he said, letting his voice carry through the small house while Sandra searched every room. "Not the feeling of a possible stroke or heart attack — that part was damn terrifying, though — but when I saw those worms, I reacted like I had never seen anything supernatural before."

From the living room, Sandra said, "Hon, you were under the influence of a hex."

"You're sure it wasn't a curse? I mean I don't want to assume right away that this is because of the Fincher case. A lot of witches hate us — or me."

Peeking her head in the kitchen, Sandra appraised his work. She reached next to the refrigerator and grabbed a broom. "Time to sweep up," she said, handing it over. "I'm positive that wasn't a curse. It acted exactly like an amateur using a hex — less controlled, less targeted."

"Felt pretty targeted to me."

"If it had stayed with you, then maybe I'd think different."

"But aren't a bunch of giant worms a bit much for a hex?"

"The hex didn't conjure a bunch of giant worms out of nowhere. It mutated normal worms that were crawling around up there. We should call an exterminator."

Max glanced up at the holes pocking the ceiling. "I think we might have some trouble explaining that."

"Giant worms, bleeding eyes, heart palpitations — no specifics to all that, no sense of control over what it would do or where it would go. This is the work of a hex."

She went into their bedroom and rummaged through the drawers while Max swept the floor. Waves of wooziness came upon him, and he would stand still until they passed. It helped to think on the case, though. Or perhaps that helped stave off any lingering panic simmering within him.

"Roy is the obvious culprit here," he said. "He has tons of motivation to stop us from trying to break the hex he put on Dwayne."

From their closet, Sandra called back, "True. But we shouldn't count out Nell. If she found out that her husband was cheating on her, that would make her every bit as likely."

"Except I haven't found anything about her that points to witchcraft or the occult. Even if she was behind this, why would she encourage her husband to hire us? He said that he wasn't so sure about us, but she clearly pushed him to do it."

"Then we're back to Roy."

"Unless his wife did it." Max swept the last corner of worm dust into a big pile. "But Jill is the one doing the cheating with Dwayne. If she wanted to hex somebody, wouldn't it be Roy?"

"Or Nell. Maybe Jill wants to get rid of Dwayne's wife, so she tries a hex and it all goes wrong, hitting Dwayne by mistake."

"If tonight is any example of her hexing abilities, I can believe that." With a dust pan, he gathered the pile and headed toward the side door. "You know, if Jill was behind all this, then after Nell insists on hiring us, she might've gotten worried that we'll figure out the truth, expose her and Dwayne and what she did. So, she tries to hex us, too."

Outside, as he walked to the trashcan, a gentle wind stirred the leaves on the ground making a noise too close to the scratching Max had heard in the walls. It made him queasy. After dumping the remnants of the hex, he breathed in the fresh air, hoping to clear away the fears lingering in his gut. But a car drove by, and his heart jumped.

"Sandra!" he called.

She bolted out the door, kitchen knife in hand, ready to strike. "What? Another hex?"

"No. Sorry. I didn't mean to scare you."

"How about no more shouting tonight?"

Max nodded. "Probably a good policy."

With a long sigh, she said, "Why did you yell for me?"

"I remembered that a car tore off down the road right before everything happened. Before that I heard sounds that I thought was mice or rats in the walls. But maybe —"

Sandra perked up. "If the hex was done with a hex bag, then it might be out here."

Without another word, they approached the house and inspected the walls. Sandra went right and Max left, both looking close at where the ground and building met as well as checking every divot, dent, and deviation from a clean, clear wall. It didn't take long.

"Over here," Max said, and Sandra hustled to join him in the backyard.

He pointed at a bulge where the siding lipped over the brick foundation. A leather, hand-sized pouch had been hastily shoved up under the siding.

"Don't touch it," Sandra said.

"I have no intention of doing that — ever."

Squatting to get a better look, she put one hand on the house. Max held back from grabbing her hand away. He wanted to — needed to feel like he could protect her from this menacing bag — but she was the expert here, not him. Stepping back, he instead gave her space and a bit more light.

After a moment, she stood, wiping her hands on her jeans. "It doesn't look like it's very secure in there. I think I can get it out easily."

"If what I heard was somebody shoving it in there and running away, then they didn't have time to do much."

"I thought the same. Plus, it's not hidden well. Just thrust up against the house. Wait here. I'll be right back." She went inside.

Max stared at the hex bag. He could feel the evil thing pulsing the air around him as if it knew he stood nearby. As if it wanted to take control of him again.

"I'm not afraid of you," he said. "All the terror I felt — that was you manipulating me. Believe me, I've felt real terror in the face of real ghosts and magic. You're just a poor imitation." Max peeked around to make sure none of the neighbors watched. But they were still at their jobs. Barely anybody around. "Talking to myself is one thing. Talking to a hex bag — I better be careful or I'll end up committed."

"If that ever happens, I'll be right beside you." Sandra returned wearing yellow dish gloves and carrying metal tongs in one hand and a large, plastic freezer bag in the other.

As she removed the hex bag with the tense care of a television bomb squad defusing a touch sensitive device, Max stayed quiet. She needed to concentrate. As much as he wanted to talk — about anything — he let her work in peace. It helped him, too. The world still dipped around him every so often. Not as bad as before, but he had yet to feel completely normal again.

With the hex bag tucked into the freezer bag, Sandra used the tongs to carry the whole mess back to the house. Max followed her through the kitchen into the bathroom. She dumped it into the tub, and he sat on the toilet to watch her at work.

Tentatively poking the back with one finger, then two, she eventually fumbled through untying the bag while keeping the rubber gloves on. It took a few tries, but when she finished, she dropped the contents into the tub followed by the bag itself. Max peeked over the edge and saw a feather, a chicken bone, a thicker bone — maybe a dog's or even a person's — a wet ball like rabbit scat, and a folded piece of paper. Sandra opened the paper. It had a casting circle design painted in red and black jagged lines. Strong, angry strokes.

"Amateur." Sandra uttered the word like a swear.

After taking off the kitchen gloves, she pulled the chalk from earlier out of her pocket. Along the side of the tub, she wrote several symbols. She then drew a circle on the base of the tub around the bag and its contents. Finally, she gathered a red candle and a white one from the closet and lit them both, setting one on the drain side of the circle and the other toward the back of the tub.

She had barely begun to chant her spell when the bones sizzled. Black flames like shadows of fire leapt up to the ceiling. It lasted less than a second, engulfing everything within the circle before vanishing with a series of crackles, leaving behind the distinct odor of burnt rubber.

"All done," Sandra said, blowing out the candles.

Max glimpsed a charred, melted mass of plastic in the tub. "Is it safe to touch that?"

"It's useless now. No magic around it anymore. It's just trash."

"Okay. Thank you. I'll clean it up."

"No. I'll take care of it. You need to find out if Roy Malone really did this. If not him, then Jill or whomever. Because that person is being reckless with magic that they don't understand." Her eyes glistened and her chin quivered. "You could have died."

He hugged her. "It's a dangerous business we're in."

"Don't do that. This isn't some retaliation from a witch or some ghost we failed to deal with properly. This is an idiot playing with fire next to lava on the edge of a volcano. If we don't stop this fast —"

"I get it. But maybe you should come with me."

"I can't. I've got to cast more protection spells on the house. Everything I've done before was against witches. I assumed if we got attacked with magic, the spells would be competent and complex. It never occurred to me we'd have to deal with this minor level of amateur."

Max grinned. "At least you're clearly feeling better now."

"More than that, hon. I'm feeling pissed off."

Chapter 10

THE DEACON GALLERY faced the Quality Mart on the corner of Pilot View Street and North Broad Street, halfway between the First Baptist Church and the Augsburg Lutheran Church. A little over a block down, the Centenary United Methodist Church poked above the trees and buildings. Lots of churches in Winston-Salem, lots of opinions, perfect for generating buzz and controversy. Jill Malone had picked a good location for her business. The place had wide windows in the front revealing a classy, spartan interior perfect for highlighting the photographs.

Max made sure to check the back of the building first — in case things went bad and he needed to get out fast. The rear exit led to a small lot with a dumpster and two slips for cars. One had a *reserved for owner* sign at the end and a new black Charger with a custom spoiler parked in front. The kind of car that would make a loud noise as it ripped down a neighborhood street. He put a hand on the hood — warm but not hot.

He walked around the block and entered the gallery properly. A small desk had been set back with two curved chairs but no receptionist. Classical music played softly in the background — Stravinsky, he thought — and a sign next to an archway explained that they were showing three local artists at the moment. All photographs were available for purchase.

After a minute, Max guessed nobody would be coming to help him, so he strolled through the gallery to look at the work. There were three distinct areas, each with its own lighting to distinguish it from the others. The gallery had limited space, so the areas were only large enough to show a handful of photographs while a select few had been blown up to reach the ceiling and dominate the display. But nothing struck Max as relevant. Photos of men and women at work throughout the city, photos of old barns that had fallen into disuse, and photos of clouds at different times and different shapes.

"Hello," Jill Malone said as she entered from a back room. She was a truly stunning woman and carried herself to say she knew it. "I'm so sorry. Our door chime died yesterday, and we haven't got the new one in yet. I had no idea anybody was out here."

"That's okay. I never noticed this place before, and I had some free time today, so I thought I'd check it out."

"Well, we're glad that you did. Are you a collector? A photographer?"

"More of an enthusiast."

She flashed a professional smile. "We're happy to have plenty of those, too. Feel free to look around. Is there anything in particular you're interested in? A specific type of photography?"

"My tastes tend to run a bit darker." He watched her carefully. "Since we just finished with Halloween, I had hoped you might still have something along those lines. Spooky stuff like something about witches or the supernatural."

"Witches? I'm afraid not."

That smile never faltered, but he swore the corner of her eye twinged. He could picture what would happen if Roy ever accused her of cheating with Dwayne. She would smile, shake her head, and deny everything. No hesitation. She would promise Roy he was being paranoid, and if he didn't look close enough, he would miss that twinge.

The rapid beeping of an office phone cut between them. Jill turned toward the reception desk like a cat hearing a bird. "Excuse me a moment. Feel free to have a look."

After she left, Max stepped to the first photograph — an aged woman standing next to the giant teapot that led into Old Salem — but he barely regarded it. Instead, he strained to hear Jill's conversation. She spoke so low that he couldn't make out most of the words, but the tone registered clear enough. Loving, warm, amused, seductive. She had to be talking with Dwayne.

That severely shortened the time Max could spend poking

around. Within the next few minutes, Jill would mention the odd customer asking about witches and Dwayne would ask what the customer looked like and Jill would give a hasty description and Dwayne would know Max Porter had been investigating his mistress. Max glanced over the photographs as he made his way toward the back office. If she had anything helpful to the case, it would be in there.

One quick listen — they were still talking and it still sounded like lovey-dovey talk. Perhaps they were ignoring Dwayne's predicament and focused on each other, instead. If Jill kept away from the subject of an oddball customer, Max might slip through. After all, why would Jill mention him when she had another round of *Afternoon Delight* to arrange? Well, Max could think of a dozen valid answers, but he didn't have the blinders of infatuation on.

The office door stood halfway open. The cramped space contained a desk covered in stacks of papers that crowded around an old computer tower. Books on art stuffed a few shelves with no clear order, and a coffee machine warmed that morning's brew next to a small trashcan overflowing with crumpled envelopes.

Too much to sift through and not enough time to do it. However, the mere fact that her office looked like a witch's chaotic collection suggested she might be more than Roy's cheating wife. Then again, Max had to acknowledge that he had been attacked with a hex only hours before. He might be seeing enemies where none stood.

But when he turned away, his eye caught a splash of color poking from a stack of bills. After checking that Jill continued cooing into the phone, he stepped fully into the office and pushed back the bills. Near the bottom, he found a flat white sheet of paper with a witch symbol painted in jagged strokes using red and black.

He didn't move. His mind looped and twisted trying to make sense of this. On one hand, he had come here suspecting he might find this very thing — proof that Jill Malone was a witch. On the other hand, nothing more than the clutter of the office supported that conclusion. She could have found this paper amongst Roy's things and took it to the gallery with the intention of digging into it without his knowledge. She had to be aware of Dwayne's problem, and if she was not the cause, then it made sense that she would put some effort into helping him. But as his mistress, she had to be secretive about it. On the other other hand, that paper sat on her desk in the open. Under a pile of bills but otherwise easy to find. Not much hiding going on there. On the other other other hand, if she was a witch and was behind all of this, then she would certainly know about Max. Why pretend not to know him? If anything, witches liked to show off how they knew more than everybody else.

Max heard the phone call end. He pulled out his own phone, grabbed a picture of the painted witch symbol, covered the paper back with the bills, pocketed his phone, and hastened down the narrow corridor which had to lead to the back alley. He heard Jill calling out, "Sir? Are you still here?" Carefully, he closed the exit and rushed a block over before doubling-back to get to his car.

He had a few ideas what to make of Jill Malone and her photo-gallery, but he wanted to hold off drawing any conclusions yet. After all, with both Dwayne and Nell being followed, there was still one other Malone that might be responsible for the hex bag attack. But Max didn't think it wise to deal with Roy alone.

Chapter 11

AFTER TWO HOURS, Max and Drummond sat in the car outside the Day's Inn off Route 52 at Exit 114. It had taken close to an hour to get Drummond back from watching Nell Fincher. Usually, Max merely had to call the ghost by name and the connection between them, the same thing that allowed Max to see Drummond, acted better than a cellphone. But this time Drummond did not respond. Max called Sandra and she used a quick spell essentially to boost the signal. That pulled the ghost's attention.

"I don't know what happened," Drummond said when he finally joined them. "It wasn't as if I was enthralled with my target. Nell has led a boring day so far."

Sandra said, "The hex on her husband has spread to all parts of his life. Maybe it's left a mark on her, too, and that energy was messing up Max's call."

Nobody felt confident about it, but the case still had to move forward. Max drove off for the motel and Drummond floated in the passenger seat. Heading north from the city, Max explained about the hex bag attack and his visit to Jill Malone's gallery.

Drummond narrowed his eyes. "I swear it's one thing to come after you or me, but putting Sandra in harm's way is a whole different matter. As for Jill Malone — I could see it both ways. She could be dabbling in magic, trying to get rid of Nell, but I ain't buying that she's a real witch of any caliber. Using hex bags tells us that much."

"I didn't mean an actual witch. But yeah, I agree. I do think that if she tried to hex Nell and botched the job, she would tell Dwayne."

"Maybe. But people do funny things when they're ashamed,

worse when they're jealous. Put the two together and you get this kind of crap."

The motel looked like a two-story shoebox with an extra growth at one end for the office. A gas station stood on one side of the building and an autobody shop surrounded by barbed wire was on the other. Further up — a storage unit building and a pawn shop. Plenty of traffic sped by for the onramps to Route 52, and the noise from the highway could not be easily masked. Far from a five-star experience.

Pointing at the motel, Max said, "According to Brenda, we want the second-floor room on the end."

"You waiting for an invitation or my permission?"

With a roll of his eyes, Max strode across the tiny parking area. It was in desperate need of repaving. He climbed the stairs to the second floor and continued down the balcony-styled walkway. Stopping at the end, he felt cool air breeze around as several cars drove by. Though he knew none of the drivers would bother looking at him, he still worried about being spotted in the open.

Max knocked on the door. No answer. He knocked again. Still no answer.

Drummond said, "You know, I could've gone through the wall and told you if he was there."

"You know, you could go through the wall now and unlock the door."

"Sure. Let's cause the ghost a lot of pain when he touches the solid world because you are too lazy to learn how to properly pick locks."

"I can pick a lock."

"I've seen you. You're terrible at it."

"I'm getting better."

"It's a good thing I'm dead because if my life depended on you picking a lock —"

"You really want to wait out here while I fumble with this thing? Maybe I get noticed by somebody. Next thing you know, the police arrest me, and since I was on television, the local news will make a story out of it. After that, well, I'm guessing all our cases will dry up, especially the good ones, and we go out of business. Isn't too long before the Sandwich Boys are back on the street, and I won't be able to help my mother with her infusion treatment payments. Everything falls apart. All because you didn't want to get a boo-boo."

Drummond's top lip lifted as he growled. He lowered the brim of his hat. "I'm not doing this for you. Got it? I just don't want to see Sandra or the boys or even your mother suffer because you're too inept to learn the basic skills of a detective."

Sliding through the wall, Drummond entered the room. A second later, he poked his head back out.

"Did you forget why you went in there?" Max asked.

"I want to warn you."

Max checked around the motel in case anybody was watching. Dropping all the wisecracks, he matched his partner's serious tone. "What's wrong? You find a dead body in there?"

"No. Not yet, at least. But Roy's definitely our guy. When you enter, walk carefully. There's stuff all over the place, and it might be important."

Wincing, Drummond reached back in, clicked the lock, and gave a short nod. Max opened the door. He stepped inside, stopping right at the entrance. Flicking on the wall switch, a fluorescent ceiling lamp lit the room in unflattering light. Pale and harsh — like the light off a ghost.

Photographs, handwritten notes, and pages ripped from books papered the walls in straight lines like the storyboard for an insane movie. Books made neat piles on the floor, but a trash can overflowed with empty fast-food bags and wrappers. A row of empty vodka bottles stood vigil nearby. The television had a fist-sized hole in it and pieces of a shattered mirror had fallen onto a small table.

Moving with care, Max turned to the first photo on the wall at his right. He pulled out his phone and started documenting the entire place. "I'll start here. You go the opposite way."

Drummond floated to the left of the doorway and passed the window. "It's all pictures here. All of Dwayne and Jill together."

"Same here. Some are taken of the Malone's house. Osorio

wasn't kidding. You can see everything."

"And Roy did."

"Yeah. A lot of these are blow-ups of the same photo. He's got notes stuck to some of them — *Thursday, 2pm, Jill said she loved me this morning.* Here's another on a photo of Jill walking into Dwayne's office building — *June 5, 11:30am, After morning racquetball, Dwayne said he couldn't have lunch with me, too much work.* It's all like that. Except this one in the center — Jill in her wedding gown."

"Look here," Drummond said, hovering halfway across the back of the room. "He's got photos of airports and old bridges, a few diners, and the paddleboats over at Salem Lake. But Dwayne and Jill aren't in any of them. No notes, either."

Max looked over the locations in detail. He pulled one of a gas station and flipped to the back. "The date's been marked — *November 2020.* These must be the first photos he took. Maybe he only suspected back then, or maybe he knew but hadn't caught them yet."

"He's been watching them for a long while."

"A lot of hate could build up in that time." Max stepped back and surveyed the room as a whole. "At least, you're right about him being our man. No more guesswork needed."

Drummond clicked his tongue. "I'm not so sure."

"What? You told me he was the guy."

Thrusting his hands into his pockets, Drummond paused to survey the room much as Max had done. But Max got the feeling that the ghost saw more than he had. Not in a supernatural way, either. Rather, with a keen detective's sense.

"Well?" Max said. "What am I missing?"

"Roy Malone has spent several years now stalking his wife. He knows she's been cheating on him. There are nude photos of her having sex with his best friend right on that wall. Roy comes to this motel room — a place he clearly is spending a lot of money to hold onto — and he does nothing but watch. Obsess. He doesn't leave his wife. He doesn't fight for her. For a moment, I thought maybe it was fetish thing. That he liked watching, but there's too much anger in this room. All that simmering hatred, yet he still doesn't do anything for years. How is a guy like that going to dig into the occult, maybe try to hire a witch or two, finally figure out how to perform a hex on his own, and then have the guts to go ahead and actually do it? Oh, and on top of that, he then attacks you and Sandra with a hex bag after only a couple days into our investigation. Years to move on his wife and friend, but us, a couple days? I'm not buying it."

Max observed the room yet again — this time taking it in with Drummond's angle in mind. But instead of a cowering chump unable to muster the courage to fight this betrayal, Max saw the evidence differently.

"This room, this work Roy has done, it's like his career — heck, his life." Max pointed to the carefully written notes and the photos pinned to the walls in organized groups. "Meticulous, methodical, and devoted. This isn't some feckless wimp who can't stand up against his cheating wife and his supposed best friend. He's been at this with patience and determination. I see a guy willing to take the time to exact revenge in as cold and dark a manner as his twisted mind can think up. I do agree with you about one thing, though — he's not one for direct confrontation. This entire room shows a serious level of obsession."

"That's two things."

"Guess I'm still not good at math. Think of it this way — Roy is hellbent on destroying Dwayne and Jill, but he's not willing to go straight at them. Somehow, he learns about the reality of witches and magic. But —"

"He wouldn't dare approach a witch." Drummond pursed his lips as he drifted along one wall, checking the photographs. "Yeah. He could've divorced his wife, cut ties with Dwayne, moved away or something normal. Instead, he's done all of this. It's a manifestation of hatred — but not only for those who betrayed him. He also hates —"

"Himself. The longer this goes on, the worse he feels. Look at what he did to the television."

"And the mirror."

"He can't stand that he isn't strong enough to have stopped them already. But he's too scared to talk with a witch."

"Or he knows how dangerous a witch deal could be. That's not a jab at you."

"I get it. And you're right. Roy wouldn't dare. So, he starts reading books on magic and works out the basics of hexing somebody. It's the perfect vengeance for him — the kind of thing that will harm his victims over and over, but it's non-confrontational, it's passive-aggressive. They wouldn't even know he was responsible for their misery."

Drummond pointed at the wedding photograph of Jill. "He still loves her. The hex is against Dwayne, not her."

"You think he wants her back? After all of this?"

"The heart can make a man do some weird things." He paused. "One big problem with this idea, though."

Max saw it, too. "No books on magic." He reinspected the piles. "These are travel books for people visiting North Carolina, and the rest are fiction. First guess is that the travel ones were for finding the locations he eventually photographed — he even tore some of the pages out and put them on the wall."

"And the fiction?"

"He spends a lot of time here. Plus, he broke the tv. Maybe they're for entertainment."

"But still nothing about magic, right? No fictional stories about witches?"

"No. Some crime novels, but mostly adventure books. There is a hard cover of *The Count of Monte Cristo.*"

Drummond snickered. "Can't say I'm surprised at the one."

Scratching the back of his neck, Max said, "We can't be wrong. Look at this place. This is the guy. You think maybe he has another motel room somewhere? Filled the whole thing with spells and such?"

"Maybe." Drummond cocked his head to the side. "Or maybe we haven't looked everywhere. Check under the mattress. These places just have a wood frame instead of a box spring. Lot of empty space in the well."

Max frowned. "You do it. You're the ghost. Take a look before I go straining to move that thing."

"It's a mattress, not a sheet of solid metal. Besides, I don't want to stick my head through there. You have any idea of how many people have slept in that? Or done other things?"

"You can say the word *sex*."

"I should hope it's only sex. Lot of odd people in this world."

"Hold on. You don't want to put your head through a mattress that you wouldn't actually be touching because of all the possibly gross things that might have happened here, but it's okay for me to move the mattress with my bare hands in which case, I'm actually touching the darn thing?"

Drummond tipped back his hat. "I opened the door, and I didn't want to do that. Your turn."

"But … except … well … fine, you win."

Moving to the side of the bed, Max tried to ignore the stagnant stench. If he hadn't argued about it, he would never have thought about people's disgusting behaviors. This would simply be a mattress like any old mattress. Instead, he dug his fingers under the bottom edge and cringed at the image of unwashed, sweaty people doing — *No. I can't think about it.*

Like ripping off a bandage, he quickly lifted the mattress and shoved it aside. It banged the bedside table and a lamp fell over. Wood slats formed the support for the bed, and beneath them, Max spotted four books. Old books. The kind he knew too well.

"All on hexes?" Drummond said.

Max nodded. "Every single one."

"Then I guess we should —"

The room door opened, and Roy Malone entered. "How dare you."

With a loud grunt that only Max could hear, Drummond slammed the door closed and turned the lock. Roy whirled around. Grabbing the knob, he twisted and pulled but the door refused to budge. Screaming in pain, Drummond leaned his whole body into the door.

Max raised his voice. "Mr. Malone, stop it."

Jumping back, Roy stared at the door, his shoulders quivering. Slowly he turned to face Max.

"Thank you." Max leaned to the side, making sure Drummond was okay. His partner, panting hard, threw a thumb's up. "I'm sure you know who I am, and I sure know who you are. So, let's not bother with the pretending ignorance part of the conversation. You hexed your best friend, Dwayne Fincher, for sleeping with your wife. When he hired us to break the hex, you tried to do the same to me. But now, it's over."

"You don't know anything," Roy said, the words whining out of him. "If you really did, if you understood what they did to me, you wouldn't try to stop me."

"We are stopping you."

"Do you see the pictures? Don't you get it? She betrayed me. She committed marital treason. And he … he was …" Roy's voice drifted away as he viewed the photos he must have known too well.

"I do understand. They hurt you like nothing you ever felt before, and you wanted to hurt them back. Punish them in a way that approached some kind of equal suffering. But the weapon you chose — magic — is too dangerous. You're lucky making the hexes didn't tear you to shreds."

"Maybe that would have been better." He dashed at his eyes.

Coughing off the last of his pain, Drummond said, "The guy sounds remorseful. That's good. He might make this easy on us."

Max put out a hand. "We can help. This hex — you don't have control over it. Not like you might think. But me and my people, we deal with this stuff all the time. Tell me how you made the hex, where you got the stone, and we can fix it all."

"You want to meet a witch? Find out where the magic is? Isn't that your thing, Mr. Television Star? Cause I don't believe for second you want to help me."

"We want to help everybody involved."

"No, no. You're hoping to do something big here. I know your type. Got on tv and started believing your own crap. But here's the thing — you are a fraud. These hexes are the real deal. You should know that considering what it must have done to you. Yeah, I see it your eyes. You're trying to trick me, get me to reveal how to do an authentic spell. Maybe get yourself back on tv to make more money off of suckers who think you can actually do something."

"The Porter Agency is legit, and if you talk with us, we can make all of this trouble go away."

But Roy laughed. A patronizing sound. No pleasure in it, either. "Why would I ever want that? The whole point was for Dwayne to suffer forever."

"Hexes are notoriously difficult to maintain. You've already lost a handle on the two you made. They've gone far beyond your intentions."

"So?"

"What about when Dwayne's hex starts crumbling into the lives of innocent people? You'll be responsible for that."

Roy's brow scrunched as he raised a quizzical eye. "Nobody's innocent. If a few people have to pay for their crimes so Dwayne can truly feel the pain he caused me, then that's the way it has to be."

Drummond said, "I'm rescinding my earlier statement about his remorse. Want me to freeze his brain?"

Max shook his head. Roy would be no good to them incapacitated. "Look, you are way out of your league here. We've already destroyed the hex you put on me, and it won't be long before we do the same to Dwayne's hex. But the harm you are causing —"

"I don't care."

"People could die. Are you willing to go to jail for killing people over two cheaters who clearly don't care about you?"

"Jail? For what? Casting a hex? Nobody's going to believe that. Not the police, anyway."

Drummond said, "He's not wrong there."

"And it ain't a crime to cause somebody bad luck. Not a single law says so." Roy crossed his arms. "In fact, the only one committing a crime here is you. I think you better leave, or I'll be the one calling the police. Get you for breaking and entering."

Max clenched his fists. "You listen here."

"Uh-oh, I think you're about to threaten me. Go on. Throw a punch. I can add assault to the charges."

"Partner," Drummond warned.

Snarling his lip, Max shoved Roy to the side. "I've dealt with far worse than you. Really, when I think about it, you're insignificant." He reached for the door.

"Look around you." Roy's face flushed as he spit out the words. "Look at my years of work. This is not an insignificant act. This has been planned, orchestrated. This is masterful."

"I think *pitiful* is the appropriate word."

As Max opened the door, Roy pushed it shut with enough force to rattle the chain lock. "Don't you dare say that. You think you know anything about magic? I haven't seen you casting a spell, creating a hex, doing anything put poking around my work."

"Good job," Drummond said. "Keep him in a frenzy. But, uh, keep your guard up, too."

Max had lowered his fists, so he straightened into a ready position and stayed vigilant. If an attack came, he would be able to block it. "I don't have to do the casting. I have a real witch on my team. You're just dipping your toes into a massive ocean, and we've been swimming for years. You haven't got a chance. We'll end your hex. Dwayne and Jill won't be bothered by you anymore."

"Careful. You don't want to go too far and send him into a murderous rage."

Snapping his hand in the air, Roy's mouth widened. "You better watch out. I hexed you once, and I can do it again."

"Not really. We stopped it pretty easy. You need a magic stone to do the heavy lifting for you."

"I'm better than any witch around. I've read the books. I've studied it all. You talk about all the others, though. Everybody thinks they're smarter. Everybody tries to keep me down. Well, not anymore. I'm willing to wait it out until the time is right, and damn if it ain't gloriously right now. You think you can best me? I dare you to try. I'll bash your head in with that hexed stone. Bash it against the bridge until there's nothing left of you but pulp. You want that? Huh? You think you're tough enough?"

"Time to leave." Drummond swished next to Roy. "If he makes a move, I'll freeze him."

Max hesitated. An animalistic urge to fight flooded his

system. But then Drummond slid in front of Roy.

"It's okay, partner. We got him."

Chapter 12

WITH EACH MILE CLOSER TO HOME, Max's spirits raised. His anger toward Roy Malone had surprised him. Perhaps the man's arrogance had caused it. The way Roy proudly admitted what he had done and his intention to keep doing it. No remorse. Not a single drop of consideration for the euphemistic collateral damage. Roy also proved to be exactly what they thought — a coward. Though he blustered through the surprise of seeing Max in his motel room, Roy never did more than yell a lot. He didn't like direct confrontation. They would have to remember that.

Thinking about that smarmy grin, Max's hands squeezed on the steering wheel. But then, he flexed his fingers outward and a genuine smile encompassed his face. Drummond was right. They got the guy.

"It's the bridges," Drummond had said the moment Max started for home.

Max had heard it, too. In his impotent fury, Roy Malone had slipped up. Admitted that the stone came from a bridge. "How many stone bridges do you think there are in North Carolina?"

Drummond's cheeks ballooned as he blew out a long breath. "Hundreds. Maybe over a thousand. This state has existed since before the original colonies were the original colonies. Lots of old British bridges."

"Yeah. But I can research the crap out of things. I'll find it."

"I know you will. While you do that, I'm going back to the Other. I think it's time to call on the last few favors I got in there before Roy's hexing gets so out of hand people start dying."

For Max, the rest of the day comprised of sitting at his laptop researching, and the research had gone well. He had several ways to narrow down the bridge possibilities that made an enormous difference. The stone had to come from a bridge where some tragedy had occurred; otherwise, it would never have become a naturally cursed stone. It also had to be accessible. A bridge spanning a wide river or on a military base would not be useful to Roy. It also had to be a bridge with some history. Plenty of tragedies happened that the world never heard about. This had to be something bad enough that, at the least, it appeared in a newspaper or developed an urban legend around it. Something either people would talk about and Roy could have overheard or people had written about and Roy could have looked up online.

That still left Max with a large number of possibilities. He spent hours whittling it down and now had three to talk about. Osorio, Brenda, and Drummond would arrive that evening expecting an answer. As he organized his notes to present everything in as clear and concise a manner as possible, he hoped he had one.

J sat at the kitchen table studying a textbook and eating the last of his dinner — reheated leftovers.

"Sorry it isn't anything better," Max said.

"No problem. I know how you get when we've got a case."

Max didn't know if he should feel proud that J could be so sympathetic or ashamed that J knew Max's tendency toward myopic behavior when deep in his research. Probably both. "I think I might be more forgetful this time around. I've got to admit it — that man really struck a nerve."

"The guy you saw today? Roy?"

"Roy Malone. Yeah. He acted so smug. The second I got home, I dove into the research. Y'know? Just sheer determination. I'm going to get him." Max tapped his notes. "Right here, it's moments like this, closing in on the bad guys, knowing that soon you'll stop them or make them pay, it makes all the fieldwork even more special."

Max thought his mini-speech would bring a smile to J's face. Instead, the young man looked uncomfortable. He debated in his head, looked at Max, then decided.

"Wait here a moment." J went to the master bedroom, spoke with Sandra, and returned.

"What's going on?" Max said.

"Just wait."

Sandra joined them in the kitchen looking every bit as confused as Max felt. J sat at the table, closed his books, and folded his hands atop them like a businessman about to announce layoffs.

"Do we need PB, too?" Sandra asked.

Max said, "He's with my mother, but I'm sure we can call him—"

"No," J said. "PB's fine. This isn't about him. This is about me and what I'm going to do after I graduate."

"You're only a junior. You've got time."

"If I think like that, nothing will get done. I'll be getting my diploma and have no future lined up. I've been thinking a lot about it, where I want to go and all that. Never really expected to have much choice, but then you came along and took me in."

Sandra covered J's hand with her own. "Best thing we ever did."

"It was for me. Got me off the streets. That would've been enough. But then you put me in school, and for the first time, I started thinking I could go places, do things."

Though it hurt to think it, Max had a pretty good idea where this headed. "You don't want to stay and work with the Agency, do you?"

"What? No. I'm looking forward it."

"Then what's wrong? You look conflicted."

Taking a deep breath, J's gaze fell on his textbook. "My teachers say I have a great shot of getting into college. Mr. Willis says my math is really advanced and Mrs. Audrey thinks I show lots of potential that schools would be excited to have. Even Ms. Cassie said if I apply for college that I'd surely get most of my top picks."

"That's wonderful."

"It's part of the reason I've been studying so much for the SAT. If I do real well on it this first time, I'll be in a great position next year going into being a senior. Also, I wouldn't have to take the stupid test ever again."

"So far, I'm not seeing the problem."

Sandra, however, looked around the small kitchen with dour acceptance. Max followed her gaze. The destroyed ceiling would probably remain that way for several months until a few more cases helped them catch up on the credit card bills. Max's cramped alcove barely functioned for an office and wouldn't change if the case work slacked off. Even the small holes in Sandra's jeans bore witness to their struggling finances.

"You're worried about paying for college," she said.

J lifted his head and the words flooded out of him. "It's not right for you guys to be burdened with that. You've spent enough on me already. But I don't want a college loan. I've read too many horror stories online about people in their 40s and 50s still trying to pay off a loan. That's insane. I've looked into scholarships, and if college is the right thing, then that's the only way I see it happening. But the scholarship world is another messed up system, too."

"It's okay," Max said. "You don't have to worry about all of this alone. I mean, first off, you are not a burden to us. We want you to go into the world and build a happy life. If it's with us and the Agency, that's great. But you don't have to do that."

"I want to."

"Great. We'd love to have you by our sides, dealing with ghosts, and helping people get out of jams with witches."

J's moment of joy disappeared. "No, not that. I don't like being in the field. I did when I first started. Parts of it I still like. But what I really want to do, I think, is get an MBA. Or if college is too expensive, I could go to a small business school. I don't want to sound mean, but you two are not good at this."

"Hold on. I've been running this business for years."

"And for years, you've been locked in a boom/bust cycle. The two of you — and Drummond — are a great team when it comes to handling the cases, but the business side of it is your weakness. I want to learn how to run a business properly. Get us to a place where we always have money to cover things like that." He pointed to the ceiling.

Max worked to keep his body from tensing up. It bothered him, but he had to admit that the boy — the young man — was right. "I guess I am a lousy businessman."

"Don't be like that," Sandra said. "He's not saying that."

"He absolutely is."

J said, "No, not like that. What I'm saying is that you all have some great strengths. You are the business, after all. But when it comes to the money details, none of us knows enough. I figure that's a place I can help. And really, you don't need me in the field and I'm better at math than any of you. Seems like it all makes sense to me."

Max chuckled softly. "As for the money, well, yeah, we don't have a lot right now. But money comes and goes. Huh. Listen to me. I guess you're right. We do run on a boom/bust kind of thing. Well, I can tell you this much — if you get into college, we'll all work together to figure out how to pay for it. Simple as that. Because like you're saying, we clearly need you."

As they talked on — restating for each other how much they cared for this family and how hard they would work to see J succeed — Brenda arrived. She saw the Porters in a family meeting and quietly entered the living room. Max could hear her moving some furniture to get ready for the meeting. Osorio came in shortly after, dropped a six-pack of cola in the fridge, and hurried to join Brenda. Finally, Drummond appeared in the kitchen.

One quick look at his partners, and he tipped back his hat. "Okay, what's going on?"

The wide grin that covered J's face brightened the room. Max thought that no matter what, J would stay with the Agency if it meant he could stay working with Uncle Drummond. It seemed strange to find such a strong family connection with a dead man, but then *strange* defined every day in the Porter household.

In a flurry, J explained the college dilemma and his desire to run the Agency. Drummond listened with a sly twinkle in his eye. Then he said, "Kid, I know you're a smart one, so I got the greatest confidence in you. But I'm going to let you in on a little secret — even if you weren't smart, anything would be better than having Max run the books."

"Hey," Max said. "I'm right here."

"You need to hear it. I value you as a partner. You're a great researcher and a good man on the job. But handling the day-to-day of a business — frankly, I'm shocked the Agency still exists."

"I see. It's pile on Max day."

As Sandra and J laughed, Drummond shifted back to work. "I went to the Other and set the last friends I have on watching Roy Malone. They'll follow him wherever he goes, and if he does anything — to us or to Dwayne or anybody — we'll know about it."

"Good," Max said. "Because we're going to break this hex."

Chapter 13

GATHERING IN THE LIVING ROOM, the only room large enough to hold a big group, Max tried to shake off all that J had said. He needed to focus on the meeting and his presentation. While glad that J had opened up, the young man's timing needed work.

As Max stepped in front of the television, Sandra lowered to the couch. J brought a chair from the kitchen and set it near the front door. Brenda and Osorio each took the same chairs they had occupied in the previous meeting. *And just like that,* Max thought — a new pattern created itself for the Agency. He shifted his papers on the coffee table, his mind sifting through the idea that by doing nothing more than sitting in the same spot twice the team had established where they would sit for years to come. Somehow, for him, that minor act solidified the Porter Agency into more than a husband and wife — and ghost — running a small business. After all these years, for the first time, he felt a sense of growth for the Agency. A sense of legitimacy he had not realized was lacking — or needed.

Drummond cut through the wall to hover in the corner near Sandra. He would have been welcome to take a more inclusive part of the room, but like the rest, he had chosen where he belonged in these meetings. Max knew the old ghost wanted the corner — giving him a vantage point that encompassed the entire room while also allowing him an easy space to avoid accidental contact with so many people. However, all of that understanding did not save Max from Drummond's mouth.

"Maybe you should warn these new members what it's like to sit through one of your lectures."

Sandra coughed out a short laugh. "While you've heard Max before, this will be a more in-depth explanation of what he's learned — and be ready, that's a unique experience. Before he gets going, does anybody have anything else to report?"

Osorio said his target had behaved in a routine manner with nothing special happening that day. J held a notebook on his lap, and at first, Max thought he had brought more schoolwork to keep atop his feverish studies. No textbook, though, and the young man's attention had remained on the meeting. It reminded Max of when the Sandwich Boys were boys — the way they would sit cross-legged on the floor, staring up at him as he told the tales he had researched, each listening with awe and delight. But when J stopped writing shortly after Osorio had finished the report and his attention went straight toward Max while he held his pen, ready to write, it became clear.

He's taking notes.

Max couldn't hold back. He beamed. Perhaps reading him in the way she always could, Sandra cleared her throat to get him started. He picked up his own notes — the ones about the first bridge — and made sure to look at each team member in the eye before starting.

"Earlier today, while Drummond and I met with Roy Malone, we heard and saw things that clued us into the idea that Roy created his hex using a naturally cursed stone from a bridge. After researching throughout the rest of the day, I'm confident we have the answer right here. I have found three bridges that meet our criteria — one of which, I think, is our best bet. But I want you to hear about the other two first. I'll go from least likely to most likely."

Drummond said, "Come on. Just because you got some new audience members doesn't mean you should milk this."

Barely hiding their snickers, Sandra and J remained attentive. But Max could see the odd looks from Brenda and Osorio. They were getting more comfortable with the idea that the original team could see and hear their ghost partner, but they still were not adjusted yet.

"I'm sorry if this might seem drawn out," Max went on, "but it's important to take the time to go through all the possibilities."

"That's right," Osorio said. "We do the same when working

with a detective new to a case. Going through it all can save a lot of time in the long run. Less second guessing. Less wrong turns of thought. That kind of thing."

"Not all detectives agree with you, but since you're the one who has the modern knowledge in that space, I think we should follow your lead."

"That's not funny," Drummond said, though he winked at Sandra.

Brenda said, "It also saves time from us asking questions about things you would have skipped over otherwise."

Holding back a cocky glance at the ghost in the corner, Max said, "I'm glad you both understand. The other reason for my approach — I'm not infallible. I might present something, and you'll see a mistake I made. That's every bit as important."

Sandra said, "Don't let him fool you. When it comes to research, Max rarely makes a mistake."

"Hey," Drummond said, "I thought you were on my side. Don't go encouraging him."

J threw his head back and laughed. The confused frowns from Osorio and Brenda only made him laugh harder. Then Sandra joined in, and the infectiousness reached everybody.

Wiping her eyes, Brenda said, "I don't even understand what's so funny."

That got them all laughing another round. But it was short-lived, and Max felt the shift back to business. He had bridges to talk about, ghosts and curses, too.

"I'm going to start with the one I think has the least chance of being our bridge. You'll see why in a moment. It's called Lydia's Bridge. The story is this — in Jamestown, a girl named Mary Lydia Jones got picked up by her date on prom night. She was a lovely gal and prom was a big deal to her. Though raining hard, nothing would dissuade her from enjoying this special night. She had been waiting for prom all year. Probably before that year, too. They drove off, and as you might have guessed, they never made it to the dance. The boy lost control of his car on a sharp curve. He died right away. But not Lydia. She crawled out of the wreckage, bruised and bleeding. Rain poured down, soaking her blood into the prom dress as she stumbled to the road. I don't know how many cars passed her by while she begged for their help. It's not even clear if she made it to a hospital. But she died from the ordeal not long after the accident. News of her death ran through the town fast, and pretty soon, folks wanted a bridge built on that curve to stop another kid dying. That's Lydia's Bridge. Not long after they finished construction, stories popped up that on rain-soaked nights, Lydia's ghost can be found trying to stop drivers to help her. Some even say she gets into the backseat of cars hoping to get a ride to her prom."

Sandra said, "That's definitely not our bridge."

Osorio leaned onto his elbows. "How can you be so sure?"

"For one, a natural curse means the person moved on while their energy stayed behind. If this story is true, then Lydia didn't move on. She's a ghost roaming this bridge. But there's plenty more against the story."

"Right," Max said. "Lydia's energy is not hateful or furious. Just sad. Maybe even a little hopeful that she'll finally get to her dance."

"But most of all — the bridge didn't exist when she died. Even if she had moved on, even if she was angry, she couldn't have naturally cursed stones in the bridge because it wasn't there."

Drummond said, "Okay, it ain't Lydia. What's next?"

Though Max knew the detective would never admit it, he heard a distinct hint of interest. Drummond loved to complain, but when dissecting his way through a case, he savored the process as much as Max.

"Next is Helen's Bridge. This one comes from the western side of the state near Ashville. A woman, Helen, suffered a terrible blow when her daughter perished in a fire. Though many tried to help console her through her loss, she could not find a way out. Spiraling in grief, she became a shadow of emptiness that eventually took her to the darkest of places. She hung herself off a bridge at Beaucatcher Mountain."

Brenda said, "This sounds like the start of another urban

legend."

"It does. Both Lydia and Helen's stories are vague enough and come packed with a mixed bag of paranormal tall tales and possibly authentic encounters that it's difficult to say. In the case of Helen, I found numerous police reports of stalled engines and other car problems occurring to motorists at the bridge. There are, of course, plenty of sightings of Helen in a long, flowing gown searching for her child, but what pulled me to this story is that there were also sightings of dark, shadowy apparitions around the bridge and in the bushes. On top of that, a few reports suggest physical contact — scratches, slaps, even punches."

Tenting his gloved fingers on his knee, Osorio said, "I'm not seeing why this is a more likely candidate over Lydia's bridge. If anything, this story seems thinner."

"I thought so, too, at first. But the more I looked at it, the more varied the stories became. An urban legend has some core event around it. Girl gets killed on the way to prom and haunts the accident site. Then we get spooky story after spooky story that support that event. All the people who claim to have seen her by the bridge, desperate to get to the prom, lost in her pain and sorrow. In the case of Helen's bridge, we have the core event but not the consistent spooky stories."

"Like when you have two suspects, and their stories match exactly?"

"Yeah," Drummond said. "Innocent people have different versions of the same thing."

"Now hold on, there." Brenda folded her hands in her lap. "Even with the various things going on at Helen's bridge, we're still talking about ghosts and apparitions, and that doesn't stick to the idea of a natural curse, as I understand it."

"Yes and no," Max said. "You're absolutely right that seeing the actual ghost of a dead person is the wrong thing for a natural curse. However, none of these reports are describing the same thing. What if they're seeing the residue of a natural curse? Not a real ghost, but rather some kind of paranormal event which their minds can't quite process, so they interpret it as a ghost."

Sandra shook her head. "We've seen enough to know that the possibilities are far more than we can imagine, so I wouldn't say that can't happen. However, hon, I've never heard of, seen, or read about anything like you're describing. That's in general. With all the studying I've done in the last few days, I've yet to find anything about a natural curse working that way."

Max put up his hands. "I figured as much. Okay, here's the last one."

"Finally," Drummond said.

"Since we've taken the time to look at why the other two can't be our bridge, I think you'll see clearly why this one is the best choice. The Bostian Bridge train wreck. First off, I'm able to find far more specifics than the other two, starting with the date — August 27, 1891. The bridge is sixty feet high, brick and stone, to the west of Statesville. It's got five arches spanning the distance crossing Third Creek. At around 2:30 in the morning, a passenger train for the Richmond & Danville Railroad left the station. It wasn't a huge train. Only six cars — a tender, baggage car, first-class, second-class, a sleeper, and a private car. That's it. Not a lot to handle for an experienced engineer, and from all I could find, the engineer — William West — had plenty of experience. Unfortunately, that kind of knowledge can cause people to miss the little things.

"See, they were behind schedule. By a lot. Thirty-four minutes. Even in the slower world of 1891, people were not happy to be over a half-hour late. Especially at 2:30 in the morning. Mr. West figured he could push the engine harder, perhaps get around 35 or 40 miles per hour, and make up the lost time. And he was right. The engine could handle it. But the rest of the train and the track was less cooperative. No more the five minutes after leaving the station, they hit Bostian Bridge and the train jumped the tracks. According to the investigation, based on speed and the 135-foot distance between the bridge and where the sleeping car hit the ground — the train had to be airborne for quite a distance before gravity grabbed it back."

Nudging Osorio's leg, Brenda said, "Already this sounds more legit to me. That's a real tragedy of a story. A whole trainload of late-night passengers dying."

"Not all died," Max said. "There were plenty of survivors. That's part of how we know a lot about the incident, and for me, what makes it less an urban legend and more a slice of truth. But twenty-five people lost their lives on that bridge. Makes it one of the worst train accidents in North Carolina ever. Now, here's where things get interesting for us. By the time a few of the survivors managed to walk back to Statesville, the day was getting started. Everything stopped, though, and the whole town came out to help with the rescue. Statesville didn't have a hospital at the time, so all the injured ended up in people's homes, and the dead were carted off to a nearby tobacco warehouse. There, they would be identified and taken care of. Remember that part — we'll get back to it."

Rapping his knuckles on the arm of his chair, Osorio said, "Man, Sandra was right. You do have a dramatic flair with all of this."

Drummond said. "I like that detective more and more."

"Not complaining, by the way. I think your way helps me see it all much clearer."

"That detective is a fool and shouldn't be trusted."

"Thank you," Max said, as both Sandra and J bit back fits of giggles. "It's nice to be appreciated."

Before any further comments could be made and Max lost control of the meeting, he dug out two grainy black-and-white photographs taken at the crash. They were shot from far back in an attempt to capture as much of the scene as possible — the bridge towering over the rescue effort, the long drop below, and on the rocky, uneven ground, the destroyed train. On one end, resting at a precarious angle, the enormous steam engine poked up. On the other, a ruined railcar tipping to one side, perhaps resting on jutting rocks, with people standing on it trying to help others out.

At least, that was what Max saw when he tried to decipher the pictures. In 1891, the art of photography barely stuttered from its infancy, and the available technology left much to be desired. Through countless hours of research, Max had grown accustomed to decerning details from such photographs, but this one posed extra challenges.

Unlike portraits or landscapes of the time where the photographer could get the subjects to hold still for the relatively lengthy period needed to make a photo, this was a living moment. One would hope that the photographers wouldn't dare ask people to hold still for a picture instead of saving lives. Given the early hours of the rescue effort, there would be limited morning light reaching down that stone-strewn crevice, making the photos darker than usual. Even if one of the photographers wanted to attempt a more detailed shot, Max thought it unlikely those in charge would allow the men to get close enough to clog up the important efforts.

He handed one photo to Osorio and one to Sandra. Giving the group a moment to look and pass them around, Max read over his final notes.

"These were done by two men — Mr. VanNess of Charlotte and Mr. Stimson of Statesville. In the weeks that followed, thousands of people showed up at the site to gawk. Some people even poked around the grounds, hunting for souvenirs and lost valuables. According to the *Landmark,* a local Statesville newspaper, the men sold those photos to these macabre tourists by the hundreds. One of the pictures — I think it was the VanNess one — was published in a paper called *Frank Leslie's Weekly* while the story itself reached all the way up to *The Police Gazette of Boston.*"

As Brenda inspected the pictures, her hands trembled. "I can almost smell the smoke and feel the soot. What an awful accident."

"Except it wasn't an accident."

Drummond perked up. "Here we go. What really happened?"

"As with any crash, an investigation occurred to figure out if anything could be done to prevent such tragedies in the future. The conclusion — a person or persons pulled out some of the spikes from the rails."

J paused his note-taking. "Why would anyone do that?"

"The Richmond & Danville Railroad company had fallen on

hard times. Their finances were a wreck, so some thought it was an effort to defraud the insurance companies. But I couldn't find evidence of that or if they even had insurance."

"Even with insurance," Osorio said, "crashing a passenger train would be stupid. A cargo train would be a loss of goods and damaged engines and that kind of thing. But a passenger train meant wrongful death lawsuits of some kind. I'm sure even in 1891 there would have been a feeding frenzy of lawyers."

"That's exactly what happened. The company tried to stave off the lawsuits by hiring numerous railroad detectives to find the culprits. While some people were detained for questioning, the detectives failed to make a final arrest. Then, in 1897, two men already behind bars made the mistake of bragging to other inmates about what they had done. The railroad company found out and swooped down with the law by their side. The two men were convicted, and more jail time was added with new sentences. But there are a lot of suspicious holes in that last part. The timing is convenient — if the company didn't find somebody to blame, they would have had to payout damages for more than they could afford. The inmates who said they heard all this bragging were less than trustworthy. And there were a lot of discrepancies about how or when these confessions of the crime supposedly happened. In the end, the case quietly went away."

Sandra said, "I see where you're going. You think some of those who died on the train hung around as ghosts for several years, seeking justice. When the case dwindled away, they were caught between being able to move on, satisfied with the culprits paying for their crimes, and being outraged at the lack of truth or caring about what happened to them. So, while the ghost may have moved on, the anger may have lingered and caused a natural cursing of the bridge."

"Exactly."

Setting the photos on the coffee table, Brenda looked skeptical. Max liked that. He wanted teammates that challenged his assumptions.

"You've certainly done a lot of work and given us a lot of

detail, but that's all history. What evidence is there of any kind of curse? While I agree that the Lydia Bridge story and the Helen Bridge story are weak for our needs, they at least had hauntings going on."

Drummond clapped his hands before pointing at Max. "I see it in your face. You've got more."

"Funny you should say that. A bit earlier, I told you all that the bodies were taken to a tobacco warehouse. Well, twenty-five bodies were recovered but only twenty-three were identified. Making it all worse, when they finally released the dead to be claimed by the families, paperwork shows only twenty-three releases."

With an incredulous gasp, Brenda said, "They lost two bodies?"

Chapter 14

THE SOUND OF BRENDA'S SHOCK helped pull the focus right back to Max. Not that he worried about losing their attention, but rather, he thrilled at hearing another person get as intrigued as he did when he learned these things. He suspected Drummond always felt the same, but that old ghost had been born and raised in the decades that prided stoicism. Osorio listened with a resolute ear that hunted for clues in every detail. He had probably been trained not to react too fast — even when hearing something important. J dutifully wrote the meeting's notes and while he may have been impressed, it wasn't the first time he had heard Max reveal astounding information. And Sandra had the burden of being Max's wife. She listened to him all the time. But Brenda was both new and lacking a filter — a perfect audience for him.

A sudden thought hit him. *Maybe I liked that television appearance more than I let on.*

"How could they lose the bodies?" Brenda asked. "It's not like this was a hurricane wiping out an entire town with hundreds of people. Twenty-five bodies doesn't seem too hard to keep track of."

"It gets more problematic. See, even at that point, long before the gawkers and the photographs and the lawsuits, the railroad company knew they had a massive problem on their hands."

Nodding his understanding, Osorio said, "Two unaccounted bodies only made it worse."

"They had probably snuck onboard which would show a lack of security on the company's part. It would be a small fact that added another nail in the lawsuit coffins. Now, it's entirely possible that the bodies were claimed, that they never went missing, and somebody made an error in the paperwork or even in the news reporting. After all, I'm dealing with articles from over a hundred years ago. But it's equally possible — and considering the curse we're investigating, perhaps more likely — that those bodies disappeared on purpose. Maybe buried in the woods nearby or dumped in a grave beneath a casket holding another body. Or any number of other ways to get rid of a corpse."

"Why would somebody do that?" Brenda asked.

Sandra said, "If those two were involved in anything supernatural, there are many reasons to bury a body. All kinds of curses to the dead."

With a professional tone, Osorio added, "There are also many everyday reasons. Gangs sending messages in the way they deal with the dead. People taking advantage of the confusion during this kind of accident might decide to finally murder that person they always wanted to kill. Hide the body with the other dead. Or perhaps the murder occurred right before the accident, and the killer wanted to hide the evidence."

Brenda crossed herself. "You all live in some pretty ugly worlds."

"The reason doesn't really matter," Max said, a bit louder to pull them all back. "However it was done, if it was done, then those two people could have moved on yet left behind their anger at the way they were treated. They may have ended up being our natural curse."

Sandra said, "This might be the bridge, but there have got to be dozens, maybe hundreds, of bridges in North Carolina that have tragic accidents around them."

"A little more patience. I'm getting there." Max paused to let Drummond snap out a sarcastic comment, but instead, the detective listened closely. "The Bostian Bridge has had a history of weird events over the last hundred-and-thirty years. It started on August 27, 1941 — fifty years after the wreck. After getting a flat tire, a husband walked off to get help while the wife stood by the car. Of course, they were stuck on the road that paralleled the railroad tracks. She then heard a train in the distance, saw the headlight approaching, and walked across the field to watch the train. But as she got closer, she heard the screams as the crash played out in front her. Screaming with them, she ran back to flag a car for help. Her husband was in the car, returning with a man from the store down the road. They hurried back to the crash, but of course, there was nothing there. And so, people have claimed that every August 27th at 2:30am, you can hear the rumble of the engine, the shriek of brakes, the screams of passengers, and the cracking of metal as the train crumples into the rocks below. If you went to the site, you might see the light of the train approaching and watch it stream over the side. There are more stories like this — the usual kind of thing surrounding a horrific tragedy of this nature, but what's notable is that they continue. Incidents in the 1950s, 1960s, all the way into 2010 and probably in the last year or so. Then there's this last one I want to share. I think this will convince you."

Drummond said, "I think I'm already there, partner."

With a confident nod, Max said, "By the 1970s, everybody in Statesville knew the dark history surrounding that bridge. Teenage boys often dared each other to hang out at the crash site at night. Then one night, three extra drunk, extra daring teenagers decided they would one-up everybody — they would cross the bridge itself. They climbed up to the top and weaved their way along the rails. About halfway across, they heard an engine. A light could be seen approaching. The boys cried in abject terror. They ran towards the far end. The boys reached the end, jumped off the tracks, and flattened to the ground. Laying there, hearing the ghost train getting louder, they probably laughed at their fear as they sat up to look. Only then did they realize that one of them had not made it back. One boy's foot got caught in the railroad ties. In his panic, he injured an ankle and couldn't figure out how to free himself. His buddies shouted at him, urging him to get off the bridge, but they wouldn't risk running back to help him. You may have guessed this part by now, but that was no ghost train. It was a real one. A modern diesel locomotive barreling down on that boy with tons of cargo lined up behind. In the investigation that followed, the coroner couldn't understand why the boy didn't run off. His ankle was fine, and there was no evidence that it had been trapped or injured in any way."

Max let that last part sink in as he gathered his notes and the photos. When he sat on the couch, he scanned the room. Now that he had finished, he worried that Drummond had been right. Perhaps he rambled too long with all his research. Not for Sandra or J — they were familiar with his way of doing this. But if he had gone too long, if he had bored Brenda or Osorio, they might lose their first teammates. And one thing had become clear with this case — having two extra hands, two extra minds, two extra everything made a huge difference.

"Well?" he finally asked.

Osorio sat straighter, his fingertips tenting below his chin. "Sounds legit to me."

"Yeah," Brenda said. "Don't forget — when I followed Roy, he went to Statesville. I didn't see any ghost bridge, but I wasn't looking for one, either. Yet it would be a weird coincidence if he happened to be going to the same town during this whole hexing business and alongside everything we've learned about him. Wouldn't it?"

"Absolutely," Sandra said. "Assuming this is the right bridge, I can start working out a specific spell to end the natural curse."

"It is the right bridge," Max said.

"You can't know that for sure."

"I do. Because of the final thing." He paused long enough for Sandra to raise an eye at him. "The Bostian Bridge is next to L. Lingle Landscaping."

Brenda said, "That's where I followed Roy to."

"Exactly."

"Okay," Sandra said. "You win. You've got the right bridge. I'll get started on the spell. Once it's done, Roy Malone's hex will no longer work. Dwayne will be free from trouble."

"Well, from that trouble, anyway." Brenda patted her legs as she stood. "Tell us what you need, and we'll be glad to help."

"Nothing, right now. I'll be spending tomorrow with my head stuck in old books."

"I figured as much. But that was our deal — I'm volunteering my time to help the Porter Agency, and you were going to start teaching me witchcraft."

Sandra stood. "You're right. Can you join me in the morning? It'll go faster with two sets of eyes."

"Tomorrow's Saturday, so yeah, I don't have to work. I'll be here."

Osorio grunted as he rose to his feet. "I wish I could help, but this is one of my weekends on. I'll be at the stationhouse for the day. If you need anything from my end, just call."

They spent a few minutes shaking hands and chatting. After Brenda and Osorio left, Max and Sandra fell back to the couch. J closed his notes, said he had more studying to do, and gave Sandra a goodnight kiss on the cheek before heading to his room.

"I think that went well," Max said.

"It did."

Drummond said, "I agree. Given every bit of evidence, this is probably the right bridge, but if we're going to go ahead with figuring out the correct spell and committing our efforts in this direction, we better check the place out. What do you say, partner? You up for a late-night drive?"

At that moment, Max had been thinking about the joyful comfort of his bed. But Drummond was right. Max knew it the second the ghost started speaking.

"Yeah, let's go," he said with all the enthusiasm of a plumber having to fix a waste line.

Chapter 15

RAIN STARTED FALLING ABOUT HALFWAY TO STATESVILLE, and when they finally pulled to the curb of Buffalo Shoals Road, the dirt and clay had become mud. Trees surrounded them, broken by a cleared area for the landscaping business — Max couldn't make out the sign from where he had parked — as well as a short, modern bridge with concrete walls stretching ahead. The road curved away further up as well as behind. After a few minutes of hard rainfall, the storm pushed eastward and lightened.

With the rain tapering off, Max got out of the car and crossed the street. Drummond floated alongside. In the quiet pattering of water falling off leaves, they stared into the thick dark.

"The Bostian Bridge parallels this part of the road." Max pointed his chin ahead. "This little creek beneath us gets much wider as you go north, and the ground drops down pretty quick."

Squinting, Drummond said, "All I see are a bunch of cows."

In the rain and dark, Max couldn't make out even that much, but he trusted the ghost's eyes in this case. "I guess the old creek bed is pasture now. If the sun were out, I think we'd be able to get a glimpse of the bridge through all these trees."

"That's a shame. If it were further away, less visible, I'd suggest we break the hex during the day. But we can't risk being seen from the road or by the farmer coming along the pasture to gather his cows. We'll have to wait until nightfall."

"That's the way it usually is."

"A fella can still hold out hope."

He turned toward Drummond. "You could recon the place right now, if you were so inclined."

"So could you."

"It's too dark for me. Too muddy from all the rain. I might slip, get hurt. Or I might spook the cows, get trampled. Might even wake the farmer, if the house isn't too far off. Could be that I —"

"Okay, you've made your point." Drummond readjusted his Fedora as if the remaining drizzle could touch him. "Sheesh."

Like a graceful ice skater, he slid forward through the concrete barrier and out over the pasture. As his pale figure moved across the air, several cows lifted their heads. Others mooed — perhaps reacting to the sudden cold spots forming above them. Max thought he also heard an old detective grumbling.

He turned away from the pasture and gazed along the road. The drizzle petered out, leaving behind quiet and emptiness. And cold. A November night was the wrong time to be conducting this kind of operation. Max crossed his arms and shivered.

No wonder J didn't want to be in the field. It took as certain kind of craziness to seek out this sort of discomfort. Then again, Max knew the heavy excitement that would arise when a case broke open. Scary at times, but thrilling, too. Maybe that was why he did it? The thrill. Maybe all the paranormal investigators and ghost hunters and such, maybe they all were nothing but another form of adrenaline junkie.

Drummond returned, breaking Max's chance to explore this thought further. Max said, "You're back? You barely glanced at it."

"I saw enough."

Max peered through the dark again. "Something out there?"

"You can't really feel it here, but the closer you get to that bridge — I'm telling you now, you can *feel* the wrongness of that place."

"I guess that confirms we found the right bridge. You didn't see a hole where a stone had been pried out, did you?"

"Never went that close. Look, we're going to spend enough time down there when Sandra's spell is ready. No need to spend more."

A shudder raised the hair on Max's arms. Could have been

the cold night air, but he knew better. "You think we should get Brenda and Osorio to come along?"

Drummond glowered at the dark pasture and shook his head. "Don't start relying on them too much. It's good to have more people to work with, to call on now and then, but in the end, it's always just us. Osorio has a career with the police — not an easy thing to navigate normally. Add in the paranormal, and he's got a tough, narrow road ahead. Brenda's a sweet doll, and I'd hate to see her get hurt. With any luck, she'll dabble in spells with Sandra but never find herself sopping wet on an Autumn night, staring into such a freakish place. You want to be the one responsible for luring them deeper into all this?"

"What the heck happened out there? You're acting, well, scared."

"A guy like me can't be scared?"

"A guy like you is dead. And I'm talking with you. I'm the one who should be scared. All the time, probably."

Drummond cinched up his coat. "Don't worry. It's just a creepy place. We've been to dozens of 'em. Nothing new."

"If you say so. I guess you're right about our new additions. We shouldn't let them get too deeply involved."

"Yeah. During my living years, I had several folks like these. They can be great assets, but if they aren't willing to drop away their old lives, then they shouldn't dive into this one all the way. Causes too many problems."

Max rubbed his arms for some warmth. "It's still really odd having more people as part of The Porter Agency."

"Why? You've got J. I suppose PB's not interested, though."

"That's different. They practically grew up in this business. Still, I guess I always thought the Sandwich Boys would be Osorio and Brenda for us, that we wouldn't need anybody else. Just you and us Porters."

"That's what you're really talking about — PB."

"Don't start becoming a shrink. You're not built for it."

Drummond poked a finger through Max's chest. "For a guy who loves to look into the past, you sure forget it all so quick. You've got to remember that PB has been his own man since he was a boy. He lived on the streets with no adults to take care of him. When he joined this family, his biggest taste of the Agency was nearly dying at his birth father's hand while atop an unfinished highway. Why would you expect him to follow in your footsteps?"

Squishing mud and the clank of a wrench hitting the pavement interrupted them. Max looked toward the sound — his car. A man hunched over behind the rear wheel.

"Hey!" Max stormed across the street.

The man scrambled away, and Max broke into a run after him. Darting into the woods, Max's feet slid on the wet leaves, but he kept upright. Though dressed all in black, the man stood out amongst the still trees. He made no effort to hide, racing along, weaving around the trunks, never glancing back. Max followed.

Another slip on the leaves, and Max hit the ground. A stone bruised his forearm as mud and rain soaked his jeans. He jumped to his feet, but the fast-moving shadow was gone. Or still. Either way, Max didn't see any hint of what direction to take.

"Crap." He spit dirt from his mouth and used a tree to help stand. Wiping mud from his clothes, he walked back towards the street. Feeling a bump already forming on his arm, he strode out of the woods to find Drummond floating by the car. "What's with you? Why didn't you help me? You could've stopped that guy a lot easier than me."

"Didn't want to spoil your fun."

"Fun? Are you kidding?"

"Of course." Drummond gestured to the car. "I stayed because I figured you could handle it and I should find out what he was doing over here. Last thing I wanted was for you to get behind the wheel and find the brakes cut."

Max hesitated. "Did you find something?"

"Underneath the rear-wheel well."

Approaching his car as if it might whirl towards him and attempt to bite his arm off, Max gently reached up the wheel well. He felt it right away — a leather pouch. Though he made sure to check it carefully, he knew what he would find before he pulled it free.

"It's a hex bag, right?" Drummond said.

"Yeah." Max inspected the bag in his hand. Then looking at the woods, he said, "That man had to be Roy Malone."

"Reasonable guess. I don't think he had time to finish the spell on that bag, but we should call Sandra to be sure."

"I'll show it to her when I get home."

"No, partner. I can't allow that. If that hex bag is active and if it's designed to interfere with your driving, then it might be too dangerous to drive. Might even do more than simply cause an accident. A bag like that could cause you untold calamities."

That seemed like a lot of conjecture, but that didn't make it wrong. Max relented without much fight. He dug out his phone and called Sandra.

Chapter 16

EARLY SUNDAY MORNING, before Max had finished making breakfast, Brenda arrived to work on the spell. Max explained about the previous night and that Sandra had lost much of it to destroying the hex bag. She thought it had never been properly finished — nothing had happened to Max or his car to suggest otherwise — but she went through the trouble of stopping the hex, just in case. By the time they returned home, they were both exhausted, and Max figured it best to let her sleep in. But hearing the chitchat in the kitchen, Sandra stumbled out of the bedroom, waved half-heartedly, and made straight for the coffee.

"Where's Drummond?" Sandra said, her voice a creaking oak from behind her mug.

Max plated some eggs and toast while tending to the bacon. "After you went to bed and he was sure nothing would come of that hex, he said he was heading to the Other. He was ticked off that his ghost friends let Roy Malone slip away long enough to attempt hexing me again. I think he plans to express that anger once he finds them."

"Even dead, I wouldn't want to be on his bad side."

Once breakfast had been eaten and Sandra had awakened fully, she and Brenda commandeered the living room to spread out the witchcraft books and get to work. Max cleaned up the kitchen, took a shower, and caught an unintended nap when he stretched on his bed, closed his eyes, and let his mind wander over the case. When he awoke, an hour had gone by.

He rubbed his face, got up, and headed toward his office alcove. Glancing in the living room, he saw Sandra leaning over Brenda's shoulder, guiding her through some lesson on the basics of creating a casting circle. He had seen her teach J some of the same before, but this struck him different. J had been a good student, but he also had a cocky confidence at times. The moment he grasped the concept being presented, he wanted to jump ahead to the next thing. Not Brenda. She was an eager student with plenty of patience. She listened to Sandra, even when she already thought she understood, and practiced hard. From that short glimpse of them as he passed in the hall, Max could tell how much Sandra enjoyed teaching Brenda.

With that on his mind, no wonder he stopped in the kitchen doorway instead of settling in his alcove for more research. He had a view through the side door leading out and saw PB under the hood of his old car. Max gave the young man plenty of credit. They had bought the used car knowing it would need some work, but it turned out more lemon than lemonade. PB jumped right in, though. He read books on automotive repair and watched YouTube videos detailing specific fixes. He'd turned that barely moving piece of junk into a somewhat reliable vehicle.

Max felt a surge of pride watching PB at work. He wanted to tell PB as much, too. So why did he falter? It wasn't some testosterone fueled fear of sharing his emotions. Heck, he never held back sharing his pride with either of the Sandwich Boys.

No answer came. So, pulling together his courage, Max stepped outside. In his ongoing attempts to be a good parent, he refused to let his own fears stop him from being there for these young men. He figured that at some point his mind would uncover why he felt nervous. He could deal with it then. For now, he only had to be there.

"You know," he said as he approached the car, "I'm thoroughly impressed with what you've done here. This car probably hasn't run so well since it came off the line."

PB glanced up from the engine but said nothing.

"Ah," Max said. "Still mad at me."

With a frustrated shake of the head, PB returned to his work. Max wanted to argue or yell or have it out. Just get it over with, let PB spew out whatever he needed to say, and they could return to the tension-free life they all tried to share. But teenagers excelled at fomenting aggravation.

Biting back on all of that, Max attempted a friendlier tone. "I'd like to talk with you, work this out between us. I know you're mad that I wasted your day, but I also know that you wouldn't be this mad over something so small."

"Wasting my life is *small?*"

Not the reaction Max wanted, but at least PB spoke. "You know that's not what I meant."

PB kept his focus on the engine. A brief wind stirred the leaves and sent a chill across Max. He ducked his head under the hood and the odor of oil permeated the air. After another short silence, PB reached to a small tool tray balanced on the edge of the car and offered a wrench.

Max backed up. "I never learned cars. Don't know a spark plug from a distributor cap. Heck, I barely know if those are the correct terms."

Dropping the wrench on the tray with a clatter, PB muttered, "Of course not."

"What does that mean?" Max heard the bitterness in his voice, but it was too late.

PB whipped up, standing tall, chest puffed, ready to throw punches. With the same flash that ignited his fury, his shoulders dropped, and his head lowered. The wind blew again, raining leaves through the air behind him.

These moments put on trial a parent's convictions — and lately, Max thought, there were a lot of them. But he held true to his own. He did not threaten PB or yell at the young man or betray what he believed was the right way to parent. He simply stood there. And waited.

Setting a clenched tool aside, PB grabbed a dirty rag and wiped his hands. "You know that I appreciate all the help you've given to me. J, too. We both understand how lucky we are to have you and Sandra in our lives. Without all of this," he made a broad gesture encompassing Max, the house, the car, their life, "I would've ended up in a gang, or I'd be a drug addict. Or dead. I know I've said things like this to you before, but I don't get the feeling you've heard me. So, listen good. I appreciate this."

Max leaned one hip against the car. He wanted to assure PB

that he always listened, that he always paid attention, but he knew better. Whenever they were on a juicy case, he tended to forget the rest of the world — sometimes that included PB and J. He nodded, hoping that would be enough to prove his attentiveness.

"Here's the thing that you and Sandra don't get — I've never really fit in. J's different. He fits in good. He's into your mystical agency scam, he's made good friends at school, and I know he's talked to you guys about going to college. If you ever doubt the impact you've made, just look at that. College. When it was just us two, the idea that J might go to college would have had us laughing in the streets. And he'll do it, too. No question about it. That kid will get in, and he'll ace whatever a school throws at him — because he's smart."

"You're smart, too."

"Not the same way. I don't belong in college. After this last day following around that lady, I can see I don't belong playing at detective like the rest of you, either."

"Then what?"

PB picked under his nails. "That's been on my mind. I know what I'm not, but I ain't got a clue what I am. I guess that's not what you want to hear. J does everything right for you, but I'm not him."

"Nobody's asking you to be J. You're not in competition with him. Sandra and I love you both. We're not judging you by the things J does. We want you to find your own path. And if I spout one more thing that makes me sound like an old parent, I swear I'm going to have to put myself in a home."

Snickering, PB said, "I know you say all that, and you believe it, too."

"That's because it's true."

"It's been my experience that people can change quickly when faced with something they don't like."

Max clamped down his worry. As plain as possible, he said, "You thinking of doing something we wouldn't like?"

PB firmed up. "I don't know where my life is going. Get it? All I know is that it won't be working here for you, and I won't be going to college. Whether you admit it or not, that's two strikes against me."

"Son, we don't keep count against you, and those things aren't strikes. We're here for you. Understand that much. Please. As your parents, we want you to succeed in whatever you choose, and we trust that you'll make good choices, so it's easy to support you."

He could see the doubt on PB's face. But he also caught a twinge of hope. The poor man had suffered so much in his early years, Max feared he may never trust people enough to fully enjoy a relationship or a friendship. Perhaps even J had trouble cracking through PB's shell.

The side door whined as it opened. Brenda stepped out. She paused, clearly trying to decide if she should speak or make a quick retreat.

"Need something?" PB asked, plastering on a friendly grin.

"Um...yeah. Sandra said I should get Max. She says she's ready."

Max looked over his shoulder. "I'll be right in." When he turned back, PB had already resumed working on the car. Max stood in the silence a bit longer, but nothing could rekindle that conversation. The most he could manage was to pat PB on the back before walking into the house. It didn't feel like enough.

Chapter 17

TOM PETTY WAS RIGHT — the waiting really was the hardest part. Max ate away at the day with little tasks — picking up extra supplies for Sandra, prepping a couple backpacks for the evening's excursion, patching some of the holes from the kitchen attack — but the hours took their leisure in passing. The minutes didn't cooperate, either. He even listened to Drummond complain about how the ghosts in the Other were all avoiding him.

"They should be ashamed. It takes a real idiot of a ghost to screw up following a guy."

"They're probably afraid to face you," Max said. "They let us down last night, and they know it."

But no matter how slow time ticked by, it continued to tick. At length, they said goodbye to Brenda as she headed off to work, they watched PB get his car running and drive off to help Mrs. Porter, and they made sure J had a decent dinner before he dove into his studies. Then the car was loaded up and off they went. Max drove, and Sandra read over the plan for her newly designed spell. Drummond made one last effort to locate his missing contacts in the Other before meeting up near Statesville.

With night descending, Max parked at the same concrete-sided bridge from the previous night. He shut off the engine and immediately heard a cow's benign mooing in the distance. As he shouldered the backpacks, Drummond arrived.

"No luck," the ghost said. "I'll find them, though. Those fools aren't ever going to move on, and that's the only way they'll get away from me."

The air still smelled of damp leaves. Max had checked WXII weather, and they predicted a clear night. He glanced at the sky

— no clouds. Clear indeed. Not much of a moon, either. He popped the trunk and grabbed a high-powered flashlight.

Moving slowly and with great care, they climbed down into the gully beneath the short bridge. Since most of North Carolina ground was partially clay, it never quite drank in the rains. More often, the ground sipped at water like a lightweight nursing a beer all night long. With the Autumn showers being more frequent, it could take days before the mud dried up.

Knowing this did not keep Max from wondering about each soggy step. They walked through a pasture, after all. Cow patties were just as likely to be underfoot.

"Maybe we should have waited at the car for the Finchers," Max said.

Drummond floated at Max's side. "Better to have everything ready to go. They don't strike me as the type that will embrace hanging out here all night."

"I don't know," Sandra said. "When I called them earlier and told them where to meet us tonight, there was something off in their response. They sounded … reticent."

"Wouldn't be the first client to act bold about magic and witches until they were actually confronted with the real thing."

"Except they've already been dealing with the hex. This isn't new to them."

"The idea of magic might not be new, but going to a cursed bridge in the middle of the night to cast a spell is definitely new."

"Still, I expected to hear a little relief or even hope from them. Being scared of tonight makes sense, too, but part of them should have been happy to know we had a plan to free them of this hex. Excited even. But they sounded reserved, at best."

Max stopped. "You don't think they're in trouble. Maybe Roy Malone got to them and when you called —"

"I'll check on them," Drummond said and disappeared.

Sandra said, "Don't worry, hon. They didn't sound like that. I didn't hear a shake in her voice or stammering words. She wasn't speaking like she had a gun to her head or anything. She just lacked the emotions I expected."

"You think maybe she's found out about the affair?"

"If so, if she's newly hurt and now wishing he would go on suffering, that could complicate the spell's chances of success."

A few minutes later, they reached the bridge. Seeing it tower above simultaneously thrilled Max and disappointed him. On one hand, this dried creek bed surrounded by tall walls of rock loomed with all the threat and danger it once posed to a group of passengers in 1891. On the other hand, it was just a tiny gully, deep enough to require a stone bridge yet barely wide enough for more than a handful of arches. Nothing overwhelmingly special.

He looked to Sandra, a wisecrack on his lips, when he saw the consternation blanching her face. "What's wrong?" he asked.

Her gaze drifted back and forth across the ground. "They're all here. They've never left."

Though Max only saw Drummond, he could imagine what Sandra witnessed. Twenty-three ghosts locked in terror and suffering their final moments. Or, if they were lucky, those souls drifted around the crash site, unable to recall where they belonged, where they should go. They wore their suits and dresses, had bowlers and canes and umbrellas, and the young boys had caps while the girls had ribbons in their hair.

Max often wondered if he would want Sandra's gift. It wouldn't be bad to see all those dead folks — he probably would get used to it — but only if they were like Drummond. Whole. Complete. But Max could see in Sandra's eyes that some of the unfortunate ghosts bore the wounds of their deaths. Broken limbs and ripped flesh would be the least of it.

Clasping her hand to offer some support, Max said, "Is this going to mess up our plans?"

"I doubt it. They've been out here so long, they don't seem to even notice us. There are others, too. People who died from the curse on this place. Over there is a woman with a '60s beehive, and that must be the boy from the '70s you told us about. So many of them." She spent a moment scanning the area before she pointed near the base of one of the bridge's support pillars. "I'll set up the spell over there. You go find where that cursed stone belongs."

They walked over to the section she had indicated. Max shivered from cold spots several times, but he also shivered from thinking about the possibility of cold spots. Either way, he knew those ghosts meandered around him, and it put him on edge.

"Well, well," Drummond said, materializing several feet away, "that's a lot of dead people. Feels like being in a hospital. Or a cemetery. Not as gloomy, though."

Max said, "How could this not be *gloomy?* They all died so horribly."

"They didn't know it was going to happen. That's why they're wandering around." Drummond tipped back his hat. "At a hospital — most of those people know the end is coming. They had time to make their peace. Heck, most people, most of the time, know Death is coming. If you don't believe me, hang out at cemetery after you're dead."

"I'll take your word for it."

"But here — every single person on that train expected to make it to the next station, at the least."

Max watched the empty land and tried to picture the ghosts in this new light. "Are they too lost, too confused, to help us? I'm sure one of them knows where our stone goes."

"Doesn't hurt to ask. I'll try."

Using a wooden kitchen spoon, Sandra dug a casting circle into the mud. "Will both of you please start looking and stop talking? I need to concentrate."

"Of course, doll. My apologies. Just so you know, the Finchers are on their way. Safe. No sign of Roy Malone in their car or following them or anything."

Max turned his flashlight onto the bridge supports and walked around them. From the start, he knew he would be inspecting them over and over. In the growing dark, he could only see small sections at a time with any clarity. Twice in his first pass, he thought he had found the gap where a stone had been only to discover a stone already there — one so dark with wet moss or mold or mud that it looked empty under the unnatural beam of a flashlight.

As he moved to the next support, he heard Drummond

making the rounds of the ghosts. Lots of *Excuse me, sir* or *Please ma'am, a word.* None of them responded. At least, not in any meaningful way that got Drummond to stop and talk.

Until he reached a spot near the back of the second pillar. Max had started his next trip around when he heard Drummond's voice shift its quality. No longer politely trying to interrupt or get attention, his register had dropped and his words smoothed out and — *oh no.* Max paused to listen closer.

"1992, huh?" Drummond said, his hat tilted at a charming angle. "Well, you don't look a day over 2010."

Max wanted to shout at his partner. This wasn't the time to pick up dates. But he held back. It wasn't the conversation Max wanted, but it was a conversation. Clearly, Miss 1992 did not suffer the same traumatic stupor as the ghosts of 1891, and if Drummond could get her to reveal where the stone belonged, it would be worth having to listen to his attempt at alluring banter.

Thankfully, Max didn't have to endure for long. Dwayne and Nell Fincher ambled through the pasture, their flashlights bobbing about. Like a rabbit bolting from a bad situation, Max hurried away from the ghostly dating game to greet the new arrivals.

When he reached them, however, he saw the fear coating every part of Dwayne. "It's going to be okay," Max said, infusing his words with as much positive energy as he could muster. "My wife is a genius at this sort of thing."

Nell held Dwayne's arm as if he were a doddering man searching for his cane. "We have faith in you," she said. "But the last few days have been hard."

Dwayne looked up at Max. The man's eyes had hollowed out and dark bags had formed beneath them. "I think this hex is trying to kill me."

Chapter 18

GUIDING DWAYNE TOWARD SANDRA'S CASTING CIRCLE, Nell gripped her husband's arm as if afraid he might be swept away. Max stayed at her side. She said, "When we met with you, we said that we had been experiencing all this bad luck. And that's all it was. But since you've gotten involved, the entire thing has turned worse. Our gas range nearly exploded. Dwayne's office had an electrical short that started a fire. Even driving out here tonight, we narrowly escaped three different car accidents. Not simple fender-benders. They would have been terrible crashes with eighteen-wheelers. We would not have survived."

Max looked closer. He noticed the lack of sleep in Nell's eyes and the shake in her fingers. "I'm sorry about that," he said. "When we confronted Roy Malone, I think he may have escalated matters, trying to beat us before we could stop the hex. But we're all here, and it's almost over."

Jutting his chin, Dwayne said, "This thing hasn't gotten us yet. I don't plan on losing right at the finish line."

"That's the right attitude."

Nell's mouth tightened, creating little ridges in her chin. "Why would Roy do this to his best friend? It makes no sense."

Max didn't answer. If he told Nell the truth, she might storm off, and the spell needed all the positive energy it could get. Besides, it wasn't his place. That was a conversation for Dwayne and Nell to have in private. At least, Dwayne looked ashamed. Maybe they really would have that conversation after this was over.

They reached the casting circle where Sandra had set two candles — one black and one green — at the north point. She gestured for Max and the Finchers to gather round. After consulting her notes and checking to make sure she had drawn the correct symbols, she gestured toward Dwayne. "I need the stone now."

Trembling, Dwayne reached into his coat pocket and produced the stone paperweight. He turned it over in his hand. "Hard to believe all my troubles came from this."

"No, dear," Nell said, "that's nothing more than a rock. It's Roy that caused this. He's the one behind it all, and you need to face that. I don't know why he's so mad at you that he would go this far, but until we figure that out, I worry that he might try something again."

"That's a good point," Max said, glaring at Dwayne. "Perhaps, after we're done here tonight, the two of you can have a long talk about it."

Sandra glowered at the stone as if it could know how she disdained it. "Please," she said, gesturing to the circle.

Dwayne offered it to Max, but Max put up both hands. "Sorry. I won't touch that until Sandra says it's okay."

Pulling the stone back, Dwayne gave an accepting nod. "I'm guessing you want it in the center?"

"Yes," Sandra said. "Where the lines converge."

After placing the stone in the indicated spot, Dwayne backed up next to his wife and clutched her hand. A burst of wind arrived from nowhere and blew out the candles.

"It knows," Nell said. "It knows we're trying to get rid of it."

As Sandra relit the candles, she threw a handful of salt over the stone. "I doubt it. There's no consciousness to this thing. No ghost attached to it. There's nothing about it that can *know* anything. Now, please, as I speak, I want you to concentrate on the stone and focus your desire for the hex to be destroyed. Not the stone, but the hex. Use the stone as this focal point, but nothing more. Understand?"

Dwayne gazed at Nell and patted her hand. "We do."

"Max, I need you to return to helping our partner in finding where that stone belongs."

"On it," Max said.

"Then we can begin."

When Max turned back to the bridge, he saw Drummond leaning his elbow against a pillar as he smiled toward an empty space. Coming up next to him, Max whispered, "You find where the stone goes, or did you get a date?"

Drummond tipped his hat at the empty space with an embarrassed cough before returning to Max. "I'm trying to do both," he said.

"Just start over on the other end of the bridge. We'll cover more ground."

As the ghost drifted off, Max shined his flashlight on the support and resumed his search. He could hear Sandra's soft, rhythmic chanting, and on occasion, the Finchers uncoordinated responses. That explained part of the difficulty Sandra faced. For most spells, a witch spoke the words of other languages, mostly dead or long forgotten by all but the most devoted. For this hex, however, Sandra had to include the victims which meant the spell, or part of it, had to be in English — an extra level of complexity.

He peeked around the side of the pillar. The edges of the casting circle pulsed a pale blue. The light reflected against Nell's wide-open eyes, her astonishment flashing back at the circle. After weeks of suffering from magic, the Finchers would finally get to see something more positive.

"Quit watching the show and do your job," Drummond said with a half-joking click of the tongue.

As Max turned away, he noticed a moment when the circle dimmed before continuing. He wanted to run over there and show Dwayne and Nell what their lack of focus had caused, but Sandra could handle them. This was all new for the Finchers, and Sandra would have planned for their concentration to be limited.

"I think I found it," Drummond said.

Max dashed across the dry creek. Drummond hovered about a foot above Max's head. Even with the flashlight pointing right where Drummond gestured, Max had to squint to discern shadow from empty hole. But it was there.

"Max," Sandra called.

He dashed back to the casting circle. The pale glow had

dimmed even more. Sandra bent forward, her hands resting on her knees while the Finchers continued to focus on the stone. He held back from chastising them. Something was wrong, but they didn't know how a spell casting should look, so they didn't know that Sandra required help.

"You need to take a break?" he asked, stroking her back.

"Is something wrong?" Nell asked, careful to avoid stepping in the circle.

Sandra snapped her hand out. "Stay in position."

Her body convulsed as if about to vomit but then relaxed. Taking a long breath, she straightened. Sweat formed along her hairline and she looked pale.

Max could see the concern on Dwayne and Nell's faces — worried more for themselves but worried nonetheless. Lowering his voice, he pressed his forehead against Sandra's and kissed the bridge of her nose. "There's water in the car. You want a moment to refresh?"

"I'll be fine," she said, a sharp quake in her speech that faded fast. "Roy might be crazy but he's no fool. Brenda had said she followed him out this way. He must have prepared for the possibility of us trying to stop all his work. Somewhere around here is another hex bag. It's not hexing any person, though. It's draining the casting energy."

"Like a security measure?"

"Right. It's blocking my spell from happening, and every time I attempt it, the hex is sucking out energy from me, too."

"Then stop. We'll find the bag and you can cast a spell to destroy it. We can come back tomorrow to finish with the stone."

She shook her head. He knew that would be her response. She said, "A hex like that — one that works on an area instead of a specific person — is actually a weak spell. It's designed to be weak so that it will pull in other spell energy if sensed. That's how it works. But something so weak doesn't need a counter-spell to be destroyed. Just open the bag and dump the contents. Go find it. Open it up. I've got to keep this spell going."

"Why? Nobody's going to be upset with postponing."

"Dwayne and Nell will. I've already started the spell. I'm creating energy, and that energy must go somewhere. The hex bag Roy planted around here is siphoning off some of it, but there's more energy than it can take. You understand?"

He thought he did, but he asked anyway. "If you stop the spell now, where does the excess energy go?"

She pointed to the center of the casting circle where they had been focusing all their thoughts and words — the stone. "If we wait a day to try this again, that hex is going to get a whole lot worse. Dwayne and Nell are going to end up dead before sunrise." Rolling her shoulders back, she turned to the circle. "Find that hex bag," she said. Then to the Finchers: "We continue."

Max hustled back to the support pillars and started examining again. Drummond darted over to him. "What now?"

After explaining the situation, Drummond flew off. Max didn't see where the ghost went but trusted that his partner also searched for the hex bag. But Drummond had done better than that.

"Max, come here."

Rushing toward the back of the support on the opposite side, Max grumbled, "I swear if I have to run across this creek one more time."

Drummond dipped his head toward the empty space next to him. "This is Connie. She died in 1992, and she's quite cute."

"Nice to meet you, Connie," Max said, glancing back at Sandra and the dim glow of her spell. "Sorry I can't see or hear you."

"She understands."

Itching to get back to his search, Max said, "We're short on time, so maybe tell me what she wants."

"She wants to help. She's been stuck here for thirty years. Not much to do but watch the cows, trains, and a bunch of ghosts locked in their misery, unable to have even a simple conversation. All of this stuff has been the most excitement in decades."

Max froze. The words, the moment, finally penetrating his

brain. "She knows where the hex bag is."

Drummond winked and lifted his gaze. "Up there."

Sixty feet above them. On the tracks. On the bridge.

"Of course."

Chapter 19

WHILE DRUMMOND HAD NO TROUBLE ascending through the air, Max faced an arduous hike around. He had no serious rock-climbing experience, so he didn't bother attempting to find a way up the steep sides. Instead, he sprinted across the low-grade incline towards the cars. He scrambled along the slope to the street, hurried down to the landscaping business, and followed the piles of gravel and dirt around to the back. Weaving through a short run of trees, he hit a steep ascent, and there he found the railroad tracks.

Coughing and sputtering, he walked along the rails toward the bridge. He strained for air, and the cold Autumn night filled his lungs like a frosty blade. He coughed more, stumbling along.

When his phone chirped, Max startled at the sound. A quick glance — his mother. Damn. He wanted to let it go to voicemail, but in her condition, he had to be careful. She might be calling in desperate need. She might require a rush to the hospital. She might be nearing her end and wanted him by her side.

"Would you be a good boy and stop at the store? I need some cookies."

"Cookies?" He tried to hold back the growl in his voice but failed.

"Don't get like that. My diet isn't an issue anymore. If I'm stuck with this horrible disease, the least I can ask for is a cookie now and then."

Standing on the railroad tracks, he clenched the phone. "I'm in the middle of work right now, and I'm in another town."

"Then send one of the boys or that wife of yours."

"I've got to go. I'll bring you cookies tomorrow morning, okay?"

Though unhappy with the answer, Mrs. Porter huffed. "Fine, fine. But if I'm dead in the morning, you'll never be able to eat a cookie again."

After he hung up, he hoped she was wrong and that cookies would still be an option in the morning. Jogging the last of the way, he tried to blot out his mother, her MS, and thoughts of her demise. Sandra struggled down below and needed him now.

By the time he had reached the bridge, Drummond hovered over a spot several feet beyond the middle. Seeing Max, the ghost snapped his fingers and pointed at the tracks. "What took so long? I found this minutes ago."

Max peeked over the edge. Stupid thing to do. Sixty feet below, looking like miniatures, Sandra and the Finchers stood around a glowing casting circle. Max's heart already pounded from racing over the area and stressing about his mother, but it kicked into overdrive at the thought of falling all that way. No wonder people could still hear the passengers from 1891 shrieking in terror. A death like that would have had him screaming loud enough to be heard for centuries, too.

The bridge did nothing to ease his fears, either. It ran straight ahead, and though it was wide enough for a train, it was barely wide enough to contain the tracks, and lacked a serious railing or safety of any kind. This was not meant for people to walk across.

"Come on," Drummond said. "Stick to the middle and you'll be fine."

"Easy to say when you can float in the air."

"Sandra's counting on you. All you have to do is walk out here and open this hex bag. I know you can do it. I've seen you face a lot worse than an old bridge. Come on, now. Pull it together and get moving."

Max shifted to the middle spot between the rails and took a few hesitant steps. Then a few more. He looked at his feet, and at times, he looked up at Drummond. Never over the side, though. Once had been enough. A few more steps. Keep moving and he would reach the spot soon.

Under his flashlight, the wooden ties crossing his path looked old enough to be the originals. It only hit him then that for the stone to be cursed by the tragic train crash, it had to have been there when the accident happened. This bridge had been around for over a hundred-and-thirty years.

He froze.

If there was ever going to be a night for the entire thing to finally collapse, this would be it.

"Don't stop," Drummond said. "You're halfway to me."

Shudders rippled through Max's muscles. He closed his eyes as his bones locked in place. A loud bubbling in his stomach threatened to send its contents barreling up his throat.

When he looked ahead again, Drummond hovered directly in front of him. The sudden appearance startled him back a step. He tripped on a railroad tie and fell. A horrid screech erupted from his mouth as his brain knew for certain he would flop too far. He could feel the air flowing around him. Soon he would plummet to an excruciating death. But as his throat caught and his heart jabbed his ribs, his backside smacked the side of one rail, and the rest of him tumbled to the solid bridge.

"You trying to kill me?" Max shouted. Then hearing his volume, he let out a breath and lowered his voice. "Sorry. But don't scare me like that."

"Get up," Drummond said. "I'll walk with you to the bag. We can talk about whatever inane thing you want to talk about. Just walk and talk. If you start to waver or go too far toward the side, then I'll suffer the pain and grab you. Okay?"

Brushing off the dirt, Max got back up. With more determination, he started walking again. Keeping his eyes straight ahead yet feeling an odd comfort having Drummond float at his side, Max thought about Dwayne and Jill and Roy and the whole mess that put him on top of this bridge in the middle of the night. "You ever cheat on a woman?" he asked.

"What kind of question is that?"

"You said we could talk about anything I wanted."

"Okay. The answer is no. Never."

"Me neither. I don't understand it. I mean I can grasp that a marriage or a relationship sours on you, and you no longer love the person you're with, but then leave. Divorce or break up. Why cheat?"

"Why ghost hunt? Why walk across a bridge like this?" Drummond pushed his coat open and stuck his hands in his pockets. "One thing I've learned in all my years living and dead — with a lot of things people do, logic has no bearing on it. We're emotional animals that crave whatever makes us feel good and run from anything painful. Don't look for sense in every action. It ain't there."

"I can't tell if that's pragmatic or bleak."

"Just honest. And look at that, my friend, we're here."

Indeed, they had traveled the entire length and Max had hardly noticed. "Thank you."

"Okay, I can hear the mushy side of you creeping in. Don't say anything else. We're men remember. Besides, I may have misrepresented how easy it'll be to get the hex bag."

Max's stomach dropped. "Why? Where is it?"

Drifting out over the edge, Drummond pointed. "Tied underneath. Not far, though."

Gentle chanting echoed from below. At least, it sounded gentle this far above. But Max pictured Sandra doubled-over, on the verge of tossing up her stomach. His poor wife suffered for real while he fought fears of his imagination.

Dropping to his knees, he muttered, "It better stay in my imagination." He lowered to his belly and wormed up against the rail. He reached over, but his hand barely passed the edge of the bridge.

Crap.

With one final breath, hoping to inhale courage beyond sense, he pushed up and over. He clutched the rail between his arm and his side, clamping his hand down tight. Once more, he reached over with his free hand. Still not enough to grab anything tied under the lip of the bridge.

"How far am I?"

Drummond raised a thumb and finger only inches away. "Roy put it there, so it's got to be possible to reach."

Max shimmied closer to the edge. The rough wood and metal of the bridge scraped his chest and stomach. His cheek pressed hard enough to water his eyes. He thrust out his free hand and wiggled it around, searching, searching.

And he felt it.

A leather pouch batting one way then the other.

"Stop flailing," Drummond said. "Just hold your hand flat and still. That's right. Now bring your hand up toward the bridge."

When he followed Drummond's instructions, Max felt the bag flap right into his palm. He seized it, yanked down twice to snap it loose, and rolled back over the rail to the safety of the center. Moaning, he breathed until he coughed. Then he laughed as he sat up. "I think that took a decade from my life."

"Don't exaggerate. You look fine. Now empty that hex bag and we can be done here."

Max untied the bag and dumped its contents next to the rail — chicken bones, tied herbs, a bit of quartz, and a strong scent of cinnamon.

"Good job, partner." Drummond drifted off the bridge once more. "I'll go down and tell Sandra she's free to finish her spell."

"She probably already knows."

"Let's be sure."

Max nodded as he stood. Sweat rolled down his back, but it felt more like soaking out the fear than dancing nerves on his skin. Still, he pointed at the shorter distance to land. "I think I'll go that way."

"Smart choice. When you get down —"

"Max Porter!" The bellowing voice slurred his name from the far end of the bridge.

Passing his flashlight beam in that direction, Max watched as Roy Malone wobbled forward. His disheveled, stained clothes and unshaven, unkempt face spoke volumes to the bender the man must have been on. Worse than that, though — in one hand, he held a bottle by the neck. In the other, he had a handgun.

Chapter 20

GUNS. Max had put off learning how to use his for too long, but in his line of work, shooting at a ghost served no purpose. Watching Roy Malone approach drunk and armed, however, Max reconsidered. He hoped he had not made a fatal mistake.

Roy moved with a relaxed gait, alcohol drowning away any fears of the dangerous bridge. Without a flashlight of his own, he stumbled over several ties, and in the short time Max observed the man, Roy came close to dropping off the side twice.

"This is all wrong," Roy said. He tilted the bottle back and guzzled. Then: "This wasn't supposed to go this way."

Though nobody but Max could hear the ghost, Drummond inched closer and whispered, "I'll go out there and freeze his head."

"You do that, and I'll have to go back out there myself and drag his unconscious body to safety."

"If we don't do something, he's liable to —"

Fire flashed from the muzzle of Roy's weapon. He had shot toward the sky. This time.

"That's it," Drummond said, slicing through the night air.

When he reached Roy, he grabbed the man's wrist. Drummond groaned loud enough for Max to hear at the end of the bridge, but the ghost did not let go. He had been touching the corporeal world more than usual, and the pain seemed to compound. Roy stared at his wrist — at first, confused; then frightened.

"Cold," he said. As if his brain could no longer connect basic motor signals, he opened his hand wide — but the wrong hand. The bottle shattered, yet the sound died fast.

"Drop the gun," Max shouted. "You'll be fine if you drop it."

Between Roy's high-pitched whines and Drummond's guttural-deep groans, Max wondered if anybody would hear him at all. But whether a result of Max's words, a sudden bout of sense, or sheer instinct, Roy finally opened his other fingers and released the handgun. It clattered against the tracks.

Drummond let go. He pressed his burning hand against his belly, coasting away from the bridge on unseen currents. Roy also nursed his hand, also drifted aimlessly, not paying attention — until his heel clipped one rail. He flailed his arms, screeching yet again, but managed to stay on the bridge. For the first time, he looked across at Max with honest dread.

"She lied to me," he slurred.

Great. Now Max had to play psychologist while shouting across the gulf of a bridge. "I know she did. But what you're doing is not fixing anything."

"No going back. I didn't get it, but when you showed, I got it. Get it? I got it now." Roy overacted laughter. "I got it good!" He peered over the side of the bridge. "She ain't ever going to do anything for me. I should've seen that from the start. Nothing I can do now."

"Don't think like that. You don't want to do anything rash."

"Nothing but take and take and hurt and hurt. She's the real witch in all of this."

A new sound cut through the cold. A quiet rumbling in the distance. Growing louder. Approaching.

Max cupped his mouth. "Roy! Get off the bridge!"

Roy looked over his shoulder at the empty tracks behind him. When his gaze wobbled back towards Max, the fear had turned to panic. He pointed into the dark. "There's a train coming!"

If the situation had been a movie, the entire thing would have been laughable. The drunk, regretful coward weaving from one edge of the bridge to the other, desperately stumbling his way towards Max, his face comically wide in terror as the click-clack of a cargo train hitting the rails came closer. Louder.

But this wasn't funny. Max wanted to rush out there and help the poor man, but he didn't move. He stood on the bridge watching, knowing that if he ran to Roy, they would both end up dead.

Roy tripped. Face-planted right between the rails. The bright headlight of the engine appeared in the distance.

"Get up," Max said, his voice barely above a whispered prayer. "Come on, now."

Lifting his head, blood streaming from his nose, Roy peeked back. He screamed. The front of that train rushed towards him, its threatening grumble like a massive storm on the rise.

When the engine's light flickered against the trees on either side, when that clear of a detail could be seen, Max knew it was too late. Roy did, too. Rather than be sliced apart by tons of rolling metal, the drunken man locked eyes with Max, yelled something that would never be heard, and then rolled across the tracks. Across the tracks and right over the far side of the bridge.

No final scream. No shouting Jill's name in a death fall. Nothing. In his last act, Roy simply disappeared from view.

Max stared at the spot where Roy had been, unable to comprehend what he had just seen. He might have stood there in a stupor until he fell victim to the train, but two things snapped him back. The blinding light of the engine and Drummond swishing into view.

"Get off the bridge!" the old detective shouted.

Max whirled around and bolted down the track. Though still afraid of teetering off the side, his fear of a train squashing him outweighed everything else. He pumped his legs, following the pale light of Drummond. The ghost led the way, and it gave Max's brain an object to focus on - a way to keep moving in the dark without plunging over the edge.

If the engineer saw a man sprinting in front of the train, Max would never know. The train never blew its horn, never slowed, never gave any sign to suggest somebody had been aware of the impending horror. Keep running. That's all he could do. Ignore the spear piercing his chest each time he breathed. Ignore the sweat and stink of fear. Keep running.

The engine's headlight created a bobbing Max-shadow that stretched along the last of the bridge. The last! Almost there. Max dug deeper, finding a final burst of energy.

The instant he spotted land, he hurled off the tracks. He tumbled down the grading, rocks and sticks pounding and poking his torso, until he clunked into the base of a tree. The train roared by. With his body sprawled on the ground, heavy gasps in his chest and a never-ending tremor in his hands, he watched boxcar after boxcar whizz by. The wheels clacking, the cars thundering. With each rhythmic noise, Max saw himself being dissected into tiny pieces.

Drummond hovered over to him. "You okay?"

"Sure," Max said, three pitches higher than he wanted. After sitting up and another deep breath, he said, "I will be."

"You need a minute before we go down to Sandra?"

Using the tree, he clambered to his feet. "I'll be fine. Let's go."

As he navigated his way back to his wife, Max marveled at the man he had become. Years ago, when he first started all of this, if he had watched another man roll off a bridge, if he had nearly died by a roaring train, he would have been a shaking wreck for hours, maybe days. Now? Less than a minute, a few gulps of air, and he returned his focus. Perhaps PB and J were right not to get too involved in this profession. Being in the field, dealing firsthand with all of this — when had it numbed him?

He reached the group at the bottom of the creek bed and noticed that he had stopped sweating and his heartrate had settled. Though he handled the situation with surprising stoicism, he felt a small prick of relief to recognize that he had been reacting on some level. Even if he could not summon the full-bodied normal reaction to Roy's death, another part of him flickered his nerves alive when he recalled what he still had left to do.

Sandra, Dwayne, and Nell all stared into the casting circle, their eyes wide and their bodies swaying. The spell had plunked them into a trance, and Max released another bit of tension — he wouldn't have to explain what happened to Roy. They never heard a sound. The glowing light of the circle blinded them to seeing much else in the night, so they never even glimpsed a shadow falling in the distance.

"Everything okay?" Sandra asked, and her face told him she knew. Dwayne and Nell might have been oblivious, but not Sandra.

"Is the stone ready?"

"Dwayne has to be the one to put it back."

"Good. 'Cause you couldn't pay me enough to touch that thing. Even now."

With eagerness, Dwayne scooped up the stone and followed Max around the back of the bridge. Sandra closed out her spell with a final chant that, Max guessed, would continue until the stone rested in its home once more. He pointed to the hole in the support pillar but didn't wait to help Dwayne. Instead, Max moved with steady purpose to the crumpled heap of flesh and bone several feet away that had once been Roy Malone.

"You really need to tell Sandra about this," Drummond said, appearing on the opposite side of the corpse.

"I will."

"Tonight. She's smarter than you when it comes to witch matters. She'll know how to best handle this."

"I promise you. I'll talk with her tonight. But I still need this jerk's hair, so if you'll stop pestering me." Max pulled out a pocketknife. A thought struck him. "Is Roy's ghost around here?"

"First thing I checked for. But no. Looks like he moved on."

Bending over the twisted mess of a body, Max found what remained of Roy's head. He held his breath against the stench of opened bowels. With fast motions, he cut loose a chunk of Roy's hair and dropped it in a sandwich bag. He shoved it all into his pocket, turned away, and spit out the bile that had rolled up his throat. Speed walking back to the group, he tried to ignore the bag in his pocket or the body he left behind.

Sandra had already started cleaning away the casting circle while Dwayne and Nell hugged. They laughed and sniffled and hugged some more. Max smiled and nodded at them, but all he felt was exhaustion and disgust.

"Thank you," Nell said. "I can see the difference already. All the worry is gone from his face."

Dwayne shook Max's hand, then Sandra's. "Yes, yes. Thank you. You've saved our lives, and if not that much, you've saved our sanity."

"No," Max said. "We did save your lives. But don't worry, we won't charge extra for that."

Nell thread her arm around Dwayne. "We should go home. Celebrate. Or maybe just try to have a normal night together. It's been a long time since we've had normal."

As they walked off, Dwayne stopped to look at Max. "I don't know if you could tell, but we weren't entirely convinced this would work."

"That's okay. It's hard to believe the world is different than you were raised to see."

"But I swear I can feel that the hex is gone. I know you and your wife did that. Thank you, again."

"Yes," Nell said. "Who would've thought you really could stop a hex? The fellow from tv."

They chuckled together and left for their car. Sandra came alongside Max with her backpack stuffed and ready.

"We should get out of here," she said. "At some point, Roy will get discovered."

"Drummond?" Max called.

From afar, Drummond said, "I'm looking over everything now. I'll let you know if you missed any evidence, but other than that one thing, I doubt the police will find much in all this mud. Frankly, they'll probably take a quick look, assume Roy was drunk and stupid and fell. Which isn't too far from the truth."

Sandra turned her head up towards Max. "What *one thing?*"

As they walked back to the car, he puffed his cheeks and grimaced. "Yeah. I didn't want to worry you with too much while you were recuperating —"

"Clearly, I'm fine now."

"I know, I know. It's time to tell you what I had to do in order to get an answer out of Madame Fein."

Chapter 21

SLOGGING THROUGH THE MUDDY PASTURE to get back to the car, then driving the long route to get home, Max detailed all that had happened at Haven House. Sandra listened. She said nothing. If she could have stood in the car, Max guessed she would have had a hand on one hip and a scowl across her brow. But he pressed on. Their marriage would never have lasted if they had gone on keeping secrets all the time. When he finished, he let the silence consume the car. Until Sandra finally spoke.

"I should kill you now and spare you whatever torture those witches have planned."

"It's not that bad. Not like I'm giving her *my* hair."

"That's not the point." She brought her leg onto the seat, resting her chin on her knee. "You're a smart man. Sometimes that's been a great asset. But it can also get you in trouble when you think you're smarter than you are about a subject."

"Like witchcraft?"

"Absolutely like witchcraft. I'm the one who has spent the last several years studying, learning, practicing in this field."

"I know that, and I respect that."

"But you seem to think that because you've encountered witches in the past, you know all you need to handle them in any situation. Your experience is making you sloppy, and that's dangerous."

Max cringed. He had been about to mention his experience, about to say that he wasn't a novice, but he already knew she was right. Surviving multiple cases involving witches — and ghosts and curses and countless other paranormal entities — had left him a bit cocky. When caught up in the moment, stuck standing in Haven House, he had found ways to justify his choices, but sitting in that car with the only good witch he knew in existence, he could see it all in a stark light. He questioned his decisions.

When they reached home, the long night hit Max hard. He showered off all the mud and grit, letting the hot water soothe his aches, and then headed straight to bed. Despite the difficulty of telling her about Haven House, Max felt the weight of it had lifted. But Sandra did not relax. She had pulled out several musty-smelling books and had three witch websites opened on her laptop.

"I've got to figure out everything that can be done to you with hair gathered in this way. Before you hand that over to Madame Fein, we need to know what to expect and if there's a way out of it."

Max offered to help, but his words muddled with sleep. His eyes fluttered to stay open. He would be no help. Besides, Sandra's anger fueled her research. Neither of them wanted Max in the path of that fire.

Monday arrived with the chirp of birds and frost on the ground. A bright sun passed through the skeletal trees and promised a crisp morning that would warm up fast. Typical North Carolina autumn. Start the day bundled tight, end the day without a coat and the windows open.

J had already left for school. Max wondered if all parents found that as their kids got older, they zipped in and out of the house on a mysterious schedule. He felt like he only saw his boys in flashes as they rushed in to grab food or change clothes, then when they rushed out to go to some event or assignment or friendly get together.

Then again, Max had learned over the years that after the close of an intense case — especially one where he could have plummeted to his death from a century-old, cursed bridge — his mind slowed the world around him. These mornings, he inhaled every breath of life, every sound, every nuance, everything that tied him to the gloriously mundane. After all, he fought the witches and ghosts and magic to protect and preserve the day-to-day lives of everybody else.

Well, that and it paid the bills.

As he opened his laptop to check the morning news, he heard tinkering metal from outside. PB working on his car. But he should have been in school.

Before Max could stand to go talk with the young man, Brenda entered the kitchen from the side door. "Knock, knock," she said. "I hope I'm not coming in too early. I couldn't sleep last night knowing y'all were breaking that hex. How'd it go? What happened?"

Sandra blundered in bleary-eyed. "Morning, Brenda." She glanced at Max. "You get dressed and make your delivery first thing."

"Oh?" Max said. "It's safe then?"

The hand went to the hip. "No, it's not safe. It'll never be safe. But for the moment, I can't find anything she can do that will harm us. I think she did the deal this way to make a point going forward. Show us that we're not in control, that the witches know more than us, and that we should be careful around them — even as I'm learning from them."

"A threat?"

"A warning. Not all witches will be as kind to us as Madame Fein."

Max thought about Madame Weir and nodded. "I'm sorry about all this."

When Sandra didn't respond, Brenda said, "I can come back later."

"No," Max said. "I'm leaving now anyway. I've just got to …" He stared at the local news website. "Did you see this?"

The others stepped behind him to read the screen. The headline read *Local Woman Found Dead in Occult Killing.* Max had already clicked the link, and a photo of Jill Malone shared space with another of her large-windowed house. Yellow police lines crossed the front while police stood around the grounds doing various duties. The article explained that the body was discovered by a freelance maid who arrived that morning to clean the house. Details were limited — the timestamp on the article suggested the body had only been found in the last few hours — but occult-like symbols had been painted on the walls in the victim's blood, and police confirmed that the victim's husband, Roy Malone, was missing and wanted for questioning.

Sandra said, "He killed her and then tried to kill you."

"I think he wanted to kill himself all along," Max said. "He couldn't have known we were at the bridge, and if he sought us out, why would he get blitzed before taking us on? No, I think after all these years of pent-up rage, he finally snapped. He tried getting revenge with that hexed stone, but it didn't stop Dwayne and Jill. They didn't get the message. Add to that a visit from me and Drummond — well, me as far as Roy understood — but he knew his chances were closing up. He has a gun with him or nearby, grabs it and kills her. Kills her because he couldn't wait any longer, couldn't take any more."

"Then he sees what he did, can't stand it, so he gets drunk and goes to the bridge to kill himself. Only we're already there. He sees you and loses it."

Brenda said, "Sounds plausible but for one thing."

"What did we miss?"

"All the blood symbols on the walls. What was he trying to do there?"

Max looked to his wife. "I've learned my lesson. You're the expert here."

"Better late than never," Sandra said, rolling her eyes with an amused grin. "The problem is that we can't know what he intended unless we know what he actually drew on the walls. Maybe he wanted to hex her ghost. That seems in line with his behavior. Maybe he didn't do it until after he was drunk, and the symbols have no real power at all. No way to know from here."

Hunching forward, Max glowered at the article. "You're kidding me."

"Afraid not."

Brenda said, "Did I miss something? I feel like I definitely missed something."

Patting her husband on the shoulder, Sandra said, "This is my job. You've got a delivery to make."

Max said, "I can drop cookies at my mother's later today. She's probably asleep now, anyway."

"Not the delivery I meant, and you know it."

"I'll stop by Haven House after."

"What just happened to you learning your lesson? Madame Fein is expecting you."

"I don't like this."

"You don't have to."

Brenda waved a hand between them. "Excuse me, but I need to know what's going on. It sounds important. And since I missed all the fun last night, you shouldn't be shutting me out now."

Sandra turned to her student. "You're in luck. While the case is over for the Finchers, we don't stop until we can safely be done. That means we have to find out what, if anything, was cast onto Jill Malone's ghost."

"And by *we*, you mean?"

"You and me. Max isn't happy because we'll have to find a way into that house that doesn't get us arrested, but he has a mess of his own making to clean up. You in?"

The wide grin dominating Brenda's face gave a clear answer. Minutes later, the two women drove off in Brenda's car. Max stood at the side door, watched them leave, and then turned his eyes towards PB. Neither spoke for a bit. Max still reeled from the news of Jill Malone, the way Sandra had hurried Brenda to go break into that house, and the knowledge that he had an old witch waiting for him. But he also had a son. PB continued repairing the engine or the belt or the plug or some other thing Max didn't understand. He did, however, understand that he stood at another parental precipice.

"Skipping school today or are you dropping out completely?" He hoped some shock value might get him somewhere.

It worked. Too well. PB thrust back from the car, his youthful muscles threatening as he stormed towards Max. This young man had come a far distance from the picked-on kid hiding in a delipidated shell of a building.

"I'm not a quitter, and even if I ain't as smart as J, I ain't stupid. I'll graduate. Don't you worry."

"Glad to hear it. Just a piece of advice — you'll find it easier to graduate if you actually go to school."

Frustration twisted PB's mouth. "One crappy day off, and you're going to come at me about it? Most kids in my class take a week or even a month for mental health stuff. I've never even skipped a class. So, yeah, I'm taking a day off. It was supposed to be a quiet, peaceful day with my car. If you leave now, it still might be."

This had not gone the way Max wanted. He saw the relationship with his son teetering over that ledge, ready to fall, and he had to think quick. "Tell you what. Walk around the block with me — just once around — and then I'll let you alone for the rest of the day. Deal?"

PB looked at his car. "Fine. I don't really have a choice anyway. If I turn you down, you'll stand there and talk all day."

"Probably."

After locking the house — not that there was much worth stealing — Max and PB strolled along the street. The morning air fulfilled the sun's earlier promise. Each breath inflated Max with a renewed, fresh sensation. There would always be problems, but that rich aroma of Nature reminded him that those problems were smaller than the Earth, smaller than the solar system, and a mere speck to the galaxy. Not so big when he thought of it that way.

Still, it took until they turned the first corner before he found the courage to speak. "I'm not trying to be hard on you," he said. "I know you won't believe this, but I'm not even trying to pester you. I'd love it if we could hang out and watch a movie or play a video game or something easy and relaxed. Every conversation between us doesn't need to be such a big deal."

"Then why is it?"

"Good question. Why do you think?"

PB had carried along an adjustable wrench, and he rolled the sizing open and closed, back and forth. As they walked, Max listened to the metal wrench, the sound tightening the pressure around him. He wanted to feed PB all the answers that would make things right and happy, but the young man had to figure this out for himself. Besides, Max didn't have all the answers, either. Nobody ever did.

A dented red pickup gathered dust on the curb ahead. Max focused on that old truck as they walked closer. If PB didn't say anything by the time they reached it, Max would —

"I guess because you're not happy with me." PB's voice cracked.

"What? I love you."

"Didn't say you didn't love me." He gained strength as he spoke on. "But you want me and J to have some defined path forward in our lives. Or something like that. J already knows the next ten years of his life. I don't. That pisses you off. Hard to go see a movie or play a game if whenever we're around each other, things get like this."

They turned the second corner, and Max fought to keep himself from reaching over and forcing PB into a hug. That young man had endured a lot in his life already, and he needed to be treated like more of an adult than his age suggested.

"I'm not pissed at you. I'm worried for you. Business has been so busy lately that I can't be here all the time, and I'm missing out on all you're going through. Maybe if we talked more, I would know already. That would be easier, wouldn't it?"

"Sure. Then you can resent me for making you choose between me and your job."

"I didn't mean it like that."

"You never do."

"What now?"

"You've got a bad habit of saying things before you think them through. It's like with J. Maybe you didn't mean it to come out that way, but whenever you talk about him and his accomplishments or how much he's helped your business and all that … forget it. It doesn't matter."

"It does."

But Max's throat choked as his mind blanked. He couldn't find the right thing to say, and each time he spoke only pushed PB further away. He needed to think.

He saw a faded-yellow house with discarded toys in the yard coming up. Part of him wanted to wait until they reached that house. Let them both simmer; let them both consider. By then, he would be able to speak in a calm, thoughtful manner. But part of him knew that waiting on an arbitrary point like a house only stalled the matter. And Max was running out of block to walk.

"All this pressure you're feeling, all this comparison to J — you're doing that to yourself." He recoiled at the way he had blurted that out. Then: "If I said something stupid to make you think otherwise, then listen to what you just said and remember that I don't always mean things the way they sound. So, let me be clear — I don't expect you to be J. I don't want you to be."

"You've said that before, but it doesn't feel that way."

"I'm sorry about that. I never meant to make you feel anything but support from us."

PB shrugged. "Can we not talk about this anymore? I don't know what I want to do with my life, and I'm not going to come up with answer in the next half-block. Maybe if you gave me the space to think, let me work on my car and have some peace, maybe it wouldn't be so bad between us right now."

They turned the third corner. Max didn't know what else to say. PB made a good point. Quite a few, actually.

When they turned the last corner and approached the house, Max knew that he had failed. Yet they hadn't tumbled over that precipice. They hadn't reached a point that would irrevocably destroy their relationship. Maybe he simply needed to do what PB asked — let him have the day off, let him think in peace.

In the driveway, PB strode right to his car and resumed working. Max held still, searching for some final word that might patch things together for a moment. In the end, he hoped a little quiet might cast its own spell on this young man — help him figure out what Max could not.

Thinking of spells brought to mind magic and witches. And thinking of witches reminded Max that he still had to go to Haven House and deal with Madame Fein. Suddenly he had the strongest desire to learn all about car maintenance.

Chapter 22

HAVEN HOUSE NEVER LOOKED INVITING, but that afternoon, it looked downright hostile. Sitting in his car, Max watched the house as if he expected all three witches to fly out of the chimneys on broomsticks and divebomb him. But that would have been too easy, too clear a threat. These witches played subtler games. Smiling like sweet grannies when in reality they held the kind of vicious power that other witches lusted after.

"It won't get any better by waiting," Drummond said, appearing in the passenger seat.

"Oh, wonderful," Max said, sarcasm oozing like syrup. "I was worried I would have to do this peacefully on my own."

"Never fear, partner. I'm here to help."

All the biting humor left him. "You can't really, though, can you? Even if you found some way to break through the ghost wards on that house, this is still my problem to face. I'm the one who made the deal, after all."

"Yeah, I'm afraid so." Drummond scratched his stubbled jaw. "But I'll still be here anyway."

Not what Max expected, and to his surprise, he felt warmed by the simple sentiment. He got out of the car. A few birds sang as a soft breeze rustled loose the last leaves before winter. Golden leaves gently drifting to the ground — beautiful sights yet reminders of an ending. They fell onto his path feeling both comforting and ominous in their timing.

Sticking his head through the car roof, Drummond said, "You actually have to walk into the house in order to meet with the witches."

Max looked back. "Unless you're offering to do this for me, you don't get a say in how I go about it."

"Fine, fine. But I don't see you going about anything at the moment."'

"Did Sandra send you to bug me?"

"Nope. I decided to be annoying all on my own."

This last statement elicited a chuckle as Max moved toward the house. Madame Novak had the door open before he set foot on the porch, and he wondered how long she had been watching him. She stepped aside to make room for him to enter, and her stern expression told him everything — they knew he had come to complete the deal, and they took it seriously.

His guts flipped. He had thought this would be a matter of walking in and handing over the cutting of Roy Malone's hair. Maybe he'd say something about their deal being over just to make it extra clear. However, the look in Madame Novak's eyes caused him to rethink this moment. He should have known. Nothing ever could be handled so simply with a witch.

"Follow me," she said, leading him through the maze of Haven House.

Though he had been in that home twice now, he still had trouble picturing the layout of the building. At every turn, he thought he knew what room they would enter or what corridor they would walk down only to find a different set of options — a door where one shouldn't have been, a row of shelving new to the walls. Without Madame Novak as a guide, he would never have found his way. Perhaps that was the point.

"Did you read about that horrendous murder?" the old witch asked.

"You'll have to be more specific. There are murders every night in this country."

"Oh, come, come, don't tease me."

With a revolted shake, Max said, "I'm sure every witch in the South has heard about the death of Jill Malone. I imagine whenever something makes the news that involves occult symbols, you all are gossiping away about it."

"Only when we don't know who cast the spell. That gets the rumors flying. I can tell you this much — those in charge are not happy. That was unauthorized magic."

"Huh. I wouldn't have pegged you and your sisters to be loyal to anybody but yourselves. I certainly can't picture you listening to what Cecily Hull decrees."

Madame Novak paused to look back at Max over her thick glasses. "You don't live as long as we have by getting up in the wrong people's business. Especially when you're a woman, a witch, and Black. Most times, people like me were lucky if all we got was burned at the stake. So don't you start implying things about which you know nothing about."

"My apologies. No offense was intended."

She smiled brightly. "None taken. Besides, what makes you think Cecily Hull is the real authority in North Carolina? Oh, she wants to be, but she's hardly the only one seeking to control everything. Power always attracts a following, and when you're talking about power over magic use, well, there's a lot of folks who would want a piece of that. In fact, I wouldn't put all my chips on Cecily Hull, if I was you. Not even on a good day."

The way Madame Novak dropped that bomb, the intention was clear. She wanted Max to be shocked, unsteady, and questioning all that he thought he knew about the current state of witch politics. She succeeded. Before he could formulate something to say, she waved him onward. "Come, come, we're almost there."

He had expected to be led downstairs again, to meet with Madame Fein in that circular chamber. But Madame Novak had him climb a spiral staircase, walk down a narrow hall lit with red neon tubes like the entrance to a night club, and enter a private study. More maneuvers to keep him off balance. However, while the destination had been a surprise, the massive clutter in the room was not. Rather typical, really.

Well-polished wood floors and walls could barely be seen from all the boxes and milk crates stuffed with the detritus of decades. Other than the usual collections of newspapers and magazines, Max noticed a long tower of plastic cups, a tall stack of muffin tins, and four cardboard boxes overflowing with cat toys. And, of course, endless piles of books older than most people ever lived.

"You can wait in here. I'll go tell Madame Fein you've arrived." Madame Novak closed the door behind her, and though Max did not hear the click of a lock, he decided it best not to try turning the knob. He didn't really want to know the answer.

The mantel of an old fireplace held a row of photographs — all three witches posing together during different eras. Most of the photos dated from the 1920s through the 1950s. Black and white darlings, carefree and full of joy, laughing for the camera.

Max turned away. He had a cold sensation running along his neck, a thought that if he looked at those photos for too long, he might see something disturbing. Maybe the photographs would move. Maybe — but he shut out any further thoughts on the subject. Too many objects in this house posed real dangers to those who didn't know what they were dealing with. Other than those three witches, that meant everybody.

What was taking so long? Madame Novak had been watching him sit in the car. She knew he was there to see Madame Fein. She surely told Madame Fein while he had been chatting with Drummond. If not, the way Madame Novak phrased things when she left the room — *I'll go tell Madame Fein you've arrived* — suggested that he had been expected.

This was more mind games. That's all. They knew he would be coming because they read about Jill Malone's murder. They probably knew from the moment the hex had been removed and certainly knew when Roy Malone had died. It wouldn't take a complex spell to sense these changes in magical energy. Max couldn't be positive, of course, but the safest move would be to assume they knew everything, that they were always watching, sensing.

Yet they still made him wait.

Near one of the two windows in the room, he saw a short shelf with two stacks of books. Reading the titles amused him. There were the plain ones — *Best Conjuring Practices* or *Spells for the New Century*. But some witches had a playful sense of humor, and he appreciated their efforts — *Witch Women, Rich Women* and *My Favorite Spells to Ruin a Bastard's Day* and *So You Want to Curse*

Your Boyfriend. As he turned away, his eye caught the last title in the second stack and he froze. It read — *Cures of the Incurable.*

This was it. The reason he had been brought to this room. The reason he had been made to wait. Like a card magician forcing a specific card to be picked, they had somehow manipulated him into seeing that book. He knew it for certain because of the first thought that hit him when he read that title — his mother.

But he refused to consider the option any further. Even if he had never made a witch deal before, he knew better than to ask one to cure his mother's multiple sclerosis. The cost extracted for such a spell would make health insurance companies look like the most altruistic institutions known to mankind. No. He never even wanted to know what these witches might ask for. It would definitely be a lot more than a few hairs from a dead man.

On the other hand, his wife was a witch. She could learn to do the spells in a book like *Cures of the Incurable.* Perhaps, someday, when she had mastered her craft, perhaps then a spell could be cast to help his mother. But only through Sandra. Any price she required would not be the kind designed to destroy him.

At length, the door opened and Madame Fein entered. Max spun from the books as if he had been caught sifting through her dresser drawers. She carried a wood tray, and sitting on the tray was a green and white box of Krispy Kreme donuts.

"Madame Fein hopes you don't mind. Madame Novak simply cannot resist getting these sweet killers whenever they have the Hot Donuts Now sign lit up at the store."

Max's stomach gurgled, but he couldn't tell whether he desired a donut or if his nerves had sent him a warning. "Thank you, but I don't expect to be here long."

"Ah. Planned to toss some hair at old Madame Fein and walk away?" She gazed around the room with a large effort that bordered parody. "Sandra's not here?"

"She's not happy with the way you've treated me."

"Because of our deal?"

"Don't act surprised. You knew very well what you were

doing."

"As did you. Nobody forced you to make that deal."

"Semantics? Are you a witch or a lawyer?"

Max salivated at the smell of those glazed donut. But taking a donut from a witch? Then again, there was no deal about donuts. But then again again, donuts and witch did not go together.

Chuckling, Madame Fein picked up a donut and took a bite. Another game. He snatched a donut and tore into it. That only caused her to giggle more before sitting behind a wide pile of papers. Max only then recognized that a desk supported the mass collection.

"The first time Madame Fein made a deal with a witch, I must have been in my teens. That was a long time ago, indeed — in a small village in France or maybe it was Italy." She flustered a moment before pulling back in her chair. "You know, Madame Fein has lived with my dear sisters for so long now that our lives have blended together. I can't say where one history stops and the other begins."

Max noticed now that the witch spoke of her past, she no longer referred to herself exclusively in the third person. Halfway to asking her about that shift, he halted. No good would come from the answer, and with witches, the possibility of bad always existed. Best to keep quiet.

Waving a hand as if dispersing an unpleasant odor, she continued, "Wherever I lived, I remember that I was ten. I remember that clearly. My mother — my dear, sweet mother — had become ill. We had a village doctor, but this was a long time ago. He was only good for headaches, fevers, and small wounds. A real illness, a disease, was far beyond his knowledge."

Using the little napkins provided with the donuts, Max wiped sugar off his fingers. "I take it you went to a witch."

"What else could I do? I wasn't going to let my mother die, and nobody else offered help. I had always been interested in the power of a witch, too. Others feared the old lady living in the woods, but I would see them sneak off to get the witch's help anyway. These same people who prayed hardest at church and were first to throw stones at sinners, they were always the ones doing the sneaking. If they could do it for whatever sinful things they truly wanted, why couldn't I go to a witch with a sincere need?"

In his pocket, Max had Roy Malone's hair — the sandwich bag placed in an envelope and folded over. He could feel it pressing against his side, anxious to be handed over, and he wanted to oblige. But if Madame Fein chose to talk for another hour, he would let her. Until he concluded this deal, she could claim all sorts of reasons to harm him with a spell. That was the point of a witch deal, after all — for a witch to gain control over a person.

"I know what you're thinking," Madame Fein said, drawing Max back to her. "I once thought the same. All people do. They distrust witches. Naturally, they would distrust any deal with a witch, too. Thus, they decide without facts that there can only be nefarious reasons for a witch to make a deal. But I learned a lot in my deal with the old witch in the woods, and today, I want you to learn, too."

"Okay. I'm listening."

"I doubt that, but I'll do my best." She wiped her mouth with her Krispy Kreme napkin, then flattened it, and set it in a box to the side. "I was the perfect person for a witch — I was desperate. We talked for an hour or two before the deal was made, and when I left, I worried I had ruined my life. But the witch had handed me a concoction that did as promised. My mother got better and lived another seven years before a horse threw her. When I finished my end of the deal — a small matter as inconsequential as the one I have asked of you — I wondered why people feared these deals so much? I started thinking about things from the witch's perspective. It became clear very fast. A witch has no other way to live. Back then, these women had to survive on their own. They hunted and grew food. They made their own clothes or, more often, stole what they needed. They had to. Nobody would sell to a witch. They were outcasts that the village still wanted around to handle the matters the elders and the church could not. This idea that a witch deal is an evil bargain designed to harm you is a fiction created by village leaders out of fear. But ask yourself — what good would it serve a witch to make punishing deals with the people she relied on for the things she could not make or steal for herself?"

"Maybe that was true back then, but you've got online shopping now. In the years since, you witches have embraced the nastier side of deal making."

"Some certainly have. And for some of the more difficult spells we wish to cast, we need things that can only be acquired through a deal. But neither is the case for you. Madame Fein feels greatly for your wife and would never want to harm her. Hurting you would harm her. Madame Fein made the deal with you to help, not hurt."

Max wanted to believe her — his life would be infinitely simpler — but he knew better than to fall victim to wishful thinking. "If you wanted to help, why make a deal at all? Why not just help?"

Pushing back from her paper-covered desk, Madame Fein cackled. "Oh, you sweet, sweet boy. Bless your heart. I'm a witch."

"But —"

"You'll have to wise up fast. You're married to a witch now, and as she grows stronger, the ways of a witch will become more a part of her. If you're not careful, you'll be making witch deals just to get a good breakfast."

He'd had enough. All this talk of his wife and his marriage angered him even as it worried him. He pulled the envelope with Roy Malone's hair from his pocket and walked it over to Madame Fein's desk. After setting it before her, he stepped back.

"Everything you said doesn't change the fact that I'm delivering this man's hair and fulfilling my end of the deal. Our business is over, and if you meant anything you've said today, you'll avoid the games and witch trickery."

"Careful how you speak."

"You should be careful, too. I know you'll be involved in my wife's life, and I can come to terms with that. But don't ever force me into another deal again. You do that, and I think you'll find Sandra a far more formidable witch than you realize."

"Ho ho. No need to threaten Madame Fein. Now, let us take a look at what you have brought."

His sudden surge of bravery washed away like a tide rolling back into the sea. When the witch picked up the envelope, Max shifted from one foot to the other. He waited and watched and wondered how the truth of the deal would be revealed. The idea that Madame Fein merely wanted to help the Porters held as much truth as a jug with no bottom held wine. When she frowned at the contents of the envelope, he knew he had read the situation correctly.

"This is not right," she said.

Though he felt the quivering throughout his body, he managed to find a firm voice. "No, no. We had a clear deal, and this concludes it. Simple as that."

"You blame witches for trickery, yet you try to trick this witch." She pushed the envelope back. "That does not fulfill your end of the deal."

"We agreed that I would bring you a cut of Roy Malone's hair, and that is exactly what I've done. Don't start with him being dead when I did it. If anything, that should make this more valuable."

"Wrong. Our exact deal was that you bring me *a clip of hair from the culprit.* Madame Fein always remembers the words of deal."

Max's forehead wrinkled. "What's the difference between *a cut of hair* and *a clip of hair?*"

"Nothing. That's not the problem."

His heart sank. "Roy Malone?"

Soaked in patronizing glee, Madame Fein said, "Do you honestly believe that pathetic man capable of casting all those spells? Or any man? Surely, you have learned that much from your dear wife. Men cannot truly use magic. Not well. Not on their own. They need help and guidance, and even then, they usually foul it up."

"But I've cast spells."

"You prove my point. Those spells have never gone well, or you nearly died in the process. Let me ask you this — why do you think witchcraft exists in the first place? Because throughout history men have always tried to control, to dominate women, and always women have found ways to control men without their knowledge. Women discovered the secrets of Nature, of its energies, of its magic. But men try to control Nature and that is why they fail so often at magic. Women work with the energies, utilizing what Nature offers on its terms, and that is why women are always the witches."

"Not Roy Malone." He said the words as if hearing them would make them truer. If not Roy Malone, that only left one possibility that made any sense. He jumped for the door. "I've got to go."

Madame Fein rose from her desk. "Indeed, you do."

As she led him out of the house, his mind buzzed with the only name that fit. She had done a good job of staying out of the spotlight, but there was no hiding this. Worse still, with the murder of Jill Malone, he knew the true culprit no longer tried to hide.

Storming toward the car, Max saw Drummond perk up. "We had it wrong," Max said.

Drummond's face dropped. "About what?"

"Roy Malone didn't cause all of this. He was part of it, but he was an accomplice and now a patsy." Max paused with his hand on the car door. He looked back at Haven House. "Only a witch could pull off all this magic."

"A witch means a woman, and there's only one woman left in this case."

"Right. Nell Fincher."

Chapter 23

SPEEDING UP THE HIGHWAY, Max weaved around cars and trucks as he headed back into Winston-Salem. Drummond peppered questions, and Max did his best to put the pieces together. It began with the infidelity.

"Roy discovered the cheating like we thought, and he even planned his revenge in his slow, methodical, never-going-to-do-anything manner. But we missed the part where he shared what he knew with Nell."

Drummond tapped his forefinger against his lips. "This whole time she let us think she had no clue."

"Let her husband think so, too."

"Why hire us then? If she's the one who made the hexes."

"She hired us because that's the bad side to playacting that you don't know something."

"Right, and she's stuck pretending to care enough to go along. Otherwise, she's got to admit she knows about the affair and that this is all her revenge."

"Her husband becomes convinced he's been cursed, and she plays the part of the concerned wife. Then they're sitting at home watching television when I appear on the screen."

"You saying she sees what's coming, so might as well put the idea out herself?"

"Somewhat. Maybe that was it at first, but when we met Dwayne and Nell, they made it sound as if she had to push him into hiring us. If that's true, she could have let the matter drop when Dwayne resisted. But she didn't. She led the charge."

"I still don't see why."

"Yeah, me neither."

"For that matter, if she's the real one who hired us, then why did she push Roy to make the hex bag used on you?"

"We must have been getting closer to success. She got Roy to set the hex bag in our siding, but she made the bag." Another part of the puzzle snapped in place, and Max smacked his hand on the steering wheel. "She's not been a witch for long. That's why she's still using hexes. Amateur stuff."

"Might be she's not an official witch at all. Just somebody who found some books on the subject and is muddling her way through. Same books she probably shared with Roy."

"The hex on her husband did grow out of control. It may have been that she pushed him to hire us in an effort to have us dispose of the hex."

"I think you're right. Why else have us meet them at the office? She knew the stone paperweight was the hexed object. She wanted us to find it. That also answers another question bugging me — why participate in ending the hex last night? But if all we're thinking is right, she wanted to end it as much as Dwayne did."

Max scanned the road ahead, worrying about speed traps and other motorists. Traps. For Roy, his entire revenge had become a trap. He had put his trust in a witch and trusting a witch never ended well.

When he found out that Nell intended to end the hex, Roy must have been furious. The whole point had been to make Dwayne and Jill suffer. So far, only Dwayne had been punished in any measurable way, and Jill had continued sleeping with the man. When Roy complained, Nell — with the makings of a true witch deep in her bones — ignored him. After all, he was just another man trying to control things. She would have the revenge, and it would be on her terms.

Roy proceeded to get drunk. Maybe he confronted Jill and they argued and the yelling turned violent. He had a gun on him. Mixing intense emotions with drinking and guns left Jill dead. Seeing what he had done, Roy figured it was time to finish everything.

He knew about the spellcasting going on that night at the bridge because Nell had told him. So, he came to kill Dwayne and Nell and then, perhaps, himself. But either through a drunken head or a simple miscalculation, he approached from the tracks and found Max first.

Reaching into his pocket, Max slid out his phone. He called Sandra, tapped the phone onto speaker, and set it down.

"Hey, hon," she answered.

"You ready for this?"

"Let me guess. Madame Fein rejected the hair you brought and told you that Roy Malone wasn't the person behind all of this. You figured out quick that it was probably Nell Fincher since she's the only one left around."

"Um, yeah. How did you know all that?"

"Because I'm standing in the Malone's living room staring at the spell she put on Jill's afterlife."

Drummond said, "Sorry to interrupt but it's not a good idea to be chatting while you're in the midst of breaking into a crime scene."

"Aren't you sweet? I'll ignore the insult that you think I'm stupid enough to do that and let you know that we had no need to break in. We called Osorio, and he told us the investigation here would wrap up before the end of the day — very few people want to be working overtime. After they left, there was one cop watching the place for tonight. Brenda smooth-talked him — I think she even got a date out of the deal — and we've been in here without trouble."

"Like I said, doll, you're one of kind. Smart, beautiful, and charming, too. Far more woman than your husband deserves."

Pressing harder on the accelerator, Max said, "Okay, so we've established that you're safely in that house and I'm no good for you. Great. How did you know it's Nell?"

From the way Sandra spoke, she clearly studied the spell at that same moment. "This is way beyond what Roy could ever do. Even if he found a book with this spell, he would've needed a witch to guide him. That meant there was a witch involved."

"And that meant a woman."

"Yes. But also, this spell is ugly. Angry. It's not a casting circle on the floor, carefully drawn. This is on a large, white wall. She used Jill's blood and wrote the symbols in sharp, furious motions. I'm sure the police will think it's madness. In a way, it is."

"What's the spell do?" Drummond asked.

"From what I can tell, Nell realized or guessed that Jill was gone. Moved on. I think she's trying to force Jill's soul back here by causing Jill's physical body to be cursed."

"Could that work?"

"No. Not that I know of. But considering how Nell botched up her hexes, I can't leave this here. I'm going to break this spell so it doesn't hurt anybody by accident."

"Sounds good," Max said. "We're following up on the rest. Talk with you soon. Love you."

When he hung up and put away his phone, he saw Drummond staring out the side window. Max thought it best to let the detective think. It also allowed him to stay focused on the road. But that didn't last long.

"Okay," Drummond said, "I'll buy into all of this. Sandra's evidence supports yours a lot. But if for no other reason, I know that witches don't lie when it comes to a deal. They'll twist the wording of the deal until it nearly breaks, but honoring those words has always been key to their survival. If that hair had been from the right person, Madame Fein would've accepted it. One question, though — why are you driving like you want to join me as a ghost?"

Max whipped onto the exit ramp. Screeching the brakes to avoid slamming into the line of cars waiting on a red light at the end, he turned his head toward Drummond. "Jill Malone is dead. Nell never had time to murder her yesterday — she was busy getting ready for the spellcasting that night. So, we can assume Roy killed Jill. But Sandra said that Roy couldn't have pulled off the spell on that wall. That means after everything happened at the bridge, after Dwayne and Nell went home, Nell either snuck out or made an excuse to leave the house. She went to Jill Malone's murder scene and attempted to curse that woman's soul."

"Okay, a bitter, angry, vengeful act. What does that have to do with you driving like a maniac?"

"There's still the original revenge left to be done."

"Dwayne Fincher."

"Exactly."

Lowering his hat, Drummond said, "We'd better hurry."

Chapter 24

MAX HAD NOT BEEN in this wealthy section of Winston-Salem since early in his career with the murder of a client, Sebastian Freeman, and all the terrible events that came with it. He found it impressive the way the city shifted from small, affordable homes to modest, mid-sized ones near Baptist Hospital to a developed area of grocery stores, restaurants, and shops, and then instantly to massive, million-dollar sprawls. A throwback to an era when people lived closer together, relied more upon each other, yet still segregated parts of their lives.

The Finchers lived off Warwick Road in a Tudor-style house with a large front lawn and horseshoe driveway. A classic 1972 Jaguar E-series sat near the entrance. As Max parked behind the two-seater, he noticed the front house door stood ajar.

Drummond had noticed, too. As he slipped through the side of the car, he said, "That ain't good."

Hearing his own thoughts verbalized, Max's burning fears that had him speeding here now froze into an icy dread. He walked toward the front door, his footsteps loud against the dimming day. In the distance, he heard cars drive along other side streets, but nobody bothered to come by this way. As if they purposely avoided the house.

"I'll check ahead," Drummond said, and swept through the walls.

When Max reached the small awning over the entrance, he waited. Through the open gap of the door, he saw a painting on the entryway wall — a portrait of Dwayne and Nell holding each other in a loving embrace. If he inspected the painting closer, would he see darkness in their eyes? Threat? Rage? He faced outward and noticed the expensive car. But only the one car.

"She's not here," he whispered.

"Nobody's here," Drummond said as he floated through the front door. "Safe to come in. And there's a lot to see."

The first meaning behind the phrase *a lot* turned out to be the sheer size of the house. The entire Porter residence could have fit inside half of the downstairs — possibly fit in the living room with only a slight overflow into the dining room. The kitchen could have serviced a small restaurant and even the mudroom had enough space to fit the entire Porter master bedroom.

"It's certainly big," Max said, strolling through one echoing room after another.

Drummond snorted. "The upstairs is just as big."

It was also lifeless. Despite the old-style exterior, the interior had been decorated with a modern, stark appearance. Perfectly clean, not a speck of dust, nothing out of place, spotless carpeting, and well-oiled woods. Everything looked ready to be photographed for a magazine spread. But none of it appeared lived in.

"I thought they would be here," Max said. "I thought we'd be able to stop her from doing anything bad to Dwayne."

"We've still got time."

"Why do you say that?"

"What other choice do we have? We've got to act as if there's still a chance to save the man; otherwise, we might as well go home and forget about him. Now, this is a lot of house to cover. How about I take the upstairs and you check around down here?"

Max pulled out his phone. "Let's not be stupid, first. I'll call his office. It's possible that Nell isn't making her big move right this moment." No answer at the office. "I'll try his cell."

"Don't do that. If she's with him, she'll know you're trying to find him. You'll be tipping our hand and we don't have much to play with."

After a small pause, he put away the phone. "Okay. Let's start searching. Anything you find, call me up. I mean anything. We don't know what we're looking for, so if it seems even remotely connected, let me know."

As Drummond rose through the ceiling, Max headed back to the living room. He checked all the framed photographs, pulling off the backs to see if anything had been hidden, and sifted through the bookshelves. On a glass coffee table large enough to be a child's bed, Max saw two leather photo albums. Since most people had gone digital with everything, these must have been for show or truly of great significance.

Opening them up, they certainly were important. Both albums consisted of the Fincher wedding photos. Everything had been captured on film including individual portraits, shots of the happy couple — Nell looked truly elated in a pearl gown with puffy sleeves and ruffled lace up to her neck — group portraits of the couple with parents and the wedding party, as well as the wedding itself. The ceremony and reception all took place in a gorgeous space that had once been a huge barn and later was converted into a warm, light-wood event hall. He turned the page and found one of the wedding invitations — ivory with gold script.

From that, Max learned the barn was part of an active vineyard, and more importantly, that Nell's interest in witchcraft began long before the betrayal of her marriage. At first glance, the border of the invitation looked like an abstract lattice design. But with a more careful inspection, Max noticed several symbols buried in the linework. Many of them looked familiar, and he swallowed dry against the thought — they were witch symbols.

The rest of the albums had photos of all the guests dancing, drinking, and laughing. Including Roy and Jill Malone. Max searched for evidence that Jill and Dwayne had started up already, but all the pictures with Dwayne portrayed a man lost in romantic love for his new bride.

That warmth — and knowing how bitter cold it would become — turned Max's attention to the portrait at the entrance. He spent several minutes observing the painting before removing it from the wall, checking the back of the canvas and the wall itself. But he came up empty. Nothing indicated any interest in the occult.

Maybe he had it wrong. Those symbols in the wedding

invitation could have been innocent — merely his eyes finding images like shapes in clouds. Or perhaps the designer was a witch and inserted those symbols unbeknownst to any who purchased the invitations. Maybe Nell still loved her husband, had no knowledge of the affair, and some other woman was involved. But whenever that thought perked in his mind, it felt off — wrong.

He recalled how Nell had behaved after they broke the curse. She showed relief, but no shock. Dwayne also looked relieved, but part of him had been amazed at seeing magic exist before his eyes. The definitions of reality and fantasy had merged in front of him, and he would require weeks, if not far longer, to come to terms with it all. But Nell simply comforted Dwayne. She had no trouble accepting the existence of the supernatural.

"That's because it was nothing new to her."

Another moment stuck in Max's mind. When they were preparing the spell, Nell had made sure to avoid stepping on the circle. Even before Sandra warned them. Nell knew. Not only did she know, but she moved around that circle with all the care and confidence of somebody who had cast a spell or two already.

Drummond's head popped out of the ceiling fixture. "You'll want to come upstairs. I found all the proof you'll ever need that she's behind everything."

Following Drummond's lead, Max climbed to the second floor, down the carpeted hall, and into the guest room — another oversized display of wealth and comfort. A queen-sized bed thrust out from the middle of the back wall, but it was hardly large enough to dominate a room that also boasted a couch and two chairs in front of a fireplace.

"Pull the bed back," Drummond said.

Max grabbed the headboard and yanked it away from the wall. A rough hole had been carved out — enough to crawl through. "Clever. She knew Dwayne would probably never come in this room, and if he did, he wouldn't have any reason to suddenly move the bed."

"It gets better. Go on in."

Though the gap had been cut for a slender woman, Max

managed to squeeze his way through — sucking in his stomach and groaning all the way. On the other side, he stood in a narrow stairwell with both walls brushing his shoulders. This led up to the attic. A false wall had been built so if Dwayne, for some unknown reason, ever got it in his head to go into the attic, he would find a shortened space and nothing else. But that man lived a pampered life. He wouldn't know what size the attic should be and would simply accept what his eyes told him. This allowed Nell to commandeer the remainder of the attic for her witch studies.

That was exactly what Max looked upon — a private sanctuary to study and explore witchcraft. She had a school desk loaded with notebooks, two long bookshelves warping under the weight of her texts, and a casting circle painted on the floor with erased chalk symbols bleeding through. Drummond hovered near the false wall and gestured to the bookshelves.

"You should call Sandra in on this, but I'm thinking Nell is still an amateur. Most of these books are on the basics, as well as some how-to type things written for the public."

Max had finished texting Sandra before Drummond finished speaking. "She's on her way." Careful to avoid crossing the circle — just in case — he moved closer to the books. Several had spine stamps from public libraries, and a few were common paperbacks found in most occult bookstores. But two books had leather bindings and the non-standard sizings of a real witch's book.

As Max reached for one, Drummond said, "You may want to wait until your wife gives the okay on touching anything in here."

Thinking of how poorly Nell's spells had gone already, Max pulled his hand back. "Let's wait downstairs."

"Good thinking."

When Sandra and Brenda finally arrived, Max and Drummond had explored the rest of the house. They found nothing else incriminating — not that they needed anything else — but Max noticed how perfect the rest of the house had been set up. Nell lived two separate lives, and if he was right about the wedding invitation, she had been this way before ever meeting

Dwayne.

"She's definitely a novice," Sandra said after looking over the secret attic room.

"Really?" Brenda said. "Hasn't she been at this for years?"

Sandra poked her fingers at some of the books as if testing a rotten piece of fruit. "The years don't matter, if she didn't put in the work. These books weren't going to teach her much of anything, and this casting circle — look at it. It's filthy. Any symbols she wrote now would be blending with old barely erased ones. It's a miracle she made any hexes work at all."

The wind picked up outside, and it moaned as it passed through the attic rafters. Max felt the cold air seeping in around them. "This was nothing more than a hobby to her. She wouldn't want to be up here in the winter, and I'll bet in the worst of summer, this place is boiling."

"Except," Drummond said, "that all changed when Roy Malone paid her a visit. Probably brought some of his photos with him in case she denied the whole thing."

"Hold on. How does a witch hobbyist suddenly get the ability to pull off hexing a naturally cursed object? How does she even know about that kind of thing? I had to go to Haven House and make an inane deal just to get some basic information, yet Nell Fincher somehow knows all about them. Not only that, but she's able to locate this rare kind of cursed object and utilize it in a hex. Does that sound even remotely plausible?"

Sandra said, "The only way it makes sense is that she had help. A witch — a real witch — must have taken her on as a student."

"She could have made a deal with a witch," Brenda said.

"Yeah, but I doubt it. Nell has enough in this room to suggest she knew better than to do that."

Drummond clicked his tongue. "Max knew better, yet he still did it."

"Hey," Max said. "We've moved on from that mistake."

Before the two could start bickering, Sandra said, "Max had a motivation — helping me."

"And Nell had a motivation — vengeance."

"Either way, there's a witch involved, and she's going to be our best bet at finding Nell and Dwayne."

With a clap of his hands, Drummond said, "Okay. We've got to go over this entire house again. Search everywhere. Any rooms specifically for Nell, search twice. There's got to be something to lead us to her witch."

Chapter 25

IN RECENT YEARS, some of the old, disused R. J. Reynold's Tobacco factories in downtown Winston-Salem had been reclaimed and overhauled. They had become offices, research labs, and spaces for numerous other purposes — including loft apartments. Standing at the head of a hallway that stretched the length of the entire building, Max inhaled the fresh paint smell and noticed the new carpeting, too. None of it, however, eased his stress as he walked to the loft of a witch.

Having Sandra at his side helped, as did knowing that Drummond and Brenda remained at the Fincher house searching for more information. The initial search had taken fruitless hours. But eventually, when all good avenues had turned out to be dead ends, Max mentioned the wedding album. In particular, the wedding invitation with a design woven into the lattice border that he thought might be witch symbols.

Sandra and Brenda leaped into the book, examining all the photographs and taking a sharp eye to the invitation. While they scrutinized each page, Max used his phone to search for people offering unique invitation services. Brenda discovered the name of the witch — Sister Sadie — nestled in a short paragraph of thanks that Nell had written near the back of the album. With that, Max's online search went fast, and they soon had the address for Sister Sadie's small business *Promises — full-service invitations and announcements.*

Max and Sandra halted at the witch's door. Best case scenario — they would find Nell and Dwayne inside. Worst case scenario — might be the same thing.

Raising his fist to knock, Max paused. Whenever he and Drummond entered a situation like this, they usually had a gameplan, a line of attack that they had agreed upon. But other than locating Nell and Dwayne, this meeting had not much else. At least, not much that Max could see.

"Are we sure about this?" he whispered to Sandra.

"It's the only good lead we have at the moment. Besides, I'm curious. I thought I knew all of the witches practicing in the area — at least, by name. I've never heard of this one."

"Yeah, but why would she tell us anything? Sisterhood through witchcraft doesn't seem like enough."

"She won't want to, but we'll get it out of her."

Max lowered his hand. "How? We're not going to rough her up."

With a knowing wink, Sandra reached over and knocked on the door. "There are lots of ways besides violence to get what you want."

The door opened. A woman in her 40s answered — tall and hunched over. She wore a white smock stained with paint. Nothing else. No shoes, no pants, no jewelry, nothing. Her sunken eyes and oblong face peeked out from behind unwashed, black strands. The first word that came to Max's mind — *haggard.* The second word — *insane.*

Max put his arm around Sandra and offered an embarrassed smile. Clearly, they had the wrong apartment and he wanted to apologize for the disturbance. But before he could utter a word, the woman lifted a hand high in the air, holding a paintbrush as if about to stab down with a knife, and stepped back to allow them in.

"Thank you," Sandra said, in an overly-pleasant voice. She gripped Max's hand tight as they stiffly entered the apartment.

What they found inside only made Max feel worse. Like most loft apartments, this one consisted of an open, high-ceilinged main room with an enclosed kitchen area. Stairs ran alongside the wall to the loft section — an open bedroom above the kitchen. It should have been a charming, fun place to live. But in the hands of this off-kilter woman, the apartment closed in around Max with dangerous intentions.

There was no furniture but one lone stool in the middle of

the main room. No books. No hoarded objects or collections. None of the usual trappings of a witch.

Instead, white paper and canvas covered the stark walls and cement floor. On every surface, casting circles had been painted, witch symbols were on display, a few sheets depicted what must have been memories of long ago — old buildings, a blurred face, even a quick drawing of a hat. A large can of red paint and another of black sat open near the stool. No other colors.

"I'm sorry if we're interrupting," Sandra said, looking to Max, urging him to help talk with this woman.

He shrugged. "We're looking for a woman who goes by Sister Sadie. Is that you?"

The woman walked over to the stool and sat. She stared ahead with a catatonic glaze in her eyes. Then her head lowered an inch before returning to its starting point.

"Was that a nod?" Max asked.

"I missed it," Sandra said. "But who else could this be?"

"I know. Except how could this witch possibly be the one mentoring Nell Fincher?"

Sister Sadie, if that's who she was, did not move or even acknowledge the conversation going on around her. Max observed her, searching for the truth, and when clearly, she would not act any further, he shifted his view across the room. More than anything else, the red and black paintings offered proof that this woman was the witch they sought.

Sandra had picked up on it, too. She walked toward the staircase where several sheets of paper had been taped against the side. "These spells are like the one I found at Jill Malone's house."

Joining her, Max said, "They're cursing a dead person in here?"

"They aren't that specific spell, but the authorship is the same. Sort of. These have a similar jagged, frantic look to them. Same as we saw on the paper around the hexed stone."

"I saw one of these sheets in Roy Malone's motel room, and Jill must have found one because she had it at the gallery."

"Look here." She pointed to a symbol at the bottom of one

circle. "That's the witch's signature symbol."

"Does that read *Sister Sadie?*"

"Signature symbols don't read actual names. And this one is all over this room. It's hers."

Max noticed that Sister Sadie had dropped to her knees with her paintbrush poised over a piece of paper. Her head arched forward, a thin line of drool slipping from her mouth, as she continued to stare toward the covered windows.

Sandra pulled out her phone. "But the spell on Jill Malone — take a look."

She swiped across the screen for a moment before handing it to Max. He saw a photo of the crime scene that included the spell painted in Jill's blood. It looked a lot like the drawings plastering this apartment. But not quite the same. Max noticed right away that the ones surrounding him had a more uneven, spiky look as if the artist slammed each brushstroke onto canvas. The spell in the photo attempted a similar expression, however, it appeared more like a facsimile than an original.

With her fingers cutting into his view, Sandra zoomed in on the bottom of the photo. "You see there?"

He did. "No signature." He peeked at Sister Sadie, but the witch remained like a statue.

"I can't answer for you how Nell talks with Sister Sadie or how she learned from her, but Nell has been learning something. That much I know."

"Considering her teacher's mental state and Nell's amateur ability, I'm thinking those lessons are slow-going and incomplete." Another look at the witch. She now hunched over the paper, her paintbrush slapping and slurring around the page. "I agree with you, hon, that this is the witch teaching Nell. But where does that leave us? Sister Sadie isn't going to tell us anything."

Snatching back her phone, Sandra said, "I'll call Haven House. Those old women have been around long enough to know every witch in the state. Probably on the whole east coast. And after what they pulled on you, I think they owe me one."

Max turned away to hide his frown. It was one thing to know

theoretically that his wife spent time talking with, learning from, and even hanging out with witches. It was another to know the specific witches in question — an entirely different thing to know one of those old witches had been toying with him, possibly setting him up for some future hardship.

He meandered up the stairs, inspecting each painting as he climbed. He had to remember that though Sandra was technically a witch, too, she strived to be a good one. She tried to drain from these witches all the information, all the knowledge available without falling prey to the corruption that came with it. A difficult task, but if anybody could succeed at that high-wire act, Max knew deep into his soul that Sandra was the one.

All his conviction, however, did not stop his stomach from twisting at the thought of Madame Fein playing more games with the Porter family. He stopped on the stairs and gazed down. Sister Sadie continued her painting with more aggressive movements while Sandra paced nearby.

"I'm fine," Sandra said, and Max could well imagine the grandmotherly tones of Madame Novak answering the phone. "Thank you. I hope you and your sisters are doing fine, too. Oh, yes, Max is doing well. We both greatly appreciate all of your help."

Turning back to the paintings on the wall, he spotted the edge of a ragged paper poking out from behind another. He flipped the top one aside and found a depiction of a man and woman locked in a kiss. Though merely a handful of slashed lines, the painting expressed the passion and danger surrounding that kiss. This wasn't merely a loving embrace. This was a *take me now before we get caught and it all ends* kind of kiss. The longer he stared at the painting, the more convinced he became it had to be Dwayne and Jill.

"I was hoping you might be able to tell me about another witch," Sandra went on. "Her name is Sister Sadie."

Even from the stairs, Max could hear the frantic yelling from Madame Novak. "Don't talk about her. Don't ever speak her name!"

"I'm sorry. I'm not trying to upset you."

"You never heard of her. Do you understand? Never."

Max didn't like to take the advice of witches — didn't often do it — but the urgency in Madame Novak's voice made him reconsider. "Hon, maybe we should go."

"But we're already here and —"

Madame Novak's voice erupted. "You're at her apartment? You're not safe there! Get out! GET OUT!"

The pure terror from that voice kicked Max into action. He bolted down the stairs and rushed to Sandra. Grabbing her hand, he wrenched her forward, lurching her towards him as he made for the door. Madame Novak's fearful yelling continued until Sandra managed to cut the call, but Max never let up. They dashed by the kitchen and turned for the exit.

Sister Sadie sprang to her feet, her eyes rolled up all white, and her mouth gaped open. A graveled hiss seeped from her throat as saliva dropped down her smock. Old garlic and stale sweat wafted off her body. With one hand, she held a painted paper like a town crier displaying a wanted poster or the King's new decree. But the other hand stretched out as if to block their escape.

With his mind locked in flight, Max ripped the paper out of her hand and hissed back at her. The shock on Sister Sadie's twisted face would have been laughable, but Max saw her rotten, sharp teeth. One bite and he figured he would be in the hospital getting tested for every imaginable disease — if he survived that long.

Sandra grabbed the paper out of his hand and held in front of the witch. "Back up now and let us out or I'll rip this into shreds."

That got Sister Sadie's attention. Her mouth shut into a drawn frown like a pouting toddler. She lowered her arms, too. But she did not move out of the way.

Max and Sandra had to squeeze by the foul woman, and when they reached the door, they heard a strange whimper. Not sad. Not hurt. Rather Sister Sadie reminded Max of a dog begging for something.

"I think she wants her painting back," he said, opening the

door.

"Here. It's yours." Sandra thrust the paper back. When the witch didn't move, Sandra bent to set it on the ground. "I'll leave it here for you."

Sister Sadie moaned long and slow as she wagged her finger all over. Her noises became staccato utterances, each accompanied by a stabbing finger — at the paper, at Max, at Sandra.

"I guess she wants us to take it," Sandra said.

"If she even knows what's happening. I don't think everything's connected up correctly in there."

Regardless of her sanity, Sister Sadie appeared to have calmed a bit. Enough for Sandra to back out of the apartment and Max to close the door behind them. They had moved slowly, afraid to startled the witch into another threatening motion. But once that door clicked shut, Max and Sandra sprinted down the hall and didn't stop running until they sat in their car, breathing hard and shaking.

Not long after, Sandra flattened out the witch's painting. Though Max could hear the adrenaline shaking her voice — and indeed, he felt the same — he admired her pluck to keep pushing on. No matter what, that strength of hers had seen them through so much.

"I love you," he said.

Sandra paused to throw him a warning. "I know that tone."

"What tone?"

She sighed. "Hon, I know we both were scared in there. Whenever something like that or worse happens to us, you feel a need to reaffirm our love. Or maybe you're worried I don't know the depths of your love and want it clear in case we die. But we're not dead. Probably didn't come close."

"Probably?"

"And now is really not the time for romantic talk."

Max reached over and held her chin. "Then I won't talk." He brushed his lips against hers, enjoyed her quiet gasp, and pressed in for a stronger kiss. In seconds, she grabbed the back of his neck and returned his intensity tenfold.

When he finally broke off, she gazed up at him. "I love you, too," she said.

"Good." He smiled. "Now we can get back to work."

Before he could say another word, she pulled him closer, tighter, and started kissing him again. They sat in their car acting like teenagers with raging hormones, desperate in their needs but holding back. Max lost his sense of time and space — everything had folded into that kiss.

But when they parted, reality returned. He could see the same crash in Sandra's eyes. "I guess we should figure out our next step," he said.

"I guess." She lowered her gaze to the painting, and her jaw dropped open.

"What is it?" Peeking over, he saw a lot of haphazard lines. No symbols, though. Whatever Sandra saw, he couldn't make it out.

Pulling out her phone, she took a photo of the painting and then tapped away a message. "Take us back to the Fincher's house. I'm sending this photo to Brenda to double-check, but I'm almost certain, and we'll need to pick her up on our way."

"To where?"

She held up the painting, and as she spoke the answer, Max saw it come together.

"It's the barn where they were married," she said.

Chapter 26

THE NEXT TWO HOURS SOARED. By the time they had returned to the Fincher house, Brenda had compared the painting with the wedding album photos. While not a perfect representation, the painting appeared to be the outside of the barn. It had the same sloping ground leading to the entrance and the same peaked top with two wings on either side — a cathedral feeling but secular.

Must work wonders for pulling in the wedding crowd, Max thought.

With the barn confirmed, everybody agreed that Sister Sadie was telling them where to go. Why she would do so was a debate that Max and Brenda engaged in until Sandra got them to focus again. Because they still had one big problem — the barn could be anywhere.

"Not quite," Max said. "We know this barn is being used for weddings and probably other events, too. From the photographs, we know it's part of a winery. So, we're not looking for a dairy farm or a soybean farm or a tobacco farm or anything like that."

Drummond said, "There's still got to be quite a few wineries in the state. You really think you can narrow it down more?"

Not only did Max think so, he did so by employing the cleverest search technique. He opened the wedding album. "The ceremony and reception were held in the same location." He pointed to the name and address on the invitation — Old Homeplace Vineyard in Thomasville.

It would take at least forty minutes to reach the vineyard, and as they closed in on Nell, a dreadful feeling pushed through Max's chest. They were going to be too late.

"We should prepare for the worst," he said. "We've been bouncing around for most of the day trying to find her, and that's more than enough time to kill a man — even if she wanted to savor it and torture him first."

Sandra said, "Unless she planned to lug a corpse all over town, I don't think she's had that long. The vineyard was open today, so she couldn't take him there until a little while ago."

"Then where have they been all day?"

"Who cares?" Drummond said. "He's so relieved to be done with the hex, she probably could have spun any story she wanted to get him to take the day off. Maybe they went to the park and had a nice lunch somewhere secluded."

Max could see that happening. "You think she wanted to give him a last chance? See if there was still some kind of connection between them worth saving?"

"I think she wanted to control the situation, keep an eye on him all day until she could get him to the barn. She may have talked with him like you think, maybe even got him thinking that way, too. It'd be easier if he willingly went to the vineyard, and a day of rekindling their love might naturally culminate in a trip to where they were wed. But add to that the lengths she's already gone to hurt him — real forgiveness is not within her."

Brenda said, "I know you're listening to that ghost talk, but not all of us can hear him. It's rude for you to go over a case with him in front of me."

"Sorry." Max quickly recapped Drummond's points.

"If you ask me, you're all a bit right. The ghost and Sandra got it that Nell's going to spend the day keeping a lock on her husband and lure him to the vineyard. This is all about revenge. The anger, the violence, we saw it all at Jill Malone's house — that was unhinged. So, Max has it right, too. Nell ain't planning on anything good for Dwayne, and we should be ready for something worse than what she did to Jill."

Sandra brought out her phone. "I'll call Osorio. Maybe he can get the police to check on a possible robbery there or something. Anything to disrupt her plans."

When she finished the call, a dark quiet overtook the car. The city drifted away, as did the smaller surrounding towns. The vineyard was tucked in the middle of a mostly rural area, far from any main roads.

Max turned onto McGee Road which curved around several suburban houses before being consumed by trees. He slowed at the entrance. The road had become gravel and dirt, and the chained gate had been cut and swung open. Forest pressed in from all sides.

Driving on the uneven ground and trying to avoid potholes that might appear in the dark shadows, Max eased them around a curve. The tiny forest gave way to a wide, beautiful stretch. To the right, a barbed wire pasture fence kept the road separate from acres of open land. It rose upward into the distance where grapevines could grow. On the left, a shed, a parking area, and a small house had been built with a manmade lake behind. In the parking area, a police cruiser sat with the engine off and the lights out.

Beyond, the gravel sloped gently downward and widened in front of the barn. A concrete path went straight to the enormous double-doors that stood open. Max parked, and everyone stared at the horror in front of them.

Stepping out of the car, the air smelled of the fresh countryside. There was that odd rural quiet noise, too — silent from all the traffic and population but filled with the sounds of insects and frogs and creatures mulling through the dimming forest. But as Max led the group down the concrete drive, as the warm lighting inside the beautifully maintained hall pressed out into the night, all the gentleness of the rural setting gave way to the blood and death ahead.

As he entered, Max saw how easily a large wedding could fit in the space. He could picture Nell and Dwayne along with a hundred friends and relatives drinking, dancing, laughing. The rooftop stretched high, and wagon-wheel chandeliers with electric candlelight spread warmth throughout. White fabric had been draped strategically to add to the momentousness of the occasion. In the back, on a small stage, a stone fireplace and chimney worked as the perfect spot for the religious portion of the ceremony. Round banquet tables would have been spread across, filled with food and conversation. It would have been a memory worth cherishing.

But now the place had an echoing, cavernous feel as it waited for the next event. Near the stage and chimney, Nell had arranged her blood-soaked spell. She had painted a large triangle on the floor and a circle inside of it. Two police officers and Dwayne each lay at a point of the triangle. All were dead. In front of each person, a wooden bowl filled to the rim with their blood. Nell sat on her knees in the center, wearing her wedding dress with a splash of red across the front. The puffy sleeves and ruffled lace had yellowed over the years, but that only heightened the disturbing stain. She had her head down as she repeated her casting.

"We're too late," Max whispered.

"For Dwayne," Drummond said. "Whatever she's trying to do, though — it's still going on."

On the walls, Nell had several of Sister Sadie's paintings displayed. Jagged mixtures of symbols and shapes created by an unstable mind. A few were more direct and gruesome — a hanged man, a headless corpse, and an evil, toothy smile. Sandra inched toward two of the paintings that appeared to match the casting triangle design on the floor.

"We can stop this," she said.

Brenda rolled her shoulders back. "Tell me what needs doing."

"Come with me. We'll set up just outside."

But Max wasn't having any of it. Why should Sandra risk injury or attack again over this case that had already ended? He ignored all the contradictions and obvious arguments his mind could rebut with, and instead, he focused on the simplicity of the matter. "Don't bother," he said. "We can break this spell easy enough."

"Max! No!"

He didn't know who had yelled at him — probably Sandra, sounded like her voice — but his mental momentum kept him from listening. He stomped to the nearest corner of the triangle, stepped over the corpse of one police officer, and kicked the blood bowl. His physical momentum kept him from stopping as he followed the blood splashing against the casting triangle.

But the blood sprayed across the air and Max's body halted at an odd angle, leaning forward and flattened as if pressing against glass. A jolting shock ripped through his nerves, locking him in place, causing his muscles to spasm and his thoughts to short out. The hair on his body stood at attention. As a long moan shivered from deep within him, the defensive spell surrounding the casting triangle threw Max back several feet. He tripped on his heels and hit the concrete floor.

"Well, bless your heart, you really thought that might work." Nell's eyes held wide open as she turned her head slowly to take in each of her guests.

Scrambling to his feet, Max shook off the lingering tingle in his back. The woman sitting in the casting triangle still looked like the gentle, loving wife he had first met days ago, but ruthlessness resided behind her grin — a grin that never encompassed the rest of her face.

"Worth a try," Max said, though he wondered if that were true considering some of his hair smelled singed.

"Many things in life are."

"But not this. You're new to witchcraft. You don't know the repercussions of what you've done. Trust me, you don't want what'll happen."

Her eyes flared. "Don't speak to me like I am some naïve little schoolgirl. You think I reached this point by accident? You think I found a witch and worked hard with her and learned from her all by happenstance? Given your reputation, I should have thought you'd be smarter than that."

"Not *happenstance,* but not a good idea, either. I've known a lot of witches, and I can tell you firsthand that Sister Sadie is not the one to be your mentor."

"You know Sister Sadie?"

Sandra took a step forward. "We've met her. Been in her apartment. Saw the state of her mind. She's not right in the head."

"She's a genius."

Max said, "I might agree with you there. She's certainly spun you like a master."

"Shut your mouth. I will not hear your lies."

"You don't have to listen to me. Think it through for yourself. How did we find you? How did we know to come to this vineyard in the middle of nowhere? Sister Sadie showed us. She drew the place so we could find it. You understand what I'm saying? She's betrayed you. Just like Dwayne betrayed you."

Nell laughed — a mocking sound harboring no joy. "You're so ignorant, you probably believe your own lies. Sister Sadie is a witch greater than all others, and she has taught me everything."

With a kinder voice, Sandra said, "But your spells have not done well, so far. That's okay. It's hard stuff that you've been trying. Much too advanced for a beginner."

"I am no mere beginner."

"You can't lie about that. Your ability speaks for itself. Relying on hexes is proof enough that you're at the start of your journey. If you listen to me, if you stop this now, then I can introduce you to real witches that will truly help you learn."

Max didn't like the sound of that, but anything that ended Nell's casting seemed like a good idea at the moment. However, Nell flushed red and clenched her fists.

"Sister Sadie *is* a real witch. Best of the lot. Far better than you and your black lackey."

"That didn't take long," Brenda said. She jutted her chin at Nell. "I didn't say anything, but I swear the first time I heard about your case, I thought you and your husband were old school crackers."

"All of you can say what you want for now. You cannot touch me, you cannot disrupt my spell, and you cannot stop the birth of the greatest coven the world will ever know. Tonight, the power I will receive, pulled straight from the energies all witches tap into, it will pour into me, give me the sight of all magic, give me the strength and knowledge of all witches throughout history — I will be a witch goddess. The Coven of Nell will claim hold on the greatest witches alive, and I will lead them. You should bow, get on your knees, pray for mercy. For this won't be the last of the blood magic I shall cast."

Closing her eyes, Nell relaxed her shoulders and opened her hands, palms up. Like a Buddhist monk meditating toward Nirvana, she appeared to detach from all around. Like a ticking timebomb, she mumbled the spell again, over and over, getting closer to blasting it into existence.

"Why are they all so nuts?" Drummond crossed his arms. "Just once I'd like to meet a power-hungry witch that can be reasoned with."

Ripping one of Sister Sadie's pages off the wall, Sandra stormed toward the exit with Brenda following. "We'll do what we can to stop her. Or maybe just slow her down. You boys find some way to help."

She walked up the incline, stopping at the edge where the concrete met the gravel drive. While instructing Brenda, she pulled out a thick piece of chalk and drew a circle. Together, they worked on the details.

Max turned to Drummond. "Any ideas on how to break through and get Nell?"

"A few. But none of them very good."

Scanning the barn, Max saw nothing practical — or impractical — that could help. His eyes landed on Dwayne. Though clearly dead, the man lacked any visible wounds beyond the slit wrist where Nell had drained his blood for her spell. A strange expression remained carved on his face — caught between remorse and desperation as if he died still thinking he could find a way out of paying for what he had done.

At the other points of the triangle, Max saw the police officers — a man and a woman. Nell had not been so kind to them. A gray powder dappled their cheeks. Their throats had been opened and blood dried on their uniforms. Max noticed their guns were holstered and locked. They never attempted to pull their weapons.

Trying to figure out how little Nell could have overpowered two trained officers, Max glanced out the open barn doors.

Sandra knelt in her circle while Brenda drew the final bits around the edge. He could see that Sandra had already begun the casting. She had reached a level of ability, knowledge, and focus where she didn't require the completed circle. Though he wanted to remain supportive in both action and thought, he couldn't deny the unwelcome shiver up his spine.

Looking beyond her, hoping his face did not betray his concerns, his view rested on the house and the parked police cruiser. "Let's check on that," he said.

"Huh?" Drummond said, following his partner toward the lot.

From the barn side, the house appeared to be a small but lovely country home. White with a classic porch leading to the front door. Walking around the side toward the gravel parking area, Max kept an eye on the dark windows.

"Doesn't look like anybody's home," he said.

Drummond flew up to the nearest wall, poked his head through, drifted fully in, and then returned. "That's no longer a home. Probably once was the family house, but it looks like the rooms are now used partly as a bar to sell their wines. The rest is offices and storage."

Since the doors appeared intact, Max decided against breaking in to have a closer inspection. Had there been evidence that Nell had forced her way in, he wouldn't have hesitated, but he doubted stacked cases of new wine and storage boxes of old taxes could help stop the witch. He turned toward the police cruiser.

Blood. First thing he saw. Even in the growing dark, the wet splotches on the gravel and the red smear on the white door near the word *POLICE* stood out. From the other side of the cruiser, Drummond snapped his fingers.

"Don't touch the car."

Max pulled his hand back — he had been about to open the door. "What is it? You got another hex bag over there?"

"No, but we found two dead cops back in the barn. At some point tonight, the rest of the police are going to find out that two of their own were murdered. That won't go down well under any circumstances. Worse when you throw in the occult angle. I'd rather you didn't put your fingerprints all over the car. This entire area is going to get picked over with extreme scrutiny."

"Oh, man, no wonder Nell laughed at us. Sister Sadie didn't betray her at all. She showed us where this was going down, so that we'd be the fall guys."

Drummond floated through the car, taking a closer look as he neared Max. "Not quite. Sister Sadie didn't betray Nell, you got that right, but she probably sent you here expecting Nell to use you and Sandra for the blood magic. They've got no reason to assume you'd be calling the police. If anything, they would figure you'd never contact any authorities because people like the police tended to think stories about witches and magic were crazy."

"Right. They probably don't know we have a connection through Osorio." Max backed away another step. "I still don't get how Nell overpowered two cops and dragged them all the way to the barn."

"I think I got an answer for that." Drummond paused — everything from the waist up still inside the car. "There's a gray dust all over the front seats."

Max thought about the police officers' faces. "You know what it is?"

"Long time ago, I had a case involving a witch from Louisiana. There's more than one kind of witchcraft, and down there, they practice voodoo, hoodoo, and all sorts of things. A lot of the spells she cast involved grinding ingredients down into a fine powder and blowing it into the face of the target."

"This is voodoo?"

"I don't know what kind of magic it is, but I'm guessing that when these cops arrived, she came running up to them covered in blood."

Max checked the car door again and the wet marks nearby. That blood could have been Nell acting frantic as if she had been injured instead of wearing the blood of her dead husband. The officer in the driver's seat would have lowered his window or opened the car door to help her, and that would be all she needed. A pile of dust blown across the front of the car, engulfing both officers with its spell.

"You think this stuff knocked them out?" Max asked.

"More likely, once they inhaled it, they became docile and open to suggestion — maybe even like zombies without the aggression. She either commanded them to walk down to the barn or she guided them there. Then it's easy. She could cut them open and get the blood or even have them slit their own throats. Any way you look at it, it's ugly stuff."

As Drummond emerged from the car, Brenda's terrified voice carried over. "Max! Come quick!"

Max held a second's look with Drummond before both shot off toward the barn.

Chapter 27

SPRINTING OVER THE GRAVEL DRIVE, part of Max's brain shouted at him to slow down. They didn't need for him to sprawl face first across a bunch of ground up rocks. But the rest of him urged his legs to pump faster. Brenda's fearful call infected him with concern for Sandra more than anything else.

Before he reached them, he could see Brenda standing over his wife with one hand on Sandra's shoulder. But Sandra did not gaze up at her student. Instead, she remained locked on her spell. Not surprising, but not encouraging either. Whatever she intended to do, and whatever consequences it had brought that caused Brenda's horrid call, Sandra had not finished yet.

With his pulse blasting through his body and his lungs burning from the short burst of action, Max swung onto the concrete and stuttered to a halt in front of them. Brenda wrung her hands, clearly at a loss for what to do, clearly clinging to the hope that either Max would fix this or that he would tell her not to worry, this was all normal.

Except it wasn't.

Three thin, crimson lines had slashed across Sandra's forehead. Blood dribbled from them, creating a trail down her nose and around her eyes. Her jaw held tight as if she forced back the urge to vomit, and her gaze held steady forward. With a slight motion back and forth like a zealot lost in prayer, she hummed a low note while tenting her fingers against the hard ground.

Max knew enough not to disturb her. Breaking her concentration could cause her to break the spell, and that could be devastating — to her, to him, to their chances of stopping Nell.

Nell.

Turning toward the barn, Max snarled his lip as he saw the woman responsible for all this suffering. She now floated above the floor, her legs crossed and a gloating grin on her face. He blazed toward the witch, muscles flexing, snorting like a bull.

"Hey!" he said, growling the words loud and strong. "You're just like all the other wannabes we've ever met." He didn't think yelling at her would accomplish much, but if anything he said got through to her, caused her a second of distraction, it could give Sandra the opening she needed. Plus, it felt good. "You probably tell yourself this is all Dwayne's fault, but that's a lie. You're just using his betrayal as an excuse. You're nothing."

Stepping into the warm barn, Max smelled something sharp in the air — an acrid, stinging odor like a pool with too much chlorine. He wished he could have some kind of magic chlorine for witches. Just bleach Nell away.

He glanced back at Sandra. The blood flowed down her face, growing heavier as Brenda tried to mop it up with part of her shirt. He had seen Sandra cast difficult spells before, but this was different. This was a battle of wills with the aid of witchcraft, and while Sandra had greater skills, Nell had nothing to lose. She would be willing to push herself and her limited abilities far beyond any sensible point — if she could control her magic at all. Given how poorly the hex bags went, Max didn't hold much hope for that. Sandra, on the other hand, cared about people, had family she loved, and probably wanted to save Nell's life, too. She was too good a person to fight dirty — or to fight with the darkest magic. It was like watching a boxing pro go against an amateur, but the pro had both hands tied behind the back.

Drummond entered the barn. "Partner, we got trouble."

"What now?"

Pointing into the air, he said, "I'm seeing a misty tendril stretching through the air and it's headed towards Nell."

They had encountered such a thing before. If their previous cases meant anything, this tendril would be some kind of connection with a ghost.

"You think she's pulling Dwayne back?" Max said. "Maybe

she wants to torture him some more?"

"My best idea at the moment — let's not find out."

All the rage roiling within him let loose. Max grabbed a wooden barstool and threw it at Nell. It smashed into the protective field around the casting triangle and splintered into pieces. To the right, he saw a small prep area. He started pitching anything he could lift at the witch — wine glasses, cardboard boxes, full wine bottles, dinner knives. The cash register wouldn't lift off the counter, but he had no trouble with a container full of wedding announcements. One after the other, he tried to batter his way through the triangle. Nothing worked.

"That tendril's right outside the barn," Drummond said.

"Thanks for the update, but if you can't help beyond telling me how greatly I'm failing —"

"I'm saying we've reached the point for a crazy idea."

Max stopped with a stapler in his hand. Another peek back at Sandra — bleeding, straining. "I take it you have that kind of an idea."

"I was watching this energy barrier every time you threw something at it. Looks like it focuses all its power wherever something strikes."

"I know. I felt it earlier. Remember?"

"Yeah, but Sandra has said over and over that witchcraft is simply taking existing energy and refocusing it. Nell doesn't have unlimited energy at her disposal, and she can't create it out of nothing. All we need to do is get the energy focused on too many things at once and you'll be able to walk right in."

It didn't sound as crazy as Max had hoped for. Certainly not something easy to dismiss. "Okay. How do we do that? Anything we push into that field is going to get thrown aside."

Drummond's grim frown answered more than Max wanted to hear. "I'll be the distraction. You wait until I've been against that barrier a few minutes."

"*Minutes?* You won't last that long. It'll throw you off the moment you touch it."

"Probably right about that. Here's what we'll do — you toss a bunch of stuff from one side, that will be the distraction to allow me to get stuck inside real good, then you wait. When I can't take it anymore, when I think I'm going to give out, I'll tell you. That'll leave the barrier as weak as we can make it. All you've got to do is step through and stop her."

"Just *step through and stop her,* huh? Any other crazy ideas on how I can do that?"

With a shrug, the old ghost said, "You can always deck her."

"Real progressive of you. Okay, fine. We'll do what we can."

Drummond slid around to the opposite side. He lowered his hat and closed his coat. "I'm ready."

Picking up pieces of destroyed chair, Max started whipping them at the triangle. One after another, not bothering to see where they hit. He could hear each one strike with a sizzle before being flung off in one direction or another. Throw, sizzle, fling. Throw, sizzle, fling.

When he heard the hard, deep bellowing of a ghost in pain, Max finally lifted his head. He saw his dear friend halfway into the barrier. Drummond roared as his ghostly form vibrated along the edges. Whisps of paleness smoked off his shoulders and back. These bits of ghost energy did not disappear, though. They hovered several feet behind as if waiting to see what would happen, if their host would survive and they could return to become part of him again. From the anguish in Drummond's face, Max didn't think the odds looked good.

He thought about shouting across the triangle, urging the ghost to let go, forget this foolish plan, and regroup. But that would diminish all of Drummond's suffering. And what if this was working? No way to tell until Max's turn to act arrived. A lump formed in his chest at the thought. Seeing Drummond's reaction to touching the barrier did not inspire confidence. If a dead man could barely hold together, what chance did Max have?

"Now!" Drummond barked. "Go!"

The universe froze. For only a millisecond. If even that. But to Max, everything locked in place, and he could see it all like one giant, world-sized painting. He saw Drummond, of course, in all the ghost's torment, but he also saw Dwayne and the two dead officers. Their lifeless eyes watched the triangle with the pity and woe of prisoners unable to change their situation. He saw Brenda mid-step as she paced around the casting circle outside. Her desire to help fraught with her lack of witchcraft knowledge left her unable to act. And Sandra — dearest, lovely, stubborn, and sure — Max saw rivulets of her blood mix with her sweat as she ground her teeth and spit out the words of her spell. Nell's lack of experience aided her in creating something far more powerful than any witch with sense would dare to cast. She held a calm, delighted expression, but Max caught the quiver glistening her lips — she rode this wave she had created, but she knew too little to realize it was a tsunami.

With all of that splashing through him, Max stepped forward.

He tensed, anticipating the electric shock of the spell. Instead, heat built from his feet and rose through his legs. Like walking through a furnace, the heat worsened until Max could feel the burn against his skin. Lifting his legs became an impossible task as the inferno thickened the air until he felt as if he waded his way through an endless desert sand. He lost all sense of his surroundings. Pain seared through him. He begged his feet to press on, his legs to take another step forward, but the agony erupting in a scream blocked out all memory of why he tried to walk in the first place.

"Max," a deep voice said. A familiar voice. Drummond. "Hold on, Max. I can see the tendril. It's here. Push harder. We have to get to Nell before the tendril does."

"Or what?" Max strained the words out, and part of him marveled that he could think straight enough to speak at all.

Whatever Drummond answered, Max lost the words as a new and vile fire raced across his skin. It sizzled and smoked. He smelled meat cooking on an open flame — his own flesh burning.

In the final seconds, perhaps because of a heightened awareness brought on through distress, perhaps because he neared his impending death, Max spotted a snake of smoke that eased through the air — the tendril. He could see the tendril. It moved at a relaxed pace as if it had no understanding of what went on around it. But when it reached the edge of the triangle, it pulled back before plunging through. It speared the barrier. It cut through with no resistance. The barrier opened itself to the tendril, and the tendril shot in without hesitation. Straight into the casting triangle and straight into Nell Fincher's skull.

Her eyes snapped open. Her head snapped back. Her arms flew out to the sides as a blinding light blasted from within her. It erupted in a sphere, pushing out in all directions at once, moving as one rapid pulse.

Max felt it sail by. His hair fluttered in its wind. When it rushed over, it took away the energy field surrounding the triangle. Just broke it apart like it was nothing more than dead leaves. The pain scorching through Max fell apart, too. Not only was the burning gone, but Max had no wounds, no charred skin, nothing. The thought that the spell caused his mind to create the pain had just formed when a second blast from Nell hit.

This one was not so friendly.

It walloped Max in the gut, digging under his ribs to graze his heart. Forcing the air in his lungs to spew out, the energy punch lobbed him backwards, lifting his feet off the ground. Chucked across the barn, Max had enough time to see Drummond thrown aside as well.

He smashed into the wood wall, and the entire barn shook. Dust puffed around the rafters and those wagon wheel lights swung on their chains. One white-cloth banner broke loose and glided to the floor. Max's head hit hard enough that he saw flashes of light dancing in his vision, and he had the ridiculous thought that he had caused the near-earthquake when he hit the wall. As his mind cleared, as he watched Nell casually lower her legs and set her feet on the ground, he understood what had happened. Not only that he hadn't caused anything but his own pain, but that the woman he now faced was no longer the same.

She rolled her shoulders back and tipped her neck from one side to the other. She scanned the barn as if seeing it for the first time. Holding herself with a new confidence, a new sense of control, she turned her mouth into a straight line. At that moment, seeing the way she had lost her maniacal fervor and simply accepted her position as inevitable, Max spotted the truth.

This was no longer Nell Fincher. This was someone far more knowledgeable, more in control, more dangerous. This was a witch with power and the motivation to use it.

This was Sister Sadie.

Chapter 28

TAKING A CLEANSING BREATH, Sister Sadie inspected her new body. "My word," she said, no longer speaking with Nell's Southern accent but rather employing rough, Slavic notes to her words. "This body was wasted on that meager woman. Definitely wasted under the attentions of her bastard husband. Good riddance to them both."

Max started towards his feet, but the witch raised her index finger and shook her head. He settled back. With a casual shift, she set her eyes directly on Drummond and gestured for him to join Max. Stunned at being seen, the ghost complied.

"Thank you," she said. "Allow me to compliment you gentlemen on your efforts to stop this moment from happening. I've always believed that my enemies deserve credit when due, and you have come the closest of any non-witch to getting in my way. It is impressive and a joy to watch."

"Gee," Drummond said, not bothering to hide his contempt, "so glad we amused you."

With a playful pout that forced Nell's features into a rarely used hint of seduction, Sister Sadie said, "Don't be like that. You never really had much chance, after all. I have been planning this for a long time, and you two only fell into it by accident, and only at the end. In many ways, you had lost before you even started."

She remained inside the triangle, and Max wondered if the protective barrier had returned. If he could grab something to throw at her — but that would require a sudden movement, and until he had a better gauge of her strength, he thought it best to hold off. He needed more information from her, and that was a path he knew he could get her to walk. Ego-driven, power-hungry arrogance led too many of the people the Porters had come against over the years. They each had their unique reasons for acting horrible, but one thing proved true to nearly all of them — they loved to brag.

"Forgive me," Max said, "I can be thick sometimes. You tricked Nell Fincher into sacrificing her body for you to take — I can see that much — but why?" He wondered if she would be fool enough to take the bait. It wasn't his best lead-in, and he feared she would see through the dumb question with ease. He should have known better.

Sister Sadie ripped one puffy sleeve off her arm, then the other. She grabbed the lace around her neck and tore it downward. It hung limp over her chest as she rubbed her throat. "That's better." Resting her eyes on Max, she cocked her head as if she had just noticed him. "You want to understand why I would do this? That's a long story, but the simple answer is this — vengeance and power."

"Those tend to be the common reasons," Drummond said.

"But there is nothing common about me."

"Maybe so, but I've met enough witches in my life and my death to say that you all seem quite the same to me."

"Careful, Mr. Drummond. You don't want to ruin our friendship right at the beginning."

Max loved how calm the ghost looked, tossing off insults without a care, when he knew Drummond had to feel the same terror that rushed through every nerve in his body. The relaxed confidence of the witch dug under Max's skin — she had something more than a body, some further plan, and the longer he managed to stall, the fewer places he had left to look at, to find something useful in stopping her. He had already tried all the big spaces in the barn. Anything that could be a weapon rested too far out of reach. Anything that could be a distraction shared the same problem.

Then we've got to keep her talking.

He knew Drummond searched as well. The fact that their behavior had become standard operating procedure for these cases would be worth a few mental health days to get over, but at that moment, he thought it best to stay focused.

"Vengeance, huh?" Max said.

"And power."

"Of course. But who has wronged you? Who deserves your wrath? Nell Fincher? What did she ever do to you? From what I could see, she idolized you, wanted to be like you."

"Nell Fincher could never be me. She was easily manipulated and terribly unskilled. She would have made an awful witch. But she is an example of how long I have worked towards this. I met her years ago when she entered my studio to ask me to design her wedding invitation. Her mother and grandmother, and possibly generations further back, all had a good appreciation for witches. They wanted a wedding blessed with all the good energy a witch could bring. Nell's mother helped her find me, and we made a deal."

"She made a witch deal with you?"

"How else would she pay for my services?"

Max thought of the symbols embedded in the border design around the invitation. "All of this was to pay that debt?"

"Not exactly. Well, yes, for me, quite exactly. But Nell did not understand that. You see, I agreed to do the work she asked if she would be my student."

"Except you never intended for her to learn much. Just enough so she could pull off this dangerous spell."

"You might be smarter than you think."

Drummond said, "How did you get any of that across? From what Max said, you were practically a vegetable when he last saw you."

With an amused grin, she bent down and set right the blood bowl Max had kicked over earlier. "That was the result of a curse. One I have suffered under since 1994. Over the years, I learned to get my meaning across. I managed to bring you here, didn't I?"

"We're pretty sure you didn't intend for two police officers to be Nell's victims."

She shrugged. "I haven't had the luxury of being specific in a long time. I made the best of what I had to work with." She moved toward Dwayne and kicked his leg aside. "If you want to know who is really responsible for Nell's demise, it's this waste of human tissue."

Observing her carefully, Max noticed she had yet to step from the confines of the triangle. While her attention remained on Dwayne and her anger, Max took a chance. He reached to his side and picked up a metallic pebble — part of a nail ripped into pieces with the shattered chair. He flicked it at the triangle. It sailed right through, hitting the markings on the ground and skidding across the spell, out the other side.

No barrier, then. At least, no barrier for Max and Drummond. Could the spell that allowed her to invade Nell's body keep her locked in that triangle? That would seem a foolish spell to be part of. Unless Nell screwed it up and Sister Sadie was trapped by accident.

"I know what you're thinking," she said, turning back.

"I doubt that." Drummond said.

"Not you. Ghosts don't really interest me much. But you, Mr. Porter, you interest me a great deal. I've watched you over the years —"

"Get in line, lady."

"You are a rude ghost. Don't interrupt me again."

"All I'm saying is that everybody in the witch community has been keeping an eye on him since the day he first arrived. You're nothing special."

Max watched the exchange and tried to see what angle Drummond played now. He clearly wanted to tick off the witch. Not a simple distraction, but outright anger her. But for what purpose.

The tendons on her neck stood out as she glowered toward Drummond. "If you wish to be hurt worse than anything you have felt this day, please, continue talking."

"Whoa, there. No need to be so grouchy."

She raised her hand, holding it out like a claw, and her eyes blazed in fury. Drummond's body stiffened as his head wracked back. His hat tumbled down and disappeared. As it reformed on his head, his eyes bulged.

"I am not like any old crone from the witch community. I've

known for ages how to keep some basic spells always in my mind. A constant chant that hums in the back of my head, ready to launch out of me whenever I want."

Despite the obvious pain he endured, Drummond managed to say, "Is that … why … you went … crazy?"

"Just because you can't be killed, doesn't mean I can't hurt you for a long time."

"Stop it," Max said. "Please. You clearly had something you wanted to say to me before my partner got ornery. Let him go, and I'll listen."

With a twist of her hand, she released Drummond. He dropped near to the floor, gasping while he rubbed his neck. "Looks like she can touch me," he whispered.

Max kept stoic but he wanted to slap his partner. That was the reason for his brash display? To see if she had any power? No. It was more than that. Drummond's actions proved she had a lot of power, yet not enough to destroy him. Or leave the triangle.

Behind Drummond, just outside the barndoors, Max could see Sandra and Brenda. Both appeared to be straining, intense, and not getting anywhere helpful. He felt like they were all poking around for a weakness that didn't exist. But he had only one plan — keep going forward. Not a good plan, admittedly, but at least it offered a direction.

Sister Sadie stepped into the center of the spell. She closed her eyes, gathered her thoughts, and appeared to calm her fiery spirit. When she finally looked at Max, he could feel her intense focus. He had to wonder if she prepared a new spell in her mind as she spoke.

"I know that you appreciate good research," she said and attempted a friendly smile across her face. She failed. "I'm sure you would enjoy spending hours digging up all you could about me. But I think it better that I tell you myself. You will, no doubt, verify what I say tonight with your own research. That is fine, too. But listen to me now, so that you may understand who the real villains are."

In as non-threatening a tone as he could manage, Max said,

"You think you can change my opinion after all I've seen tonight?"

"I think you are a rarity in this world — a fair, thinking man."

He didn't want to feel flattered, didn't want to admit his desire to hear her story, but some part of his mind knew the truth. That same part helped him as he said, "I'll listen as objectively as I can."

"Good. Because you will know who you should be afraid of and why. You will know how I had little choice in my actions and what choices you now face. Most important of all — at least, to you — you will find out why you are still alive."

Chapter 29

SADIE RICHE HAD BEEN BORN IN POLAND during the winter of 1948 — a fact that Max found hard to believe. The crazed woman he met in the loft apartment could not have been more than forty years old. But watching the ease with which she had adapted to the body of Nell Fincher suggested the clear possibility that she had performed this spell before. Perhaps numerous times.

She explained that though World War II had ended, plenty of suffering continued. Her parents — Jews by birth though agnostic by belief — had survived the Holocaust only to be faced with intimidation and ostracization by the townspeople they once considered friends years earlier. Faced with constant threat as well as starvation, they sold what little they owned and took on a nomadic life.

"During those early years, I thought everybody lived like I did. New towns, new countries, new people to meet all the time. As I got older, I learned better what the world was like. I also learned how there were other worlds existing right under the noses of the everyday people. The homeless world was my first, of course. But as is obvious, I eventually came across my first witch. Her name was Mother Charity. I was fifteen. My parents had passed away that summer, and Mother Charity took me in. She gave me all the foundations a witch needed and then presented me to the witch community."

Max tried to listen. Not only out of respect — and fear — but because he hoped to glean some nugget of information that would help stop Sister Sadie from success. But his mind kept wondering why she wanted to tell him this. It had to be more than the unconvincing reasons she had offered. Sure, he had lured her into it, trusting her need to self-aggrandize, but this seemed a bit much.

"You strike me as the kind of man that never had trouble making friends or fitting in," she went on. "I was not so lucky. Perhaps because I never went to a regular school, and I rarely spent time with people my own age. I don't think I properly learned how to behave around others in a way that they would understand and accept. From the start, I was made unwelcome by the other witches. My peers, my elders — it did not matter. None of them offered to help me become one of their kind."

"I'm sorry that happened to you," Drummond said with a sincerity that shocked Max. "I didn't live long enough to see the end of the war, but I remember what people were like. Say what you want about today's youth, but they got a lot going on to prove we were far from *The Greatest Generation.* We were tough SOBs, sure, but not always as kind as we should have been. Especially to those who didn't quite fit the mold."

Some unspoken communication passed between Sister Sadie and Drummond. Max watched this with a mixture of awe and a certainty that he had missed his partner's true aim. Not that Drummond had lied. The truth rang hard with each word he had spoken. But rather, Max could think of no logical reason Drummond would offer any aid to a witch — especially emotional aid — unless doing so helped with a plan to stop her.

Bending forward, Sister Sadie pressed on the smooth floor. "I can remember washing floors by hand. Did laundry, too. A weak coven in France took us in. Even with our addition, they lacked a full thirteen, but we were in no position to argue. Like in the fairy tales, I was made to cook and clean and work hard just to be allowed to live under the same roof — in the attic, no less. Nobody would speak with me, let alone teach me anything. But being in a coven, no matter how weak a coven, gave Mother Charity access to their libraries. Mr. Porter, I know you understand this — the value of books. From those slim offerings and from her own failing memories, Mother Charity further educated me in the ways of witchcraft. By the time I had my eighteenth birthday, I had mastered the core of what all witches know."

Max stretched his legs and leaned down on an elbow. He hoped it appeared to be a casual move to get comfortable as he became more and more interested in her story — and he was truly interested. But he had an ulterior motive. He had repositioned to put his body closer to the triangle. He didn't think she would notice, and if he could maneuver a few feet more, he might get near enough to make a play of some kind. That was the hardest part, though — he still didn't understand what he could possibly do.

"I suppose I don't need to tell you about Alexander. You don't really need to know the details of my first love and how my fellow coven sister stole him from me. All the pain and hardships I dealt with, all the cruelty I fell victim to — none of that matters. Not anymore. Here is what I want you to know of that time — I was young and angry, but most of all, I was already more powerful than any of my sisters. That is not bragging. At nineteen, I proved it. Mother Charity had passed away, and I wanted out. But like all covens, once you join, you never leave. There was only one way to get free. I had to end the coven. One night, while everyone slept, I went into the basement and cast my first spell using blood magic. It slaughtered them all."

A glossy gaze filled her eyes. She was lost in these memories, adrift in years of pain. From the little he had heard, he guessed she had been alone most of her life. Perhaps this was the first time in decades that she had an audience. It hadn't taken much to get her started. Max couldn't recall a time when stalling had been so easy. And the longer she talked, the more he could inch towards her. He had to be close enough to move fast, to reach her before she could raise her arm and cast a preset spell.

"I tell you all of this so that you might grasp how I felt a few years later. I had taken all the valuables I could find in the coven house and ran. The police never paid much attention to us. I think they were afraid of us more than anything, but eventually, a dozen dead bodies gets noticed. They were small-minded people, though. The corpses were disposed of and the house abandoned. If anyone thought a single one of us was responsible or could have escaped, they never voiced their thoughts. Or if they did, the rest of the town shut them down. It was easier to forget us and tear down the house. Cover it over with dirt as if it had never happened. Back then, we Europeans were masters of burying the past. When I arrived in America, I was another street urchin with no past, no future, nothing but money hidden in the lining of my coat and a strong desire to find witches worthy of me."

From what Max could tell, Drummond had picked up on his intentions. Either that or the ghost had his own plan. Because Drummond ceased goading Sister Sadie, and instead, stroked his chin while leaning forward, feigning great interest yet drifting away from Max. As he pulled her attention, Max grew bolder, scooting further than he had dared yet.

"Did you?" Drummond asked, his voice yanking full focus from the witch.

"You know I did. Though barely in its adolescence, this country has become a beacon for all who wish to take control of their own lives. For some, it has brought great success. Others, utter ruin. The witch community is no different. But they are old and have blood ties reaching back to countries long forgotten. It did not surprise me that I found many of the same pathetic attitudes and willful ignorance amongst the older covens that I faced back in Europe. The difference here, I did not need them. I decided I would start my own coven, and as I traveled the country in search of the best place to call home, I came here. I met three witches who brought me to their special home. You know it well — Haven House."

Max froze at the name.

"Perhaps now you are starting to see the full picture. Madame Novak, Madame Fein, and Madame Weir. They were older than the type of witches I had sought, but their enthusiasm for my goal was infectious. They had been a coven long ago and wanted to start anew. I was excited for a future with them. But that did not last."

Drummond snorted a laugh. "Gee, you mean to tell me that you can't trust a witch? What's this world coming to?"

"They thought it would be one of them that would lead our coven, but I made it clear who amongst us held the real power. Except I made a mistake. In my experience, witches were always a selfish group. Oh, we unite into covens, but that was a means of gaining more power than we could attain on our own. Even in a close coven, a tight-knit coven, each witch seeks to serve her own needs above all others. My mistake — I assumed all witches acted this way."

"Right. Those three have been together for longer than most have lived."

"I tried to divide them, but I could not play them against each other. When we finally fought it out, as powerful as I had become, I learned that I could not handle all three at once. They subdued me, locked me beneath Haven House, and forgot about me. Foolish old ladies. They believed I no longer threatened them. But from the moment my captivity began, I worked towards my escape. I listened to every visitor that came to use the books at Haven House. I left my body and floated through the rooms to read the books myself and observe the quality of witch that frequented the place. Until finally, after many years, I met Jessie. A young woman. Eager to learn."

"I can see this play out," Drummond said, still gaining distance from Max. "You contact her like a ghost, entice her with promises of great power, and con her into sneaking you out of your prison."

"Not exactly. She did not break into Haven House. She did not have to. As an apparition, I taught her the spell I needed her to make — the same one I stand upon now."

"Surprise — she went home, used the spell, and you zapped right into her. Took her body over."

"Only Jessie did not follow my instructions well enough. The results were … messy. I lived in that wretched, confused state, until the day Nell entered the loft."

Max had reached the closest he dared without being noticed. The time to act had arrived. Since she clearly avoided leaving the triangle, that seemed the best area to exploit.

In a single, grand motion, he popped to his feet and launched forward. With a start, she whipped her head towards him and attempted to raise her clawed hand. He had the advantage. Arms out, he rushed to tackle her, knock her out of the triangle, and hopefully, end this nightmare evening.

But she moved faster than he could. Both arms raised. Both hands bent into claws. And Max lost all momentum. His body lifted off the ground, an invisible force clasped around his head and throat. To his side, he saw Drummond locked in the same grip.

"Are all the people of today idiots?" she said. "Nell and her useless friends were a dream of stupidity. I had no trouble casting a few spells to bring Dwayne and Jill together. They wanted it long before I meddled. Nell's interest in witchcraft primed her to seek out a witch's solution. Her pathetic attempts at a simple hex, however, worried me she would fail at the transference spell." She clutched Max's head tighter. "But then you went on television for a harmless Halloween piece and suddenly Nell came to me, afraid and crying, and I knew that all would work for me."

The blood bowls rattled, and a glowing light pulsed out of each one. Sister Sadie glanced down and smiled. "Finally," she said.

The way she said that word, the heavy relief in her eyes — Max wanted to smack himself. All that time, he had thought they were stalling her. But the truth — *she* had been stalling. For reasons he would have to learn later, the spell had taken its time to finish, and until it did, she could not leave that triangle.

Damn. If he had attacked earlier, he could have stopped this. When she held Drummond the first time, she had probably used all the magic energy she held — or at least enough to weaken her further. But Max had thought himself so clever. He had thought to keep stalling her because that always worked in the past.

"Gentlemen," she said, as bits of light sprinkled upward from the bowls and swirled around her. "I want to thank you for coming tonight. I knew I had Nell in my hand. I made her study hard for this. I knew I would stand here to begin the coven I was destined to create. But when I destroy you, I will gain the respect of all witches. Nobody will care about Cecily Hull or her lapdog, Madame Ti. It will be Sister Sadie's name they bow to with reverence."

"Really?" Drummond groaned. "You forgot one thing?"

"What is that, dead man?"

"Me," Sandra said at the open barn doors.

Chapter 30

THE NEXT MOMENTS HAPPENED SO FAST Max could only remember them like a dream. Sandra shot forward, rising off the floor like a jet lifting into the air. Streaks of light flowed behind her, and in their glow, Max spotted Brenda — eyes rolled back, arms down and facing out, mouth agape. As the thought struck that Brenda had emptied her energy into Sandra like a booster battery, Sandra blasted into Sister Sadie.

The two flew straight against the stone chimney in the back wall. A thunderous crack rippled the air around them. Sister Sadie gasped at the hit. Max dropped to the floor, released from her grasp. When he checked on Drummond, he saw the ghost had also been freed.

"We've got to help her," the detective said.

Max looked at the two women wrestling in flashes of light twelve feet in the air. "How?"

With a rapid motion, Sister Sadie flipped Sandra around, taking control from behind as she viced her arm around Sandra's neck. She raised her free arm, flexed her fingers into that horrible claw, and pointed those razor nails at Sandra's chest. Dropping her mouth in silent pain, Sandra's entire face widened.

"The spell," Drummond finally said. "Destroy it."

Pushing onto his feet, fighting the woozy sway in his head, Max hastened to the casting triangle. Though only a few steps away, it seemed to stretch before him. Or perhaps time did the stretching. He didn't care about the answer — only that it took him too long. Each step weighed down his body with worry. He heard the grunts of physical fighting and the electric sizzle of magical fighting above but didn't dare look. Only getting to that spell mattered. If he failed, if she died, choked out in seconds because he could not move fast enough —

But he didn't have to complete that thought. Blitzing over the first line in the casting triangle, meeting no magical resistance, he discovered that shining ember of energy — hope. He kicked over two of the bowls, their blood splashing across the written symbols on the floor. The third bowl, he chose to stomp on, cracking it into several pieces.

Sister Sadie cried out. Her hands flailed wildly.

"Regroup!" Max charged towards Brenda and Drummond followed.

He spun back, expecting to catch his wife in his arms, but Sandra had not moved. Let loose, she had formed a circle by cupping her hands above her head, and with a blazing rage in her eyes, she thundered a blistering noise. Electricity arced out of Brenda, across the entire length of the barn, and into Sandra's circle. Sparks spattered from the wagon-wheel lights, shorting them out. But the sunlight radiating from Sandra brightened the entire barn.

The last thing Max saw as he shielded his eyes — Sister Sadie's sheer terror.

The light brightened more. Blinding. Burning. Until everything went dark.

Chapter 31

MAX HAD TO CONCENTRATE in order to open his eyes. They stuck together as if gooey from deep sleep. Once he managed to peek through a slit in his lids, he waited for them to focus. His brain took a few extra seconds to comprehend what he saw. A wooden ceiling with rafters, a burnt wagon-wheel chandelier, and an unconscious ghost bouncing up there like a lost balloon. All lit by the amber flickering of a small fire.

He tried to sit up, but his stomach muscles tremored more than helped. Twice he attempted this small feat, and finally resorted to rolling onto his side, placing one hand flat on the cement, and pushing himself into a seated position. A quick scan of the barn — Sandra lay crumpled by the fireplace, scorching marked the blast high above her, Brenda had fallen at the barndoors. The firelight came from the casting triangle and dimmed even as Max watched. No sign of Sister Sadie.

Two grunts and he folded onto his hands and knees. A pause to let his brain catch up with his body, then one final heroic push, and he stood. A bit unsteady, but he stayed upright.

Sandra. He thought he had spoken her name, but the whispery noise coming from his mouth said otherwise. Taking in a deep breath, one tainted with the smoke of an unnatural fire, he called out again, "Sandra!"

Lurching toward the raised platform with the fireplace, Max blotted out the dead bodies, the burning witchcraft, and the blood spilled across the floor. All of that was past. He only cared about his wife.

When he reached her, she looked lifeless, her body twisted from the fall. Choking back the negative thoughts racing through him, he pressed his fingers against her neck while he watched for her chest to rise. He didn't have to wait long. She breathed. Her heart pumped.

Gently, he maneuvered her legs and arms into a more comfortable position while brushing the tears from his face. She was fine. Whatever she did to that witch, she was fine. She had survived. The words kept repeating in his head as he scooped her into his arms and carried her out of the barn.

But when he reached the fresh air, he stopped. The fire behind him died, leaving him in the dark night. Rain drops plunked onto his cheeks. Just a few. A threat of things to come.

He set Sandra down and pulled Brenda the short distance to join her. Sitting next to them, he let the rain strengthen and waited. Nothing in the sky indicated a terrible storm — just a typical evening rain in North Carolina. With any luck, the cool water would wake up one or both women, and they could get into the car with ease. Max didn't want to leave Drummond floating in the barn, but the ghost would come to no harm there. When he awoke, he would understand what had happened and join them when he could.

The raindrops thickened and became more frequent. Max closed his eyes to listen — the rapping of rain against barn a unique, rhythmic chant. But he heard something else. At first, he thought it was an injured cat mewling for aid. The longer it whined, however, the more human it sounded. He couldn't be sure until he heard a voice call out.

"Help. Please, help me."

Max didn't need to see. He knew that voice right away. Nell Fincher. Something about the vulnerable nature of her call told him that she was Nell once again. Sister Sadie would have rather died than sound so weak — especially to Max.

While he had a rough idea of the vineyard's layout, he never had the time to explore. With the moon obscured by storm clouds, he had to follow the beam of a flashlight and listen for the quiet cry. But the whimpering seemed to come from everywhere.

He headed to the right where a grass lawn stretched downhill toward the manmade lake. A white platform stage had been set up — barely large enough for a band to perform during events or even a wedding ceremony on a clear, summer day — but Nell's voice disappeared. He climbed back up. The rain fell in earnest now, and the drops hitting the ground, the trees, the house, the barn made it even harder to hear a single sorrowful voice.

"Nell?" he called out.

Stepping onto the gravel drive which had small puddles forming at various spots, he played his flashlight toward the barn. Sandra and Brenda still lay unconscious. They were getting soaked, and he considered dragging them into the barn for protection but rejected that idea. Magic often left a residue of energy, especially around big usages. He didn't want to find out what such a thing might do to those wonderful women if he brought them closer to the event. Besides, getting soaked should wake them up.

As he turned the flashlight away, he brought it down. At the foot of the concrete section, the chalk of Sandra's casting circle dismantled before him as cold water slowly washed it away. A morbid, fatalistic thought tried to form in his head, but Nell's cry pulled him back.

The sound came from behind. He was sure of it. Squinting as he walked up the endless drive that would eventually spit out onto a paved road, he took cautious steps.

"Nell? Where are you?"

He stopped, the rain chilling his face as it pattered on his head. What if this was a trap? A Siren call to lure him away from the safety of his wife and team.

"Please. Somebody."

No. That sounded like true pain, true need. Still, if he waited until Drummond awoke, the ghost could fly around and locate Nell. He could recon the area and tell them if she waited to ambush the first unlucky fool to offer help. But Drummond might be out for hours. Sandra and Brenda, too. If Nell needed serious medical help, she might not last that long.

A part of him asked, *So what?* But he wiped that out of his brain. No matter how horrible her actions, Max didn't think she deserved to die. Nobody did.

Don't lie to yourself, his pesky brain said.

Fine. Some people deserved to die. Few but some. And not like this. And not by his hand. He refused to become a death penalty judge, let alone the executioner — even if only through his inaction.

He could hear his brain revving up another simple argument. After all, he had faced down enough criminals attempting to use magic and enough witches who pushed the boundaries of their abilities. Some of them died in the process. Some partly by his hand. But those were survival situations. Before things had reached such a dire point or if they had lived through their altercations, he would gladly have had them live, had them in jail or pay in some other witch community way. That wasn't simply a happy wish. The Porters had succeeded many times that way. Ghosts moved on, witches gave up magic, curses were lifted. There was no reason Nell had to die out here tonight. Not anymore.

"Hello?" Nell called. "Are you still there?"

Max couldn't be sure how long he had stood debating in his mind, but he heard her much clearer now. Just ahead. On the left. Moving faster, bouncing his flashlight from tree to tree, across an old shed, over a face, onto the long … *a face?*

Holding still to keep the flashlight steady, he brought it back over the path he had been looking. In seconds, he found her. She stood off the gravel drive, her feet steeped in mud. Her arms were tangled in the barbed-wire pasture fencing. Deep cuts ran along her skin as if she had been clawed by a bear — some ending in deep punctures, some ending in barbs, some oozing blood. Thick crimson stained her skin even as rain tried to rinse it away, and black scorching spread out from where Sandra's attack had made contact.

"You?" Nell said with grating disgust.

He lifted the flashlight and saw her scowl. It was a brave showing considering her circumstances. But she could not hide the mascara running down her cheeks. Even the rain could not hide that for her. She had been crying. He didn't think it was from her physical pain.

Stepping closer, he said, "Don't move. Let me see if I can get you out of there."

She squirmed back, sinking some of the barbs deeper and releasing one with a blob of blood. Her foot slipped in the mud, and she scrambled to keep from falling — causing the wire and her body to tangle even worse. But she did not cry out. Her eyes seethed at him.

"You've ruined it all," she said.

"I'm not the one who lied to you. Or did you plan to sacrifice yourself to Sister Sadie all along?"

"Betrayal. Dwayne betrayed me. Sister Sadie betrayed me."

She spoke from another world, and Max supposed that being taken over by a half-crazed witch might send a person's mind to some strange places. But then she tried to point at him, pulling her skin further apart. When her arm wouldn't raise, she let it drop and settled for lifting her lip.

"I don't begrudge Sister Sadie. She has suffered in that old body. I know. I was there. When she took over my body, I was sent into hers. She didn't have to do that. She could have given me nothing at all, let me become a ghost adrift on the currents of another existence. But she wanted me to understand, and I think, to forgive her." Her face darkened as she looked off into that other world her mind inhabited. "Not like Dwayne."

The idea of leaving her there, rambling into the night as she soaked through with blood and rain, felt full of poetic justice. But it also felt cruel.

"Tell me about Dwayne," he said, inching toward the twisted metal fencing. As long as she stayed in her own mind, he thought he could free her arms little by little. Once no longer stuck, maybe she would allow them to call an ambulance, get her some help.

"He never tried," she said, a slight hitch in her throat. "Sister Sadie cared what I thought of her, wanted me to understand, to forgive. But Dwayne — he was a cockroach. He wanted to hide. And why? That's what I really needed to know. How could he do this to me?"

With one more step, Max stood next to her. "I wish I could tell you. I'm sure you were a good wife to him."

"The best. I devoted myself to him and his happiness. Even when I was too tired, I put up with his needs. I may have spent hours taking care of the house and dinner and bills and whatever, and all I wanted was to sit down, have some quiet, read a book. But he needed to bitch about people at work or figure out what to do about a certain case. So, I would sit there and listen."

"He was self-centered." Max pulled gently on one piece of wire.

"Self-centered people think the world revolves around them. But Dwayne thought the entire galaxy, maybe even the universe, bowed at his feet. That's why he cheated. He couldn't accept that a deity like him should be limited to only one woman. He had an appetite and saw no reason to deny what he wanted."

There were only three wires along the fence — upper, middle, and lower — but she had them yanked together and snarled around her arms. He tried to nudge one arm to the side and release another barb from the middle wire, but when he did, the barbs from the upper wire cut deeper into her flesh.

She lolled her head back, letting the rain spatter on her cheeks. With a childlike glee, she opened her mouth. A moment later, she lowered her head and spoke clearer, her mind back to this world.

"I could have forgiven him. I think I really could have done so. If he had slept with some bimbo at a conference or maybe a secretary at work. An anonymous piece of youth that made him feel more manly or some crap like that in his head — I could have forgiven. But Jill? Our friend? That was unacceptable. That required payment. Vengeance."

Her constant movements, though small, caused more damage to her arms. Opting to focus on the wires themselves — if he could untangle those, then maybe he could free her with minimal harm — Max discovered that she had scraped the back of her waist into several barbs. She could have arched away. But she didn't. As if using the barbs to scratch an itch, a bone-deep itch, she had shoved herself harder into the pain.

"It's not your fault," he said. "You're not responsible for what Dwayne did."

She laughed. "I'll pay for what I've done, though."

Thinking of the dead bodies in the barn, Max nodded. "You didn't need to go so far. When the police find —"

"The police? I don't care about them. It is Sister Sadie I'll have to pay. I've failed her. I shouldn't have fought back."

"You fought her?"

"When the transfer occurred, I was angry. She never explained to me what would happen. There was flash of light, and I awoke inside her old body. I was in that loft covered with her paintings, and I knew right then that she intended for me to stay there, but that had not been the plan. Not my plan. I had expected to be by her side always, not some stepping stone toward the creation of our coven. I panicked. The line connecting us still existed and would do so until the spell finished completely, so I tried to grasp it, tried to pull myself back to my body. Do you know what it's like to betray someone? I betrayed her as much as you think she betrayed me. I pulled hard on that ethereal line, and each time I did so, I slowed her spell."

All of Sister Sadie's jabbering, her stalling — some of it had been waiting on the spell itself, but Nell had caused things to worsen. Sandra did her part in fighting the spell, too, but at some point, she had switched into the spell of attack that saved them all. Yet if Nell had accepted her fate, Sister Sadie would have completed the transference long before Sandra was ready.

"Huh," he said. "Can't say I'm going to thank you. None of this would have come close to happening if you hadn't started making hex bags, but in a weird way —"

"I won't be responsible for Sister Sadie's demise. I can't be."

Max didn't think there was any chance Sister Sadie had died. If for no other reason, he knew Sandra would not have tried to kill her. Banish the witch, perhaps, but not kill her. More likely, though, he suspected Sister Sadie had been returned to the prison of her old body.

"Honey," Sandra called in a weak voice.

Through the rain, Max saw his wife standing by their car.

Brenda stood next to her, desperately trying to light a cigarette in a rainstorm. Behind them, the barn loomed like a shadow in the dark. And in the shadow, a dead man and two dead police officers had already started to rot on the floor.

Putting out her hand, Sandra said, "We need to leave. The police will take care of her."

Max looked back at the wire and the bloody wedding gown.

"Stop," Nell said, lowering her head. "Let go of the fence."

With his hands shaking from the cold and wet, he tried to twist another barb loose.

"You're hurting me," she said, but she no longer sounded in pain. "Please, leave me alone."

He gently set the wire back before stepping away. "I'm sorry."

"You should be. I hired you to save Dwayne and look at him now." She let a weak chuckle pass her lips. "I never thought you were the real thing. I had heard rumors about you, but when I saw you on tv, I thought you were a joke. I wanted you to give Dwayne false hope, to make him suffer more. But Sister Sadie knew. She had set you up to fall — another way I never really knew what the plan had ever been."

"If you're here when the police arrive —"

"It's only Sister Sadie that matters. The police can arrest me, and I'll confess to everything. Maybe in prison I'll be safe from her anger, but I doubt it. She will blame my weakness for her loss tonight, and she's right. Even if I serve an entire prison term and live to be released, she will awaken from wherever she is, she will find me, and that first night of freedom will be my last. I have to pay."

The finality in this admission, the surety that her end would come at the hands of an insane witch, lodged into Max's chest. He could imagine Drummond floating next to him. The old ghost would click his tongue or flick the brim of his hat. *You can't save everybody,* he would say. *Especially when they don't want saving.*

He would be right.

"Treat your wife well, Mr. Porter." Nell shouted the words to make sure Sandra could hear. "She's a witch now. Can't deny that. And you've seen what an angry witch can do."

She laughed — witch cackled, really. Max backed away, afraid to take his eyes off her, afraid she might rip herself off the fence and lunge at him, all blood and dirt sopped up in madness. Her shredded wedding gown hung like the remnants of her sanity, and seeing her devilish smirk as she warned him of his own wife, he wondered at what point she had lost control. Was it love for Dwayne from the start that had spiraled her, or was it his betrayal that set her off?

Max's feet squished in his sopping shoes as his teeth chattered. He continued backing up, part of him wishing he could have helped her more, part of him glad to be done with her forever. At least, he hoped so. Dealing with witchcraft meant never knowing if a case truly ended. He rolled his foot on a rock but kept his steady backward pace until he felt a comforting hand on his neck.

Sandra.

"Come on, hon," she said. "Get in the car. Brenda's got it warming up. Let's go home and get dry. We need to forget about tonight."

Chapter 32

THE TRIPLE HOMICIDE AT A THOMASVILLE VINEYARD would have kept the news salivating for a full week. But adding in a tragic love story, an occult angle, and two dead cops — the story stayed alive for nearly a month. It only helped the local stations that Nell Fincher happily gave interviews while looking crazier than Charles Manson on his best day. Several reporters thought she faked her lunacy in an effort to plead insanity, but she proved them wrong when she pled guilty and asked to serve the maximum. The judge required her to repeat her request several times and checked with her lawyer to make sure he heard right. He couldn't understand. But Max did.

Nell wanted as much jail time as she could get to avoid a witch. Slim protection from Sister Sadie, but better than nothing. Not so crazy, after all.

Strolling back to the house from his mailbox as a cold winter wind threatened to start the season earlier than usual, Max thought about how nice the latest batch of inane and pointless cases felt. No witches trying to kill him. No ancient curses or old grudges to hang over him. Just a few simple matters that could be handled in a few hours — *Is my grandpa's ghost in the house? Can you act as a medium for me? Should I stay away from the Ouija board my brother is using?* Even Drummond didn't seem to mind.

Max wondered if firefighters felt this way about rescuing cats from trees. After dealing with a five-alarm blaze that came close to killing all their buddies, a few days of cats in trees might no longer feel like a burden.

In fact, the only burden he dealt with of late was making sure his mother got a box of cookies each week. She had been livid when he forgot to bring them during the case, but he had a difficult time explaining that he was trying to stop a witch from murdering people, casting blood magic, and transferring her soul into another witch. He figured best to act like a thoughtless son and let his mother stay mad for another month.

"Got a few minutes?" PB said, still working on his car.

Despite the plummeting temperature, Max figured PB wouldn't stop until he had that car running the smoothest possible. He tried not to be offended, tried not to think that the only reason PB insisted on tinkering in the early-winter weather was to avoid conversations with Max in the small house. But here PB stood initiating a talk. Hard to argue with that.

"Everything okay?" Max asked, lowering to the concrete step at the door. The cold surface went straight through his jeans and into his rear, but he wasn't about to complain. He wanted to listen.

"Yeah. Fine." PB peeked over at his car, and Max got the distinct impression the young man was summoning his courage.

"I'm glad to hear it." Trying to ease whatever tensions PB held, Max stretched out and crossed his legs while leaning an elbow on the lip of the door. Another icy chill ran from stone to skin. "What do you want to talk about?"

A breath. Then: "I've made up my mind about the future."

More serious than expected. Okay. Max sat up again, resting his elbows on his knees. "I'm here for you. Tell me."

Another pause. Finally: "Well, I got this car going pretty good, now. It's good for getting to school and hanging out around town, but by the time I graduate and summer hits, it'll be reliable for a longer ride."

"I take it you plan to go on a trip. You got a specific place picked out yet?"

"No. And I'm not going to."

"Ah. The open road."

But PB shook his head. "Not like that. I'm not going on some summer vacation where I drive around for a few weeks, get drunk, and think I've had a great experience." He looked down at his hands. "I'm leaving. I'm going to explore, maybe hit every state I can reach, go on a real journey, and I'm going to talk to people and see how they all live, and maybe — hopefully — I'll figure out how to get what I want."

"And what's that? What is it you want?"

With the most solemn expression PB had ever shown, he stared straight into Max. "Contentment."

Max had to admit that he wasn't surprised. Well, that wasn't entirely honest. Truthfully, he had expected PB might want to drive off for a time. He hadn't expected such a poetic, romanticized plan. Yet, if he continued to be honest with himself, Max was a bit surprised at the depth behind that single word — *contentment.* Not *happiness* or *love* or any of the usual suspects of big emotions that people chart the course of their lives by. Rather, PB sought something far bigger, far greater, and far more valuable. Contentment. Peace.

Though Max knew he would need to tell Sandra and that they both would need time to let it all sink in, he also felt PB waiting for some kind of response. Max gave the best he could muster. He stood and wrapped his arms around his son.

"I'm going to miss you awful bad, but I think you'll do great out there."

PB pulled back. "Really? You're okay with this?"

"Of course."

"But I'm not going to college. Not ever."

"That's up to you. There is no single right path that we all have to follow. There never has been. People like to think there's a set route, that if we graduate high school, go to college, get a good job, then everything will fall into place and we'll have a good life. But that's not true. That does work for some people, but others have a different road to travel. Heck, look at me and Sandra. You think we set out to be what we are now? Look at your own life. You're barely an adult, and you've lived more than many people do from birth to death. So, if you think you can find some measure of peace by exploring the country, or even the world, then do it."

PB's eyes welled up as his shoulders slouched. He hugged Max tight. "Thank you."

"Don't lie to yourself, though. It won't be easy. Keeping that car gassed up, getting food, finding your way — that'll be rough, at times. You'll need money."

"I know how to survive."

"Contentment takes more than that." Max patted PB's shoulder and pulled away. "But I think you'll do great. I ask just one favor."

"Sure. What is it?"

"Call us. Once every week. Doesn't have to be a long report. Just call so we know you're okay."

"You got it," PB said before returning to his car, a new bounce to his step, a new grin on his face.

Max entered the house with a grin of his own. It faltered, though. He had only started to feel like he might have a clue how to be a good parent, yet soon PB would be driving away. Didn't seem fair. In the kitchen, J sat at the table buried in another school textbook. Well, at least he still had J for a couple years. But not many.

I'm going to miss those boys.

He needed to clear his mind. Focusing on a little work would help, but if he sat in his alcove to go through the mail, he would probably disturb J's studies. Careful to move as quietly as possible, Max strolled to the living room. A small casting circle had been set up on the coffee table using a piece of paper and two candles. Sandra sat on the couch with Brenda and explained all the basic elements of casting a spell. Brenda knew this stuff already, but after experiencing Nell and how bad things could get when poorly-trained, both women agreed that strengthening their understanding of the basics, the foundations of witchcraft, would only serve them well.

"This house is getting smaller by the minute," Max grumbled and turned toward the master bedroom.

Plunking down on the corner of the bed, he sorted the junk mail from the handful of actual correspondences — a few bills and a "thank you for clearing our haunted house" card. He then used his phone to check his email. There he found a message from the local news. Max set all else aside. As he read, his jaw dropped, and he let out a hearty whoop.

Sandra and Brenda came in a moment later. "What's all the noise?" Sandra asked with a laugh.

Waving the phone, Max said, "A local crew wants to do a special all about Nell Fincher and her connection to the occult. They want me to be one of the main talking heads."

Brenda acted as if she whiffed sour milk. "I thought you didn't want to do anymore tv."

"Sometimes we have to do things we don't want in order to find peace on the other side."

"Huh?"

Scrolling to a section of the email, Max turned his phone toward them. "Look how much they're offering to pay."

Brenda's eyes widened. "Oh." She looked to Sandra. "You better get in on this."

"No way," Sandra said. "The last thing we need is a witch on television. I do that and before you know it, they'll start televising witch burnings for ratings. I'd rather leave it to Max to represent us."

Having said her piece, she angled the phone so she could read the offer. Max saw the slight lift of the corner of her mouth.

"Just one more time?" she asked.

Max kissed her. "I promise. I really don't want to do this, but with that money —"

"Honey, it's okay to admit you like it."

"I don't know. But I'm sure that with money like this we could help J with college, we could get a better car for ourselves, and PB — we could give him some cash to fund his trip."

"What trip?"

"I'll tell you later. This is great." Max stopped, stunned by the thought that hit him. "You know what else we could do? We could open a real office again."

Sandra laughed. "Don't spend it all three times over. We've got to have an agency left for when J starts handling the money."

"But a place downtown where you and I could have our own desks, our own space, and a bookshelf for Drummond so he won't have to hang out here all the time."

"Honey."

"Okay, maybe not an office yet. But we'll get there."

Sandra took his hand. "I see some real happiness sparkling your eyes."

"No, no," he said. "It's the start of something else."

"What's that?"

He thought about PB traveling from one state to another in search of himself and his purpose, and Max squeezed Sandra's hand. He didn't know how to explain the swirl of emotion racing through him, and the one word that came to mind would not carry the weight he wanted it to. But it would have to do.

"Contentment," he said.

She rested her head on his shoulder and placed one hand on his chest. He could feel his heartbeat against her hand, so she must have felt it, too. Such simple gestures. But she told him with that hand that she did understand, maybe even shared what he was finding. He kissed the top of her head. Yeah, contentment. He could live with that.

Afterword

As always, I hope you have enjoyed spending some time with Max and the gang. For those of you who have read any Max Porter before, you know what's coming, so I won't delay. Here's what you want to know…

You've probably guessed this already, so the answer is yes. The Bostian Bridge train wreck really happened. There were, however, only twenty-three deaths. The two missing bodies were a fiction of my creation. All the other non-paranormal details regarding the crash are true, including the numerous people who came out to see the site days later and bought pictures taken by two newspaper photographers. While it seems a bit morbid, remember this was in the late-1800s. No television. No radio. Certainly no internet. I don't think we've changed that much either, really. We can simply watch our horrors in the comfort of home.

The other two bridge stories are urban legends which, like all good urban legends, are based on some truth. However, while those deaths did occur, stories like Lydia's Bridge can be found in practically every state in the Union. Probably every country in the world.

Finally, the Old Homeplace Vineyard in Thomasville is a real location. The parents of fellow author and good friend, Darin Kennedy, as well as his sister and brother-in-law, own the business. In addition to weddings and wine, every year after Thanksgiving, they run an event called the Jingle Mingle, where local crafts people set up tables to sell their wares inside that beautiful barn. Being a relation, Darin also gets a table to sell his books. Being a good friend, Darin gives me some tablespace, too. We've been doing this for years.

It so happened that at the time of the 2022 Jingle Mingle, I was working on this book and looking for a place to stage the climax. Sitting in that barn for two days, I had no choice. But I did ask his sister if she wouldn't mind me bloodying up the place and casting witch spells in the barn. Once she understood that I meant it only in fiction, she was happy to play along. So, if you are ever in Thomasville for the Jingle Mingle, be sure to thank her!

Acknowledgements

Even after sixteen novels in this series, there are always people that deserve some thanks. Among them are Mari Morgan for a stunning cover and Darin Kennedy for his continued friendship. Big, big thanks to Jill and David Stone for allowing me to fictionally commit murder and magic in the barn of their beautiful vineyard. Another round of big thanks to Jordan Harris for taking the time to sit with me and explain all the pains of living with MS. Of course, my forever thanks to Glory and Gabriel. Without them in my corner, I'd never have made it this far. And finally, my deepest thanks to you, my reader. Your love for Max and the gang as well as all the other books I write has privileged me with a career I once merely dreamt of.

Thank you.

About the Author

Stuart Jaffe is the madman behind the *Nathan K* thrillers, *The Max Porter Paranormal Mysteries,* the *Ridnight Mysteries,* the *Parallel Society* novels, *The Malja Chronicles, The Bluesman, Founders, Real Magic,* and much more. He trained in martial arts for over a decade until a knee injury ended that practice. Now, he plays lead guitar in a local blues band, *The Bootleggers*, and enjoys life on a small farm in rural North Carolina. For those who continue to keep count, the animal list is as follows: one dog, two cats, two aquatic turtles, and four chickens. As best as he's been able to manage, Stuart has made sure that the chickens do not live in the house.

www.ingramcontent.com/pod-product-compliance
Lightning Source LLC
Chambersburg PA
CBHW030530310726
48979CB00010B/1858/J
9781963517095